ACCUSED

FREE JUDGE REBORN™
BOOK TWO

MICHAEL ANDERLE

LMBPN Publishing
2375 E. Tropicana Avenue, Suite 8-305
Las Vegas, Nevada 89119 USA

Version 1.00, February 2026
ebook ISBN: 979-8-88878-978-0
Print ISBN: 979-8-89354-337-7

DEDICATION

*To Family, Friends and
Those Who Love
to Read.
May We All Enjoy Grace
to Live the Life We Are
Called.*

— Michael

CHAPTER ONE

<u>**Tuesday, December 19, 2090**</u>

Kara Greims' life looked a lot different than her last five-year plan had predicted.

For one, she now spent most of her time in Neo Los Angeles, the sprawling megametropolis that covered a significant portion of California's coast. Her permanent address remained in the Central NorMetro area of North Texas Mega-Metroplex, formerly known as Dallas, so the population density was a familiar constant. The architecture that formed the backdrop of her daily life had shifted significantly.

Part of her missed NorMetro's open blue skies and dusty streets, but she was becoming accustomed to NLA's Japanese-influenced skyscrapers. She couldn't say she loved the ubiquitous, flashing neon advertising of the animated billboards covering the façades of those skyscrapers. Still, she had to admit it provided excellent cover for her as often as not.

Needing cover was another one of those things she'd never expected to factor into her daily routine, but such were the necessities of being a vigilante.

Kara Greims was a lawyer, and a damn good one. She specialized in corporate law with a focus on anti-corruption and anti-trust regulatory concerns. She had begun to make a name for herself with Harper & Associates back in NorMetro, working her ass off in an attempt to make a difference in the world.

She liked to think she had done more than most, but the truth was the system didn't always work the way it was supposed to. Too often, guilty parties walked away either scot-free or with nothing more than a slap on the wrist. Money made the world go 'round.

All of that had changed six months ago, on a hot, dusty day in July.

Kara would never forget that day. She had started by losing an insurance case in court, where she'd failed to secure reparations for her elderly client who had lost the use of her legs in an elevator accident. It had been clear as crystal that Jamie MacNamara had been negligent in his maintenance, but the judge had ruled that Mr. MacNamara had done sufficient due diligence and the tragedy was a freak accident.

That would have been bad enough. Kara had left the court-house to let off some steam at the gym before she punched a hole through a wall instead. While sweating it out on the treadmill, she'd received a call from the Mid-Wilshire precinct of the Neo Los Angeles Police Department with news she could have gone her whole life without hearing.

Her brother Jacob had been killed.

Jacob Greims had been a software engineer trying to make a living in the pseudo-Japanese metropolis alongside his fiancée, Maria Reyes. They'd been planning a wedding for next spring because Maria hadn't wanted to fit a wedding dress over her emerging baby bump. She was due any day now—her and Jacob's Christmas present to one another.

Instead, barely a month into Maria's pregnancy, Jacob had taken his beloved fiancée off his emergency contacts and out of his will, doing his best to shield her from any connection to him.

Kara had been called in to confirm the identification of Jacob's body and handle his affairs. She had also discovered in short order that Jacob had been moonlighting as a vigilante...and not just any vigilante.

Jacob had been a Free Judge of the True Vehmic Court, an ancient society created almost a millennium ago to fight corruption and injustice. When the guilty weaseled out of the consequences they were due in the mundane courts, the Judges of the Vehmic Court stepped up to deliver justice with a supernatural bent. The names of those deemed worthy of judgment appeared by magic in the *Book of the Guilty*, with their actions recorded in the *Book of Deeds* for the Free Judge to, well, judge.

Six weeks and a day. That was the time you were given to turn yourself in and face the music if the Vehmic Court was involved. If you did the right thing, you would serve your sentence fairly. If you continued to evade justice, the Free Judge paid you a visit.

Jacob had held the position since the death of their father, Oskar Greims, several years earlier. Upon Jacob's death, the position passed to Kara.

Naturally, all of this information had hit Kara like a cargo zeppelin going top speed, and she refused to apologize for the gallows humor in the comparison. Finding out that your brother had been a vigilante judge, jury, and executioner for years on the same day that you found out he was dead was a kick in the pants that sent you into next week.

On top of that, it was all too clear that Jacob had been murdered. He'd been right to hide his connection to Maria, too, because no sooner had Kara landed in NLA than she also became a target. The man at the center of the intimidation tactics, Willie Marrow, had been Kara's first case of final judgment, which she had delivered in a container yard in the wee hours of the morning three months after Jacob's death.

In other words, Kara's life had become a whirlwind she'd

never seen coming. It had calmed down marginally after Willie Marrow's death, but it hadn't "gone back to normal."

Kara wasn't certain she knew what normal *was* anymore. Her world now included the real-life existence of magic, including her personal supernatural powers. She could blend into her surroundings so well that security cameras didn't see her. She could shrug off blows and cuts as though she were made of steel. Kara could also make you believe you'd heard something back the way you'd come.

She had the talking skull of a nineteenth-century linguist and jurist as a guide to her new abilities and responsibilities—namely, the skull of Jakob Grimm, her great-great-something-or-other. Somehow, that no longer felt like the weirdest thing in her life. Probably because Jakob could now inhabit the body of a white cat when he felt like it, and that still took the cake.

This morning, Kara was awake before the sun and on the roof. She'd taken to coming up here whenever she could make the time. She was still living in Jacob's old apartment, which was only five stories tall, but the perch was more private than anywhere else she'd found. Except for the one gargoyle-studded roof in downtown NLA, but that was too far to go in the mornings.

Grimm was curled up on her lap. It wasn't *too* cold this morning, but there was a definite chill in the air. Kara wasn't complaining. She remembered all too well the Minnesota winters of her youth. This was nothing.

"You're brooding again." The cat's mouth didn't move, but the voice emanated from the lithe white feline.

Kara shrugged one shoulder. "Seems like a good morning for it. Wouldn't you agree?"

"Far be it from me to discourage a good brooding session, but I must insist it be productive. What are you pondering?"

Kara let her gaze wander over the flashing, flickering billboards that dominated the view of any given part of the NLA cityscape. Even at five-thirty in the morning, you could navigate most of the megametropolis' streets by the light of the ubiquitous advertising. Blackout curtains came standard in every domicile because they were a necessity if you wanted to get any sleep.

"I've killed three people in the last three months, and I'm about to kill a fourth. It's almost become routine."

"You have been busy," Grimm agreed. "It's not often that Judges are handed a list of candidates for final judgment as long as yours, especially this early in their tenure."

Kara managed a tiny laugh. "I'm glad you talked me out of targeting more than one at once."

The cat stretched and licked a paw. "I *do* hope your tenure will be a productive one. I *also* hope it will be *long*."

"Point taken. It's just hard to accept that I'm doing all I can."

"You have made great progress, Kara. With each judgment, you hone your skills. Your last target was particularly clean."

"Thank you."

Kara drew a deep breath and let it out in a long sigh. The "last target" Grimm was referring to was a fellow lawyer who'd been getting away with murder—not literally, but in terms of arguing defendants' charges down when they *really* shouldn't have been.

It was one thing to fight unfair charge *increases*, which was something Kara saw every day back in NorMetro, but letting career criminals and gang members back on the street in a matter of weeks instead of years was an interesting career choice. The longer Kara spent in NLA, the more it felt like the real Wild West. She'd felt safer walking the streets of NorMetro, even with its more relaxed attitude toward firearms.

Kara had offered the dirty lawyer ample opportunity to repent and walk away from his enabling ways. He'd spat in her face. The one time she'd met him in person before final judgment, she'd expected him to *literally* spit in her face.

Now, he was resting six feet under, and Kara's body count stood at three. The only one she was legally linked to was the death of Willie Marrow. She'd left no evidence behind for the other two. Her name had been cleared in Willie Marrow's case, but she'd decided that racking up a list of cleared murder charges would eventually look nearly as suspicious as an actual list of legally confirmed kills.

"I'm starting to feel comfortable in the outfit, too," Kara admitted. "It's becoming a second skin."

"Good." Grimm-the-cat stretched, settled in, and purred. "The less time you spend distracted by your accoutrements, the more you will focus on your work."

"I still haven't found a good name, though."

Grimm opened one baleful eye. "I remain stymied as to why this is a priority. You do not need a name. You are supposed to be anonymous."

Kara deliberately avoided his glare. "If I'm ever caught by someone in person, I need an alias," she explained. *Again.* "If I don't pick one out ahead of time, I'll make something up on the spot, and it *won't* be good. I'll end up 'the Maroon Mantle' or something equally dumb."

"Why not keep it simple? Red Hood?"

"Trademarked. I'm a lawyer. I *especially* don't want to fight a copyright suit."

"You could always use the German. *Rotkäppchen.*"

"Gesundheit."

"That joke was not funny the first time, nor any time since."

Kara stroked the cat's fur and did not think about it as stroking Grimm. "I'm only half joking. Even I can't quite wrap my tongue around some German consonants, and I'm actively working on it. It needs to be snappy. Easy to remember. Also, I'm not convinced of the fairy tale angle."

"Used correctly, fairy tales inspire terror as much as wonder."

"You're not wrong, but Little Red Riding Hood has definitely had its teeth removed over the last couple of centuries. I don't think it counts anymore."

Kara had stumbled into the association with Little Red Riding Hood mostly accidentally. She'd drawn a parallel between Willie Marrow and the Big Bad Wolf, which had automatically cast her in the role of Little Red. When she'd gotten home that night and laid eyes on the red leather outfit hanging in the armory, the moment had resonated like a gong sounding her fate.

She'd worn the armored bodysuit on most of her sorties since. It was mainly made of supple leather with thin pieces of tough metal riveted between leather layers. The chest piece would stop a very small caliber bullet on its own, and with the Kevlar vest she'd added underneath, Kara felt well-protected against small arms fire. Anything larger, and she had bigger problems to worry about than her outfit standing up to the task.

Beyond functionality, the bodysuit was a stunning work of art. It came with a hooded jacket—hence the comparison to the children's story—with a flared hem that went almost to her knees. The hood came to a point over her forehead and covered her face on both sides. It even had a face mask she could hook into the inside of the hood, which left only her eyes exposed. Paired with the matching gloves and boots, when Kara looked at herself in the mirror, she saw a superhero.

Anti-hero, maybe. I'm still technically breaking the law by committing extrajudicial executions. I don't think superheroes can call themselves "super" if they break the law.

"You're still brooding."

Kara shifted guiltily in her chair. "You can't prove anything."

"I don't need to. I am the master, you are the student."

Kara raised an eyebrow. "Next, you'll be asking me to carry you around in a backpack while I hop, skip, and jump through swamps."

"That is a reference to a film. Your brother made the same reference but refused to allow me to watch the film in question."

"You sound very put-out by this."

"It is hardly fair to make literary references when the recipient cannot appreciate the context. It is extremely discourteous, in fact. I demand this be rectified."

Kara struggled to keep from laughing. "You demand to watch *Star Wars*."

"We did not *have* films in my day, and none of those who have been entrusted to my guidance since the advent of cinema have taken it upon themselves to allow me to encounter this new medium. I wrote books, for heaven's sake! It is only sensible that I be allowed to witness this evolution of the narrative form!"

A snicker escaped, and Kara clapped her hand over her mouth to stifle it.

"You are laughing at me." The cat hopped off Kara's lap and stuck its tail in the air as it slunk toward the edge of the roof. "See if I assist you the next time you come across a German word you can't find in the dictionary."

"I'm not—Grimm, I'm not laughing *at* you..." Kara gave up and guffawed. "Okay, fine, maybe I am. But only a little! And only because it's *adorable* that a centuries-old skull is offended by the fact that he's never seen *Star Wars*."

She stood and followed Grimm toward the fire escape she used to get down. "Look. I have a subscription to a classic films database through my old law school email address. I'm sure *Star Wars* is included. How about a movie night? It's not too late yet, and I don't have anything going on tomorrow anyway."

Grimm paused on the lip of the roof and looked over his shoulder. The cat's tail bent at the top in a question mark. "Really?"

"Really. I can even make popcorn and poke some into your jaw, if you want."

The cat sneezed. "No, thank you. I would prefer to lick the bowl in this form. Besides, moving my skull would disturb the melted candle wax."

Kara shimmied over the edge and dropped to the fire escape landing with barely a *clang*. The first time she'd made this climb, she'd sounded like a cat on a hot tin roof. Now, she sounded like a cat burglar. "So? I've been meaning to clean that up, anyway. It's getting a little ridiculous."

The cat leapt from the roof to the railing, then sat and licked its paw delicately. "I would request that you do not."

"Would that reduce your power? I didn't realize the candle *wax* was connected to your magic, only the flame."

"You are correct. The wax is immaterial to my capacity."

"Then… I'm missing something."

Grimm-the-cat hadn't stopped grooming himself. "I like it."

"You like it," she repeated, and narrowed her eyes. "Why, because it *looks* good?"

"It is part of my cultivated aesthetic, yes."

Kara rolled her eyes. "Oh my *God*, Grimm. Next you'll be asking me for a black choker with a red rose on it, and some pipe organ music to play while I'm gone."

"That would be lovely. I'd request Buxtehude, if you please, dear *Rotkäppchen*." Grimm leapt to the next floor down.

Kara snickered all the way down to Jacob's apartment.

They had made it two-thirds of the way through the movie when Kara's phone went off. She scrabbled for the device, which was hidden under a blanket and the handful of popcorn she'd thrown at Grimm when he'd yowled the first time a TIE fighter came on-screen, having stuck his claws deep in Kara's thigh.

When she unearthed it, she attempted to swipe the notification open and was stymied by the grease on her thumb. She growled, wiped it on a stray napkin, and tried again. The message was from Maria, and it was four words long.

Junior's on his way.

Kara rocketed off the sofa. Popcorn scattered across the floor, along with a startled cat. Space opera continued to play in the background while Kara dashed for the bedroom, hauled the closet open, and pulled a suitcase off the overhead shelf.

"What is going *on?*" Grimm demanded. His tail was up and puffed to twice its normal width.

Kara threw the suitcase on the bed and wrenched the zipper open. "Maria's in labor!"

"Well, why didn't you say so?" Grimm hopped up on the bed and climbed into the suitcase.

Kara turned with an armful of clothes quickly gathered from the dresser and raised an eyebrow. "You're not coming."

He licked a paw. "Why not?"

"Because I'd have to bring your skull, and that would mean breaking the wax off it. We had this conversation less than two hours ago."

Grimm huffed and hopped back out. "I do not appreciate the disrespectful assumption that the birth of a child in the lineage of the Free Judges of the Vehmic Court would not rank more highly than my personal aesthetic preferences."

Kara tossed the clothes into the case. Normally, she was a fastidious packer. Tonight, she wanted to get to the airfield an hour ago. "I don't hear you disagreeing."

The cat disappeared into the room hidden in the back of Kara's closet, and Kara chuckled under her breath as she continued to pack.

CHAPTER TWO

Kara splurged on a jet to New York. Zeppelins were more affordable, having been the gold standard for long-distance travel for the better part of two centuries. Still, the popularity of the faster jet planes had surged over the last couple of decades. In Kara's parents' time, taking a jet was an expense attainable only by the super-rich. Now, a seat on an airplane only cost two or three times the same flight on a zeppelin, and it cut your travel time in half.

Kara only took airplanes when she had to. Traveling by jet was much louder and much less comfortable than traveling by zeppelin, especially if you didn't fork over the fee to fly in business or first class. You were paying for speed. In this case, Kara was eager to get to New York as quickly as humanly possible.

I need to ask Grimm about teleportation, she silently groused as she chewed a piece of bubble gum. Descent in an airplane meant the entire plane went from sky to ground, rather than the calm descent in the docking elevator used at zeppelin mooring stations. Kara wasn't convinced the chewing gum helped, but people swore by it.

Still, her mild grumpiness evaporated the moment her feet hit the ground. Maria had texted Kara right after contacting her doula, which meant Kara had made it to the airport and across the country less than six hours after Maria had gone into labor. Kara wouldn't have a nephew yet by any means, but not being greeted with a phone call from Maria's birthing team could only mean good things. *No news is good news.*

Kara practiced deep breathing exercises while she waited in line to rent a car. She wanted nothing more than to jump the queue, grab a set of keys, and take off into the night, but even in the wee hours of the morning, the New York airport was packed with people.

Doesn't help that it's almost Christmas. She flashed a grateful smile at the rental kiosk attendant as the brunette slid a clipboard across the counter for Kara to fill out and sign. *Everyone wants to get to their destination before Santa shows up or the cookies run out.*

A minute later, Kara pushed the clipboard back to the other woman, who nodded and tapped the information into the computer on the desk. After Kara swiped her credit card, she was given the keys to an Audi.

Kara's eyebrows rose. "I didn't ask for a luxury car."

The other woman shrugged. "We're short on stock. 'Tis the season. No upcharge for you, ma'am. Enjoy."

Kara twirled the keys around her index finger, then palmed them. "Thanks."

With her suitcase in tow, Kara navigated the parking lot until she located the sleek, silver car she'd rented. It wasn't *quite* a sports car, but Kara was glad that New York hadn't been buried under six feet of snow like Minnesota typically was by this time of year. One foot would suffice.

Kara pulled out of the parking spot and headed for the exit. *Maybe I should take some stunt driving lessons, too. Might come in handy if I ever have to chase a target that isn't on foot.*

The drive was uneventful. Kara listened to the radio, which

spouted a DJ-less playlist of Top 40 hits at this hour of the night. It took a few hours to pass out of New York City's sprawl, but eventually the spaces between buildings grew wider until trees popped up between them like nature's advance guard.

At last, as the late winter sun finally tinted the clouds a warmer gray with its anemic rising, Kara made the last turn in the thick pine forest that led her to the safe house where Maria Reyes hid. She had followed a single set of tire tracks for the last two hours, the only set of tracks that had turned off the highway into the trees.

That's a good sign. She locked the car behind her and trotted up the snowy front path. *One set of tire tracks, one set of footprints. Hopefully, that means Athemis still doesn't know she's here.*

Athemis was a splinter group of the Vehmic Court. It had broken off not long before Jakob Grimm's lifetime, believing that the supernatural court was too lenient toward its adjudged. Athemis—or as it had been known at the time, the Wolf Court— held that the guilty should receive no opportunity for repentance, and should be cut down as quickly and lethally as possible. They had hacked away at the True Court's forces for hundreds of years in an attempt to supplant it.

It was Athemis, acting through Willie Marrow, that had killed Kara's brother. Athemis had tried to kill her on multiple occasions already too, and they'd made threats against Maria. Kara had no doubt that if they found out Jacob's son was being born, they would come after him the first chance they got.

A pained yell from inside broke Kara's rumination. She took the front steps in a single bound and wrapped her hand around the cold doorknob. She waited a moment for its metal to warm to an unnatural level, indicating the magical scanner had recognized her, then turned it. The door unlocked and swung open, and Kara slipped inside.

The safe house was more of a cabin, nestled in the thick forests of upstate New York. It belonged to the Vehmic Court, although its ownership was obscured by enough shell companies to be a Matryoshka doll that would make any Russian toymaker proud. Grimm had assured Kara that the cabin's numerous magical wards and shields protected it from the casual observer. Satellite images showed nothing but forest, and unless you knew where the turnoff was, you would drive right past it.

Inside, the two-room cabin was warm and cozy thanks to the fire roaring on its hearth. It had every modern amenity, although the appliances were a few decades old and the décor left a lot to be desired. Kara grimaced at the bear's head mounted over the mantle, and did not wonder why Maria had rigged up a curtain around the bed.

The living space showed the signs of Maria's quiet existence hidden away from the world, as well as her preparations for her new baby. The corner of a crib poked out from the side of the curtain, and several soft toys sat waiting in a basket on the low coffee table. Two books on parenting were stacked beside the basket. Both were well-thumbed and bristled with bookmarks.

The yelling that had preceded Kara's entrance subsided to panting and a quiet groan. Maria's midwife, Elaine, murmured behind the curtain in a low, sweet voice, telling Maria she was doing fantastic and to keep breathing. Maria answered in a litany of whispered Spanish that Kara caught enough of to stifle a snicker.

Elaine spoke up. "Kara? Is that you?"

Kara had just removed her boots. She came around to the edge of the curtain. "It's me. How's it going?"

"As expected," Elaine replied. "You can come in, if you like. Maria said so earlier."

Kara twitched the curtain aside. The double bed was rumpled and covered in towels. Maria sat at its head, leaning on a pile of pillows with her feet flat on the mattress. Her dark hair stuck to her skin with sweat, and her face was flushed. Her eyes were closed, and she was breathing heavily.

Kara smiled. Even though Maria looked exhausted, Kara recognized the "glow" everyone talked about when it came to pregnant mothers. Maria looked more *alive* than anyone Kara had ever seen. "Hey, mama. Ready to kill Jacob yet?"

Maria's dark eyes snapped open, and she briefly showed her teeth. "If he wasn't all the way across the country, I'd have already resurrected him so I could kill him again. Twice."

Kara winced. "That bad, eh?"

Elaine was a motherly woman with ample curves and a pixie cut of white-blonde hair currently hidden beneath a plaid bandana. She chuckled. "First babies are often challenging. Maria's doing brilliantly, and Junior should be along any time now."

Kara frowned and checked her watch. "It's been almost twelve hours."

"Don't remind me." Maria grunted.

Elaine's smile didn't falter. "We had a slow start. Maria called me early, in the grand scheme of things, but the forecast was calling for plenty of snow, so it was a good call."

Kara grimaced. "Delivering a baby on your own would be awful."

Elaine nodded. "The forecast turned out to be an exaggeration, but better safe than sorry."

"Absolutely," Kara agreed. "Do you need anything? What can I do?"

"More hot water," Elaine suggested. "Based on the timing of the contractions so far, another one should be along any minute now. We'll meet Junior soon."

As though on cue, Maria groaned and gripped the rucked-up blanket beneath her. Kara swallowed hard and zipped away to the kitchen. She'd seen plenty of pain and suffering in the court-room, and the last six months had been a crash course in pain and suffering of a different kind, but Kara wasn't sure she could do what Maria was doing now.

Carlos Daniel Reyes took his first lungful of air at 10:23 AM on Wednesday, December 20, 2090. He followed it up with a yell that rivaled his mother's of the preceding hours, but he was quickly pacified with the offer of cuddles—and more importantly, food.

"He's in perfect shape," Elaine reported as she settled the newborn onto Maria's chest. "Everything's in order and looking good. How do you feel?"

"Like I've been run over by a convoy of semi-trucks, but I'm on top of the world." Maria cradled her infant son and bent to kiss the top of his warm, damp head, which was covered with a thick thatch of dark hair.

"Any concerning pains anywhere?"

"Not yet."

"That's what I like to hear. I don't see any new bleeding, and the placenta was intact. In my experienced opinion, you'll be right as rain. I'll stick around for the day, as we planned, just to make sure. Kara, you're staying afterward, right?"

"Yes," Kara called from the kitchen, where she was washing the buckets they had used to gather the towels before tossing them in the washing machine. "I have a week off to start with. Then Maria and I will decide what to do from there. Rumor has it her mother plans to come for a while."

"Good." Elaine fixed Maria with a stern look. "You're the most independent-minded new mother I know, and I've met plenty. But especially if you insist on living out here in the middle of nowhere, you *need* help to get through the fourth trimester. It's not that you *can't* do it on your own, it's that you *shouldn't.*"

"I know." Maria's eyes were closed, and her head remained bent over Carlos'. She breathed deeply, drinking in the scent of her newborn baby. "I'm not an idiot. I don't feel like walking for at least the next three days, for starters. Kara's gonna be waiting on me hand and foot."

Kara saluted with a soapy hand. "Yes, ma'am!"

Elaine chuckled. "Glad to hear it. I'm going to help Kara with the washing up. You tell us the second you need anything, but for now, just rest. You've more than earned it."

Maria slept on and off through the daylight hours, between feeding Carlos and managing to get some food down herself. The three women shared an easy but hearty supper of chicken noodle soup around her bedside. Then Kara and Elaine got out some air mattresses to set up their spots to sleep.

"Still good, mama?" Elaine asked Maria.

"Still good. Can't believe this little one is here. It somehow doesn't feel real, but also the most real I've ever felt anything." She laughed. "That doesn't make any sense."

Elaine smiled. "Makes perfect sense to me. Live in these moments. Drink them in."

Maria kissed Carlos' forehead again, then settled back into the pillows. "Yeah. Yeah, I will."

Kara's gaze was drawn up over Maria's shoulder to the snow-crusted window above her head. All she could see beyond were the white-tipped pine trees, which made her think of winters back home in Minnesota with warmth and comfort in her heart, but a twinge of fear wiggled in like a worm in an apple.

Maria couldn't stay here forever. Not with a newborn, not on her own. And Athemis was out there, waiting for her. Kara had to come up with a better plan to keep Maria and Carlos safe.

I should have been working on that for the last three months, not chasing down dirty lawyers and common criminals. What was I thinking?

Kara slept fitfully that night, tossing and turning even though the air mattress was plenty comfortable. Part of it was that Carlos woke regularly to feed, and Kara wasn't used to the noises of roommates, let alone the noises of a newborn. The other part was the insistent conviction that something wasn't right.

Early the next morning, as dawn was breaking in a clear sky, Kara bundled up against the cold snap and went to get more wood for the fire. Instead of heading for the woodshed, she circled the cabin and ventured out into the nearest trees, calling on her enhanced senses to gauge whether anything was amiss.

Winter birds chirped quietly farther into the forest. A fox, disturbed from its den by Kara's footsteps crunching in the new snow, scampered over the drifts and away from the big, scary human. A light breeze whispered through the branches, sending a shower of powder over Kara's toque and scarf.

Kara returned to the cabin, having neither seen nor felt any sign of trouble. She gathered an armful of quartered logs and stood at the cabin's front door, giving the trio of cars sitting at the entrance, buried in snow, a final once-over. Then she went inside, stamped the snow off her boots, and stoked the fire.

Later that morning, while Elaine was giving Maria and Carlos each a full checkup, Kara went for a longer walk. Hands in her pockets, she strolled between the trees and breathed in the crisp winter air, exhaling a long stream of steam that clouded in front of her face.

"Maybe I got used to the big city," she mused. Even her voice sounded too loud for the peaceful silence of the snow-covered forest. "Maybe I'm just not used to *quiet* anymore."

She also realized this was approaching the longest period in the last six months that she'd gone without actively working on a Vehmic Court case. Even during the periods when she'd returned to NorMetro to pick up casework from Jack Harper or to check on her apartment, she'd spent time thinking about or planning her next or current Vehmic Court task. Since getting the message from Maria, she'd barely thought about her Free Judge work at all.

That wasn't to say she hadn't thought about the Court. She

had, at length. Her involvement with Athemis was the entire reason she'd started feeling on edge. But out here in the snow, hidden from the rest of the population, where the most important thing in existence was the tiny new life Maria had brought into the world…

"I don't wait well," Kara told a brightly colored bird perched on a branch far above her head. "I get impatient. I always want to be doing something."

She chuckled. "I suppose I could shovel out our cars. Elaine has to get back to the city at *some* point."

Kara trudged back through the snow to the cabin, brushed snow off the shovel leaning on the wall, and set to work. The hours of training she had put in over the last six months were paying dividends. Most of that time had been spent doing footwork and movement drills with Cedric and Cindy, and target practice with Lawrence, but her body was stronger and more finely honed than ever. She made quick work of the snow surrounding all three cars and was barely breathing hard when she set the shovel back against the wall.

Kara shook snow off her hat and scarf before returning inside. She hung her outerwear on the coatrack, tapped packed snow off her boots, and let the remaining tension melt out of her shoulders as she approached the fire.

"You went after that snow with a vengeance," Elaine commented from the kitchen, where she was making lunch. "Everything okay?"

Kara shrugged. "Needed something to do. Also, figured you might not want to get stuck here when you tried to leave."

Elaine chuckled. "I appreciate that. I have other clients to see, although I leave myself a couple days of margin in the winter whenever possible, just in case."

"Smart. I've gotten used to living in cities, where you're more likely to be delayed by a traffic jam than inclement weather, unless it's tornado season."

Maria grimaced. "Or wildfire season. I don't miss that part of living on the West Coast."

The three women laughed and groused about the weather over the sandwiches Elaine had made, then Elaine packed her kit. She went over Maria and Carlos' care plan one more time, ensuring Maria and Kara knew what needed to happen and what was cause for alarm. Then she bid them both goodbye and disappeared out into the winter afternoon.

Quiet settled in, punctuated by the crackling fire and the suckling of Carlos having his lunch.

"Have you thought about what you want to do next?" Kara asked Maria.

Maria shook her head, then caught herself and smiled sheepishly. "All the time, actually, but I haven't made any decisions. If I'm honest, I've been avoiding thinking about it too hard. I don't want to break the spell, if you know what I mean."

Kara watched the little black-haired head nestled against Maria's chest. His eyes were squeezed shut, and one little fist waved aimlessly in the air. "I think I do know."

Sunday, December 24, 2090

Four days passed in whatever counted as "routine" when you were caring for a newborn. Maria and Kara slept when they could and ate when they were hungry, just like little Carlos. Kara kept up with the dishes and the fire, and Maria gradually worked up to getting out of bed for longer periods.

Elaine visited on the third day, as planned, and confirmed that mother and baby were thriving. Meanwhile, Kara's phone remained mercifully devoid of urgent messages. She was deeply glad she hadn't decided to start another final judgment countdown before Christmas. She would have been climbing the walls by this point.

It snowed twice more, blanketing the cabin and its surroundings in thick, white quilts of tiny, flaked crystals. Kara walked the grounds twice a day, keeping an eye out for anything suspicious, and was relieved each time she found nothing. She didn't trust Athemis further than she could throw them, but so far, the Vehmic Court's wards were holding firm.

She curled up on the air mattress on Christmas Eve with the firelight flickering over her eyelids. Maria and Carlos were asleep and had been for some time. Kara had finished an evening perimeter check, brought in more logs for overnight, and had filled the kettle for coffee in the morning.

Kara had tucked a couple of small presents into her bag when she'd left NLA. She had bought them months before, and they'd been waiting to come along whenever the call arrived. She planned to surprise Maria with them in the morning. Based on the basket of knitting she'd discovered in a corner, Kara would be receiving a scarf at some point, whenever Maria was able to finish it.

You have to be really bored to take up knitting from scratch with nothing else to occupy your time. I gotta get Maria out of here. How she hasn't gone crazy by now is beyond me.

Monday, December 25, 2090

"Kara. *Kara.*"

Maria's hiss cut through Kara's dreams like a knife. Her eyes snapped open. The first thing she saw was the fire, which had died down to embers. The next thing was the gray light coming through the windows. Morning, but only just.

"What?" she whispered. "You okay?"

"I hear someone outside."

Adrenaline shot through Kara like the world's strongest coffee. She was on her feet a heartbeat later, the quilts thrown off the air mattress like a deck of cards. She landed without a sound, sank into a crouch, and listened. She heard nothing, but the snow was so thick outside that it muffled everything within, too.

Kara yanked on her thick wool socks one at a time as she hopped toward Maria's bed. They had removed the curtain to make movement easier in the small cabin, so Kara had an uninterrupted view of Maria sitting up in bed, nursing Carlos.

"What did you hear?" Kara whispered. The cabin was otherwise silent. Kara counted herself lucky the floorboards didn't creak.

"Footsteps in the snow," Maria whispered.

"Could it be a deer?"

Maria shook her head. "Too regular to be an animal, and too close to the cabin. I've gotten used to hearing deer. This wasn't a deer."

Both women twitched as something *thumped* outside. At the same time, the marks on Kara's arms flared hot. Beneath the long sleeves of her nightshirt, the stark black lines would be sharpening into existence like a mirage on her skin. Athemis, without a doubt. The magic marks of the Vehmic Court wouldn't respond otherwise.

Kara gritted her teeth and dove into her suitcase. *Shit.* She'd been working on finding Maria a new location closer to civilization, with the goal of moving her and Carlos as soon as Maria felt up to it. Athemis attacking in the middle of the night was very near the top of Kara's "please no" list, beaten only by full-scale Armageddon or a prolonged power outage.

Kara motioned for Maria to scoot closer to the wall. "Stay away from the windows," she warned under her breath. "I'll go outside and check."

"What if there's more than one of them?"

Kara grimaced as she donned the thermal suit she'd brought with her. It wasn't as much protection from blades or firearms as the leather suit she had at home, but it was much warmer. It would have to do. "Then they're in for a Christmas surprise." She grabbed the pair of knives she had hidden beneath the thermal suit and strapped their sheaths to her thighs. "And they're definitely on the naughty list."

Maria stared at her. "You're getting into a knife fight in the snow on Christmas Day. Of course you're making jokes. Sometimes you're so much like Jacob, I can't believe it."

Kara cracked a smile. "It's the only way to stay sane, with the way my life has gone lately."

She tied her boots tightly and slipped on a pair of snow goggles. Judging by the lack of forced entry, the Athemis operatives outside either thought she and Maria were still asleep or they'd disappeared into the forest. She was betting on the first. While Athemis displayed an annoying level of intelligence, when they went after someone, they were a bit like a dog with a bone.

"Wish me luck," she told Maria, with one hand on the doorknob.

Maria held Carlos close and bit her lip. "Good luck."

Kara opened the door.

CHAPTER THREE

<u>**Monday, December 25, 2090**</u>

Kara was not immediately assaulted. That was nice. She closed the door behind her and magically sealed it with a gentle grip. This was one of her brand-new powers, *verschliessen,* which allowed her to lock or seal simple devices. It didn't work on electronic locks—*yet*—but for basic tumbler locks and latches, it provided an extra layer of security in quick order that would last up to an hour or until she canceled it.

I wish I had time to seal all the windows. Although I suppose the power doesn't stop them from physically breaking in.

Kara cautiously stepped forward into the thick blanket of snow. She had uncovered both her and Maria's cars yesterday, but enough snow had fallen overnight that you couldn't tell. The sliver of a moon was below the horizon, but the sky was clear and full of stars. Thanks to Kara's enhanced vision, the night was as bright as the day.

No footprints were visible within her field of sight, and she heard nothing but the muffled silence that accompanied thick snow. Not even a hint of a breeze drifted to make the snow-covered trees creak.

The utter lack of noise made Kara wonder if they'd heard correctly. Maybe the *thump* had been a tree branch cracking under the strain of the snow, or snow falling from a tree.

But Maria heard footsteps.

There had been enough sun between the snowfalls that there were thin layers of ice within the snow. Kara was stepping as carefully and gently as she could, but her footsteps weren't silent. If Maria believed she'd heard footsteps, the chances were good that she had.

Especially when she's been living on tenterhooks for months. Kara set her jaw. She wasn't sure what it would take to get Athemis off Maria's back for good, but she knew the price would have to be high for her to flinch.

Kara's enhanced vision caught a flash of movement behind a snow-caked pine bough. Too big to be a bird, not big enough to be a bear, and it didn't bound out from behind the tree like a deer would.

Got you.

Kara settled her weight evenly on her feet and let her senses play over the surroundings. Normally, she could sense the people around her to such a degree that she could easily predict their movements. Another gift of the Vehmic Court...one that didn't seem to be working at the moment.

Just like the day on the sidewalk with Cedric. The head goon had a device that protected him from my powers.

Kara sighed under her breath. *No sense prolonging this any further.*

She pivoted on the ball of her foot, bent her knee, and sprang forward. The powerful movement drove her through the knee-deep snow all the way to the tree line, where she skidded on her heel to pull a sharp left turn around the pine.

At the same time she rocketed around the tree, she slammed her left hand out at neck level. Her audacious opening gambit was rewarded. The blade hidden in her sleeve went through the operative's throat with a wet, muffled *shk,* triggered by the impact.

Kara took no more than a second to look the man over. Just shy of six feet tall, he was well-built but on the wiry side. He wore a balaclava with his cold winter gear, and any lingering doubt that he worked for Athemis was dispelled by the abundance of nasty weaponry attached to his outfit.

The symbol doesn't hurt, either. Kara's upper lip curled as she noticed the subtle embroidery on the jacket. The symbol of the True Vehmic Court was a wheel of arrows where each arrowhead was one-sided. Athemis had bastardized the symbol, removing the connecting ring and adding barbs to each arrow. If you didn't know what you were looking for, you would assume it was an esoteric fashion designer's logo.

Kara knew. The marks on her arms flared as she delivered swift justice to the man who had dedicated his life to revenge. Her action was deemed noble by the magic binding her to the Court.

Hopefully, I'll be able to hide this body well enough that I don't have to prove it to anyone else. Hard to be a vigilante from prison.

The light left the man's eyes as blood gushed from his throat. Kara dropped him in the snow, reset her wrist blade, and pressed herself against the tree. Her attack hadn't brought anyone else running, but this man's footsteps only led away into the forest. He hadn't been the one Maria had heard by the window.

A crossbow bolt whistled out of the darkness and struck the tree where Kara's head had been a split second before. Kara completed her hasty somersault and came up running. No sooner had she thrown herself behind another tree than she dashed toward the shadow creeping around the corner of the cabin.

Kara tackled him full-on, bowling him over in the snow as though she were the football player in the family instead of Jacob. She rolled off when he slashed up at her with a long knife that glinted in the starlight, then twisted back and caught his second slash on the blade she snatched from her thigh.

The clash of metal on metal rang through the silence like deadly sleigh bells and nearly disguised the *crunch* of boots on snow behind them. Kara vaulted to her feet and lashed out with one boot. It connected with the temple of the man she'd been fighting, and he went down hard.

She didn't wait to see if she had incapacitated him. The third person, a woman judging by the build, was sprinting for the door with something glinting in her hand. In Kara's peripheral vision, she caught three more shadows moving in the trees. They would have been invisible in the starlit night if not for her enhanced senses.

Six-on-one. They sent six *people to take out two women and a newborn baby. I guess that tells me what they think of me.*

Kara couldn't chance the woman getting through the door. She trusted her abilities when it came to mundane criminals, but Athemis operatives had a frustrating habit of upending her expectations.

Kara flipped the knife around in her hand and whipped it at the woman. Her aim was true. The blade pierced the back of the woman's hand and threw her off course with its impact.

Whatever she held sparked as the blade drove through the woman's hand and into it. The woman screamed in sudden pain. Blood dripped to the snow, black on white, and a moment later she went down too, convulsing.

Kara pivoted to face the three shadows emerging from the tree line. The guy she'd kicked in the head hadn't moved, but that wasn't a guarantee he was out of the fight. Kara's arms were burning with intent in a way she'd never felt. Even the night of Willie Marrow's death, when she had executed a man who'd killed a Free Judge, those tattoos hadn't been this warm.

Two more men and another woman. All wore the same black outerwear, complete with balaclavas. The woman and one of the men had handguns at their waists, but all three carried melee weapons. The woman wore a weird backpack that obscured her silhouette, and Kara was confused about its purpose until she realized it was a baby board.

The bottom dropped out of Kara's stomach at the same time as a fire lit in her chest. *They came for Carlos. That's all they want.*

"Well, that's not happening," she muttered. "You'll kidnap my nephew over my dead body."

The man leading the slow charge chuckled. "That's the idea, sweetheart."

His voice grated on Kara's nerves. It was strident and reedy, even in quiet tones. He sounded like he chewed gravel on a recreational basis and chased it with battery acid.

Kara unsheathed her second knife and sank into a fighting stance. Three-on-one was hard enough in the gym with Cedric, where she practiced footwork and movement drills for hours on end. It would be even harder in the real world, especially with the uneven snow beneath her feet.

She needed to even the odds. She clenched her jaw, reached for the ripple of magic that felt like it skated around the back of her skull and along her cheekbone, and threw an *ablenken* past them into the forest. The resultant wolf howl in the distance made a shiver crawl up *her* spine, even though she knew she'd caused it.

The woman glanced over her shoulder, but the two men didn't flinch.

The man in the lead adjusted his grip on his knife and chuckled. "Your tricks won't work on us. You're going down. I'd say we'll make it painless, but...we won't. And that's nothing compared to what we have in store for the bitch inside."

His buddy, off to his left, chuckled. The sound made Kara's gut twist.

Kara stood her ground. "You're supposed to be seeking *justice*," she spat. "What part of torturing a new mother is *just*?"

The black-clad woman flinched and glanced to the side, where her colleague still twitched in the snow.

You're not convinced. They needed someone with maternal instincts to take the baby safely, but that means you're not as ruthless as the others. You're the weak link.

The lead guy, whom Kara was tempted to call Mr. Asshole, snorted. "There's no such thing as justice. Only power. We don't give a damn about your fairy bullshit. We're just following orders."

Kara didn't respond to Mr. Asshole. Arguing with him would be pointless. She wasn't here to change his mind. She was here to protect Maria and Carlos.

Instead, she sent another *ablenken* into the trees while watching the three assailants approach. This time, the wolf's howl was closer and was echoed by another one behind the cabin. Kara bit her tongue. The echo hadn't been her. There was a real, live wolf out in the woods, and chances were good it was heading this way.

Too bad talking to animals isn't in my toolkit. Then I'd ask it to help.

Kara darted forward, splitting the distance between the two men. Mr. Asshole struck with his blade, but Kara slid away like a baseball player at the last second, ducking under his knife and careening into his buddy's ankles.

The second guy toppled. Kara was ready for him with her wrist blade. She jammed it into the soft flesh of his belly, aiming the spring-driven knife under the edge of the ballistic vest she suspected hid beneath the thermal layer. She guessed correctly. The hardened, triangular knife punched through the winterwear, glanced off the vest's ceramic edge, and stabbed into his abdomen.

The man choked in pain and tried to stab down at Kara's neck, but she rolled away, dragging her blade sideways as she did to gut him like a fish. He hit the snowbank as she twisted out from underneath him, and the unpleasant smell of ruptured intestines assaulted their nostrils.

Kara left him clutching the wound and bounced back up on her feet in time to block an incoming strike from the first man. As they traded blows, more howls pierced the silent forest. The woman wearing the baby board nervously glanced between the cabin and the woods. Her knife hung limply in her hand.

Kara mustered her focus to throw another *ablenken*, creating the sound of a four-legged creature approaching from behind the cabin. The magic was difficult while engaged in hand-to-hand combat, but when she'd started training with Grimm, she couldn't have even *walked* and thrown sounds at the same time.

The woman's breath caught, then started again, much quicker and shallower. She took one step back, then another, and when the next howl sounded, she turned and ran.

Kara briefly wondered whether she would make it out. The scent of dead bodies would doubtless draw the wolves. Whether they would hunt the prey on the run, Kara had no idea, but if she got lucky, the wolves would make the corpses look like they'd died of "natural" causes. Kara might not have to hide them.

The man got in a lucky strike, slicing through Kara's sleeve and drawing blood. The wound barely stung, thanks to the *stählen* ability that Kara was pumping every spare ounce of concentration into. She likely wouldn't even scar.

Mr. Asshole snarled. He was getting frustrated. Kara was almost disappointed. Athemis didn't train their operatives as professionals. This guy struck her as nothing more than a gun-for-hire, and not one with any sense of pride in his work. She could work with that.

"You picked the wrong side," she told him plainly. "Didn't your mother ever tell you that crime doesn't pay?"

"The world doesn't run on one-liners," he snapped. "You're not a superhero."

"Never said I was. You guys are the ones with inflated heads.

I'm just trying to make the world a safer place. Not sure what *your* bosses want out of life, but I'd wager it isn't world peace."

"Survival of the fittest," he growled. "We hunt the unworthy."

"Who decides who's worthy?" Kara cocked her head as the wolves' howls sounded their closest yet. "Never mind. Rhetorical question. If you'll excuse me, I think we have company. You should say hello, one hunter to another."

Kara abruptly broke off her sustained attack, throwing Mr. Asshole off-balance. She stepped aside, allowing him to see the wolf Kara had been able to hear approaching, which bounded into the clearing. He drew back, eyes wide, and Kara took the opportunity to leap forward and drive her knife through his eye.

He screamed, dropped his knife, and fell to his knees with his hands instinctively covering his face.

Kara sprinted past him, yanked her glove off, and gripped the freezing doorknob. More wolves were padding past the tree line now. Their panting crawled up Kara's spine as she prayed for the magic to work faster and let her in.

The knob pulsed in her hand, and light flashed around the door frame. Kara twisted the knob, opened the door only far enough to slip inside, then closed and resealed it with a new *verschliessen.*

Kara pressed her back against the door and let her head fall back against the solid wood. Her breath heaved, and her hands and knees trembled. She'd left her knife in the man's eye socket, not believing she had time to yank it back out. From the agonized sounds coming from behind the door, she'd been right.

Kara opened her eyes again after a score of heartbeats. Still with her back to the door, she looked at Maria across the room in bed. She was unharmed, and in the exact position Kara had left her, but even in the darkness of the cabin Kara could tell the Latina woman had gone pale as a sheet.

"Are you okay?" Kara asked.

"I have never been more scared in my life," Maria whispered.

She clutched Carlos to her chest with his head tucked under her chin. "*Dios mío,* what *happened* out there?"

Kara tried to ignore the horror movie Foley track continuing outside as she crossed the cabin to kneel beside Maria's bed. She considered sugarcoating the incident, but only for a moment. Maria didn't know about the Vehmic Court, but she knew her late fiancé had been involved in something dangerous—and that Kara had taken up the torch in his stead.

Kara couldn't tell Maria the full truth, not yet. Not without risking supernatural retribution for oath-breaking, which would mean Kara's swift and unavoidable death as far as she understood the terms. Still, Maria had endured more than almost anyone Kara knew, and she deserved the closest thing to the truth that Kara could give her.

Kara looked Maria squarely in the eyes, drew a deep breath, and slowly let it out. "I just killed five—" A high-pitched scream echoed through the night from much farther into the forest. Kara winced, sighed, and started again. "I just killed *six* people—although if you want to get technical about it, wolves probably killed two of them, maybe three. Regardless, they're dead because of me."

Maria held Kara's gaze steadily, even though her eyes were wide. "Were they the same people who killed Jacob?"

"They worked for the same people, yes."

"Were they after you, or me?"

Kara hesitated, then bit her lip. "Neither. They wanted Carlos."

Terror turned to horror in Maria's face. Just as quickly, the horror metamorphosed to unbridled fury, and the new mother clasped her infant son tightly as steel filled her gaze. "They will *not* have my son."

Kara shook her head. "Not if either of us has anything to say about it, no. But we need to get out of here as soon as we can. This place isn't safe anymore."

This declaration didn't faze Maria. She only nodded. "Where will we go?"

"I'm taking you both back to NLA with me. It's the only place I can keep you safe for now. We'll leave everything we can here. When the people who were sent don't report back, I'm sure more will come to find them. We don't want to be here when that happens. I'll come back to get what we leave behind, but you and Carlos *must* be safe."

Maria nodded again, then bent her head over the baby's as sudden tears rose to her eyes. "Why do they want Carlos?"

Kara put a hand on Maria's shoulder. "I don't know, but it doesn't matter. I will keep you safe. I promise."

CHAPTER FOUR

<u>**Monday, December 25, 2090**</u>

The remaining hours before dawn crept by. The grinding and cracking of teeth on bone, and the suckle and slurp of viscera consumed nauseated both women inside the cabin.

"At least we know nobody's getting by them to us any time soon," Maria murmured, although green still tinged her face.

"I hope they clear out with enough time for us to get out." Kara was busily packing whatever necessities she could fit in her car alongside Carlos' baby seat. She was doing so quietly, although she doubted the wolves could gain access to the cabin. If they remained curious, or weren't entirely sated by the half-dozen meals of muscle and organ meat she had so graciously provided them...

A shudder ran down Kara's spine, and she swallowed against the wave of nausea that rose in its wake. Nature took its course. Even wolves that hunted at their pleasure wouldn't turn down a free dinner. Plus, it *would* make her life easier in the long run. She might not have to bury their attackers' remains, which was good, because the ground was frozen and she was short on backhoes.

Kara chanced opening the door an hour after dawn. Silence

had fallen outside with the coming of the sun, but she wanted to give the wolves ample time to find somewhere else to be before she risked crossing their paths.

Her stomach did several more unpleasant flip-flops as she surveyed the carnage. The hungry beasts had thoroughly savaged the bodies of the Athemis operatives. Some of them might be identifiable through dental records, but the wolves had consumed most of their flesh.

If we're lucky and can disappear everything from here before the snow melts, thanks to the wards, it's possible no one will ever find what little remains after the scavengers have their way.

Part of Kara disliked leaving anyone to such an ignoble end, even cold-hearted mercenaries. The other, larger part of her recognized that this was a situation where practicality won out. She had a newborn nephew to protect above all else. Athemis agents knew the risks of their job when they signed up, no doubt —although she had to admit, ending one's life as a wolf's supper probably hadn't been in the disclosure forms.

Kara gritted her teeth and ignored the bloody mess in the snow. She grabbed the snow shovel and began the backbreaking work of clearing off her car and forging a path between it and the cabin. She wished she had rented a truck or an SUV at a stretch, but there was nothing for it. She would have to hope the winter tires would get them out of the forest, and that the trees had kept some of the snow off the road.

She muttered, "This could be interesting, but I'm not complaining. Snow hides a multitude of sins."

It took Kara the better part of an hour and a half to clear enough snow for them to escape and to pack the car. When she finished, she sat to polish off the remains of the breakfast Maria had made them while Maria fed Carlos.

"Are you okay to travel?" Kara took her last bite of scrambled eggs.

Maria nodded. "We'll be fine. I wouldn't want to fight anyone or run a marathon just yet, but I can sit in a car."

"We'll make pit stops whenever we can. I remember what Elaine said about needing to use the bathroom."

Maria snorted. "I appreciate it."

The new mother sobered as her gaze went from the door to her son, lying in the car seat and ready to be tucked into a blanket before heading out in the cold. "Sometimes, in the last six months, I have wished that Jacob never got us into this mess. That we were back in NLA, and he was the one bringing me home to our new house, with the nursery covered in fairy tales.

"Instead, we are running for our lives, and we don't even know why."

Kara's heart ached. She bowed her head. "I'm sorry, Maria. I wish I could tell you. It's not fair."

Maria didn't answer. Instead, she drew a long breath and let it out slowly. "I don't like not knowing what's going on, especially when it threatens my son. But I trusted Jacob with my life, and he trusted you. I trust you, too.

"But, Kara…when you can tell me, please do."

Kara lifted her head and met Maria's gaze. The woman's dark eyes were full of pensive sorrow, and her brow and lips creased with anxiety.

Kara took Maria's hand. "I promise I will." *Grimm's not wiggling out of this one. I need to tell her.*

<u>Tuesday, December 26, 2090</u>

Kara wanted nothing more than to collapse into bed the moment they crossed the threshold of Jacob's apartment. The drive back to New York City had been stressful, especially with the extra tension of keeping her enhanced senses alert for

Athemis operatives lurking in the forest or following them on the road.

That paranoia had jumped again when they'd reached the city proper. Kara had begun to doubt her senses were working properly by the time they reached LaGuardia Airfield, since she hadn't detected anyone. It struck her as strange that Athemis would have sent half a dozen operatives and no backup.

Despite Kara's suspicion, they had booked tickets for a same-day zeppelin to Neo Los Angeles and boarded without incident. Maria and Carlos slept on the long flight, but Kara was wired. She'd kept tabs on every passenger she could see, and let her awareness drift over the ones she couldn't. Nothing felt amiss.

Then again, Athemis didn't tend to act in public. They'd tried to kidnap her in broad daylight once, but they had used a device that would allow them to bypass Kara's *ausklammern* field while keeping it active for passers-by. Every other attempt on Kara's life had happened in one of NLA's innumerable alleys.

Regardless, Kara had kept her guard up until she locked the door behind them in Neo Los Angeles. Even then, she'd helped Maria unpack and ordered dinner before she allowed herself to slump onto the couch and close her aching eyes.

"Kara."

She cracked an eye open. "Yeah?"

"I think I need to know what's going on."

Kara held Maria's unswerving, pointed gaze for several heartbeats before she closed her eye again and let out a long sigh. "I know. I agree. Give me…five minutes."

Maria didn't answer, which Kara took as a not-entirely-thrilled agreement. Kara drew three deep breaths, then hauled herself off the couch and stumbled into the apartment's single bedroom.

This had been Jacob's room, once upon a time. Kara had taken down and packed away most of her brother's things by now, but sometimes she still felt his presence here. Whether she was imagining things, she didn't know. If fairy tales were real, maybe ghosts were too.

She didn't have time to think about that today. Instead, she opened the closet, pushed aside her carefully hung collection of court wear—blouses, pantsuits, blazers—and fished a key from her pocket. The key bore the same symbol that was magically tattooed on Kara's arms, the wheel of arrows that signified the True Vehmic Court.

The key slid into its hidden keyhole, and the closet's back panel slid open. Kara stepped through into the apartment's inner sanctum, the hidden room that functioned as an armory and library as well as Grimm's home.

She relocked the panel behind her. Normally, she left it open, but she didn't want to risk Maria walking in before Kara could talk to Grimm. She'd been putting off this conversation for far too long, and now she had no choice but to hope the hidden room was sufficiently soundproof to avoid accidentally breaking her magical oath.

Kara sat across from the polished skull on the table, which was covered in wax from the candle stuck to its crown. She struck a match from the ornate box beside it and lit the wick.

The flame caught, then flared. "Welcome home, Kara."

"Thanks. How much can you sense within the apartment?"

"I know Maria and the baby are here, if that's what you are asking. I thought you planned to bring them back when the child was a few months old."

Kara grimaced. "I did. That got completely upended yesterday. Also, Merry Christmas."

"*Fröhliche Weihnachten* to you as well. What happened?"

"Six Athemis operatives found the safe house in the middle of the night on Christmas Eve. They'd come to kidnap Carlos. I killed five of them, and the wolves got the last one."

Grimm was silent for a full two seconds before he whispered, "*Mein Gott.* How did they find you?"

"I have no idea. As far as I could tell, the wards were still functional. I didn't see any tire tracks leading in. They might have snowshoed in from the forest and camped out for days, for all I know. I did regular perimeter checks while I was there and didn't see anything."

"This is very bad."

"You're telling me." Kara rubbed her eyes. "None of them got close to Maria or Carlos. I didn't say who they were or what they wanted, but… Grimm, I can't keep hiding everything from her. She needs to know."

"I agree."

Kara blinked at the skull. She would have raised an eyebrow, but she was too tired to do anything but stare. "You're not gonna fight me on this? What about the whole 'keep the secrets of the Court on pain of death' thing?"

"Friends of the Court may know of the Court. It is up to the discretion of a Free Judge and their guide to decide who may be inducted as a Friend of the Court. Maria Reyes is the mother of the current heir to your position. If I may use a phrase your brother taught me, she's a shoo-in."

Tension eased from Kara's shoulders as though she'd sat in a hot tub. "I thought I was gonna have to argue myself blue in the face to push this through. Does that mean I can go tell her now?"

"Yes, but begin by telling her of the Court's existence, then inform her that she will need to be sworn to secrecy to know everything. If she agrees, bring her in here, and we'll continue."

Kara wearily nodded. Someday, when she wasn't exhausted, she would overhaul the Court's paradoxical, self-referential by-laws. *You can't tell anyone about the Court, but you can't not tell a Friend of the Court about the Court until you've told them about the Court… God. It gives me a headache.*

She pushed her chair back and stood. "Back in a minute. Or two. Or twelve."

"Good luck."

"Thanks."

Kara emerged into the living room and headed for the kitchen. "You're gonna want a drink for this," she told Maria. "What do you want?"

"Water's fine."

"Coming right up."

A moment later, Kara handed Maria a glass of water and returned to her spot on the couch. Kara drank deeply from the second glass, set it on the coffee table, then squared her shoulders and faced Maria. "Ready?"

Maria rocked Carlos' car seat, which sat on the coffee table. The newborn was snoozing inside it, contentedly curled up in a blue blanket. "Yes."

"Okay. Here goes." Kara drew a deep breath and dove in. "I am a vigilante investigator, judge, and enforcer for a supernatural court that judges criminals who evade the justice system. It's called the Vehmic Court, and it was founded over a thousand years ago. I inherited the position from Jacob, who inherited it from our father, who inherited it from our grandfather. If I don't have a kid before I die, Carlos is next in line."

She paused for breath and to gauge Maria's reaction. The woman had paled, but her expression was still serious, not incredulous or disgusted.

"The people who've been chasing you—and me, and now Carlos—are called Athemis," Kara continued. "They're an offshoot of the Vehmic Court that believes the True Court is too merciful. They believe justice should be swift and without opportunity for repentance. They've been hunting down the Free Judges of the True Court for centuries."

"They killed Jacob," Maria murmured.

Kara nodded. "And they've been doing their best to kill me since I showed up in NLA."

Maria's hand tightened on the edge of Carlos' car seat. "They want to kill Carlos." It wasn't a question.

Kara grimaced. "I don't know that for sure. One of the agents who attacked the cabin had a baby board, which suggests they wanted to *kidnap* Carlos, not kill him."

Maria's upper lip curled. "Over my dead body."

"I believe that *was* the idea." Kara's lips twitched in a wry smile. "I don't know what they want with Carlos. Maybe it's as simple as them wanting to raise him in Athemis' values. Who knows? There's ancient magic at play here. It could be anything."

Maria quietly took Carlos out of the car seat and curled up in the corner of the couch with him on her chest. He woke at the movement, blinked his big, dark eyes a few times, then snuggled into his mother's embrace and relaxed.

"Magic," Maria repeated.

"Magic," Kara confirmed. "Real, honest-to-God magic."

"I wondered how you locked the cabin door when the keys were on the counter."

Kara exhaled with a tiny laugh. "I can also influence people and security cameras to ignore me, and make small sounds happen far away as a distraction. I'm working on creating light next."

"Is that also how you got so good at fighting?"

"Yeah. Magically enhanced reflexes and senses come in very handy when you have to go from being a lawyer to being a superhero overnight. Plus, my skin is tougher, so I'm harder to injure."

"Fewer awkward trips to the emergency room that way."

"And fewer insurance claims."

Maria made a face. "That would be worth the magic alone."

Kara let a moment pass, then put a hand on Maria's knee. "I gotta say, you're taking this well. You don't seem fazed."

Maria half-smiled. Her head was bent, with her gaze settled on Carlos. "I never *really* believed magic was real, but...I suspected, sometimes, as a kid. Suddenly, a lot of things make sense, and not only about the last six months."

"I'm glad to hear that, because now I have to ask you to take an oath of secrecy."

Maria looked up from her baby and raised her eyebrows. "Who on Earth would I tell?"

Kara raised her hands, palms up. "Beats me. I trust you, but the magic binding the Vehmic Court is… Let's call it *strict.* Now that you know, I need to introduce you to Grimm. After you take the oath of secrecy, we can tell you more."

"Who's Grimm?"

Kara stood. "Come with me."

Maria settled Carlos in her arms, rose, and followed Maria into the bedroom. She made a soft sound in the back of her throat as they crossed the threshold, which made Kara wince. *Jacob's old room… Should have thought of that. No time now. I'll apologize later.*

Kara pushed the dress clothes aside again and slid the pocket door into the wall. Maria gasped at the reveal of the secret room packed with weapons and books, but she didn't hesitate to follow Kara in.

Maria's gaze wandered over the shelves and racks. "I had no idea this was here. It was here the whole time, right? You didn't put this in?"

"I did not," Kara confirmed. "Neither did Jacob, but we'll get to that. Maria, this is Grimm. Grimm, meet Maria."

Maria frowned. "There's no one here—"

"Guten Abend, Fräulein Maria."

Maria started so hard that Kara was worried she might drop Carlos, but the new mother's grip on her baby was stronger than anything. She regained her composure in record time, although she *did* lean on the sideboard full of weapons for support.

"Is… Is there a speaker in the skull?" Maria's voice wavered.

Kara laughed. "Props to you, Maria. I didn't even *think* of that one. No, there isn't."

"If by 'speaker' one means 'a person who speaks,' then I must disagree with you, *Fräulein* Kara," Grimm responded. "I am the disembodied spirit of Jakob Wilhelm Grimm, bound to the bone which housed my mind while I lived, and from this vessel I speak still."

Maria shifted her hold on Carlos to support herself with one hand on the wooden cabinet. "*Madre de Dios.* I am talking to a ghost."

"According to certain taxonomies of the spirit and the fey, yes," Grimm agreed. "It is a pleasure to meet you. I have heard much about you, and all of it has been exemplary. I take it, by your presence, that you have consented to becoming a Friend of the Court."

Maria hadn't blinked since Grimm spoke, and even though her countenance sobered, she wasn't about to start now. "If that means I'm pitching in to help Kara any way I can, then yes. She mentioned something about a vow of secrecy. I don't think that'll be a problem. No one would believe me anyway."

Grimm chuckled. "That's correct, although you might be surprised. After all, *you've* taken the revelation of the existence of the supernatural quite well."

"Like I told Kara, I've suspected as much for years. This is a shock, but more a shock of confirmation. My worldview hasn't turned upside down."

"In that case, let us proceed with the oath-taking."

Two hours and two cups of tea later, Maria nursed Carlos in the hidden room's single chair while Kara perched on the side cabinet. When Carlos had finished his snack, Maria put him on her shoulder to burp him, then glanced over the books and documents spread across the table once more.

"Let me make sure I have all of this straight. The Vehmic Court, through magic, determines who is worthy of final judgment based on their deeds and whether they've been evading justice through the regular courts."

"So far, so good," Kara confirmed. "I can also write a name in the *Book of Deeds* and see what it comes up with. If it agrees with me, that name will appear in the *Book of the Guilty.*"

"Which means it's not all-knowing," Maria pointed out. "It also must have criteria to decide who counts. Otherwise, anyone who's stolen a cookie from the cookie jar would end up on the list."

"Historically, petty criminals have not merited the attentions of a Free Judge," Grimm explained. "The True Court focuses on those who do lasting harm to others, and as you said, *actively* evade justice."

"In other words, my name isn't gonna show up for Kara to hunt me down if I steal baby formula, but the executives who jack up the price of that formula so they can have bonuses big enough to buy two yachts a year might find themselves brought to her attention."

"Precisely."

Maria nodded slowly. "But Athemis…they wouldn't do the whole 'six weeks and a day' thing for those executives, right? They'd show up and slit their throats or gun them down."

"Very likely."

"And the reason we don't like that is…"

"It doesn't give them the opportunity to make it right," Kara replied.

Maria raised an eyebrow. "They've had *plenty* of opportunities to make it right. If they were interested in making it right, they wouldn't be where they are now."

"That may be, but it's not a guarantee. Anyone can have an eleventh-hour heel-face turn. Not to get too holiday spirit on us, but that's what *A Christmas Carol* is all about. Some people need more of a kick in the pants to figure out they don't *actually* want to be on the wrong side of history."

"From the sounds of it, though, most of the people who end up in here—" Maria tapped the *Book of the Guilty,* then went back to gently tapping Carlos' back. "Are quite content to stay exactly where they are."

"True. The ratio of executions to surrenders is pretty damn high throughout the Court's history. But we can't assume. That's what makes it fair."

Maria considered this. Carlos let out a milk burp in the middle of her contemplation. She wiped the corner of his mouth with the edge of the blanket over her shoulder, then rearranged the infant so he was resting on her chest. "All right. It's not a perfect system, but it's not a horrible one. It's a *lot* of weight on one person's shoulders, though."

"Tell me about it." Kara scrubbed her hands down her face. "Looking back, I understand why Jacob and my dad were so damn stressed all the time. I thought it was work. I guess I wasn't *wrong,* not entirely."

"As I have told Kara, in the Vehmic Court's prime, more Judges shared the load," Grimm added. "One Judge typically held jurisdiction over a reasonably large geographical area. On occasion, for certain targets, multiple Judges might collaborate."

Maria frowned. "But since Athemis has been hunting down all the other Judges, Kara's responsible for the whole world?"

"In theory, but hardly in practice," Grimm replied. "Kara is primarily responsible for the area in which she lives, just like any other Free Judge would have been. In this case, that is Neo Los Angeles."

"An entire megametropolis all to yourself. Congrats, Kara."

Kara sighed. "Somehow, I suspect Judges from centuries past had a lot more uninhabited land in their area of influence."

"The population density has certainly risen," Grimm agreed. "Also, *Fräulein* Reyes, it is worth noting that the decline in the numbers of Free Judges is not solely thanks to Athemis. The global population continues to rise, and the individual birth rate is low. Lines die out as a matter of course."

"Fair point. I imagine most Judges die in the line of duty, too, and since people have kids much later in life than they did back then…"

"That is an additional factor, yes. I have been gently suggesting that Kara ought to make the acquaintance of at least one gentleman caller."

"Grimm!"

Maria snorted at Kara's incredulous dismay. "Well, Kara, if you don't want it to fall on Carlos' shoulders…"

Kara glared. "I also have to manage to stay alive for at least eighteen years. Given the average lifespan of a Free Judge, that's gonna be quite a feat. It's not like I can keep my head down."

Maria tilted her head. "That's a good point. What would happen if Kara didn't pursue criminals, Grimm?"

"The Court would eventually deem her derelict in her duty. Once upon a time, that would be grounds for dismissal and death, given the importance of maintaining secrecy. Since Kara is the final remaining Free Judge… She would lose her powers until she took up the mantle once more."

Kara added, "And Athemis wouldn't stop hunting me, so it's not like that would be much of a vacation. Trust me. I've thought about it."

But not very hard. Justice has always been my passion.

"Speaking of Athemis…" Kara crossed her arms. "Grimm, we need to find another safe place for Maria and Carlos. If the last one was top-secret, this one needs to be a black site."

"That could be a problem."

"I don't like the sound of that. Why?"

"The Vehmic Court accumulated numerous assets over its existence, mainly thanks to bequests from wealthy or landed patrons, or by seizing its targets' ill-gotten gains. Unfortunately, as Free Judges have died or been killed, many of those assets have been wrapped into their estates and have ultimately been lost to the Court."

Kara narrowed her eyes. "That's not what you told me before."

Grimm sighed. "As I have mentioned, my power and influence grow the longer we work together. I am gradually gaining access to more information. What I told you before was what I knew. Now I know differently."

"So, you're saying we don't have *any* properties? Nowhere we can send Maria and Carlos?"

"Nowhere that would be suitable for a newborn and a nursing mother. Any properties sufficiently remote as to be inaccessible to Athemis would be equally inaccessible for the delivery of goods. Surmounting that obstacle would result in Athemis acquiring a trail to follow."

Kara scowled. "Just like they did with the New York site."

"Precisely."

Silence fell in the small room, broken only by the sleeping baby's soft snuffling. Eventually, Kara knew the quiet would break. Babies never stayed quiet forever. Soon, the whole building would know there was a baby here, and word would spread.

"What about the fey?" Maria asked.

Kara cocked her head. "What?"

"The fey," Maria repeated. "Fairies. Grimm, you talked earlier about how the Vehmic Court gets its magic from the world of fairies. Something about a contract to serve justice in the real world so the fairies wouldn't have to settle things themselves."

"That is correct." Grimm sounded as confused as Kara.

"Why don't you ask if they have a place I can hide? I'd put up with crazy *Alice in Wonderland* stuff for however long I needed to, if it meant Carlos was safe."

Kara turned her gaze to Grimm's skull. She would swear the empty eye sockets were staring back while they both considered this.

"It seems like a good idea to me," Kara slowly mused. "We might have to experiment to make sure staying in fairyland doesn't mess up Carlos' development, but if it doesn't… I can't imagine a safer place for Carlos when it comes to Athemis."

"Faerie is not a safe place," Grimm cautioned. "It has threats beyond your ken."

Maria nodded. "No doubt. Still…"

"Couldn't hurt to ask," Kara concluded. "Grimm?"

The skull was silent for a long moment. At length, it replied, "I will make contact. I make no guarantees, but you are correct that there is no harm in asking."

CHAPTER FIVE

<u>**Wednesday, December 27, 2090**</u>

Most administrative offices of Neo Los Angeles' municipal government closed for regular business between Christmas and New Year's, but business ground on with a skeleton crew nonetheless. There were always those for whom the *de facto* holiday season meant little to nothing, and who would happily ensure the vital work of local government continued during those winter weeks in return for time off of their choosing.

In the last six months, Kara had become intimately familiar with the idiosyncrasies of these offices and their denizens. Some of the names she knew weren't there, off visiting family or taking time to rest, but others waved and smiled as Kara passed through the halls.

"Hey, it's NLA's most vigilant lawyer!" came a deep, hearty voice from down a side corridor.

Kara paused, then hung back until Chidi Jackson caught up with her. The big man had shoulders that could carry the world and a voice that could silence any courtroom. His warm brown eyes matched his skin. He kept his tightly curled hair very short, and its equally rich brown was beginning to be shot through with the same silver that covered his chin and jaw. He wore rimless glasses and a cardigan, and Kara always thought he looked like a strange cross between a linebacker and a librarian.

She'd never met a friendlier man, least of all one who'd been employed in the correctional services. Chidi had worked as a bailiff for many years until he stepped back into a less active position. Now he helped ensure NLA's municipal government ran like a well-oiled machine, circulating between departments as a sort of itinerant admin assistant and security guard.

He had confided in Kara once that he'd started law school. "Could have gone all the way, but I knew I needed to be in the trenches. Needed to be where I could make the most difference."

Kara could empathize with that. Ever since her teenage years, she'd been hell-bent on taking a bite out of the injustice running rampant in the world around her. It took all kinds to make progress in that arena—lawyers, bailiffs, and even vigilantes.

She smiled at Chidi. *If you only knew just how 'vigilant' I was.* "Hey, Chidi. I thought for sure you'd be home this week."

He grinned and clapped her on the shoulder. "My sister and her kids left last night to make it back to Cincinnati in time for her ex's family gathering, so it's just the cats and me. I get plenty of time with them as it is, so I figure there's no reason I can't put in a few hours while the place is quiet. Help folks catch up on their to-do lists, you know."

"That's very kind of you."

"Nothing to it. It's what we do, isn't that right?" Chidi chuckled. "Although I heard from George downstairs that he hasn't seen you for the last couple of days, either. Did you finally take a break?"

"Sort of." Kara motioned down the hall. "I'm headed to get coffee, then to talk to Sumati. Walk with me?"

"Any time."

The tall Black man fell into an easy step beside Kara and stuck his hands in his cardigan pockets. "What's *sort of* mean? Did that taskmaster from NorMetro have you toiling away in the paralegal mines over Christmas?"

Kara laughed. Jack Harper, her boss at Harper & Associates back in the North Texas Metropolitan Area, kept her supplied with as much work as she wanted. He'd funneled every anti-corruption case that came across his desk in her direction, which had gone a long way to bolstering Kara's reputation in NLA's legal community.

"Actually, I became an aunt. I went to help out and visit, and I brought mom and baby home with me. That's why I'm headed to see Sumati."

Chidi's face lit up. "Please pass on congratulations from me! My sister's little ones are in grade school now, but I still remember their baby days. I never could get enough of the way their heads smelled."

Kara chuckled. "I know, right? Although to be honest, given how much bodily fluid we have to clean up on an hourly basis, I think the cuteness is a survival mechanism designed to keep us from giving up."

"You know, my sister said the same thing." Chidi's laugh was a belly laugh by default, deep and booming. Kara always thought he would make a brilliant Santa Claus. "Am I right in thinking these are the same folks you took guardianship of last year?"

The first time Kara had encountered Chidi's uncanny knack for knowing things he shouldn't, she'd politely finished their conversation and hightailed it home to write his name in the *Book of Deeds.* To her immense relief, the Vehmic Court had found nary a hint of malfeasance in the man's past. He was clean as a whistle and wholly trustworthy, two essential qualities for someone with access to so much confidential information.

People talked to Chidi because they trusted him, and Chidi guarded secrets better than Fort Knox. He'd talk to *you* about your secrets, but no one else—no matter where on the grapevine he'd heard the details to begin with.

Knowing this, Chidi's oblique reference to Maria and Carlos didn't give Kara pause. Kara *had* applied for emergency guardianship of Maria last year, even though she hadn't wanted to.

Jacob had done his level best to sever any official ties between himself and Maria, trying to keep her out of Athemis' sights. He either hadn't known about the magical protections afforded to her by her connection to him, or he hadn't realized they would end after his death. To keep those magical wards intact, the Vehmic Court had required Kara to take guardianship of Maria and her then-unborn child, even though this would be a flashing neon sign to anyone keeping tabs on legal filings through less-than-legal channels.

Kara hoped the guardianship would facilitate an application for protective custody. What she *truly* wanted to do was hide Maria in a basement or a panic room until Carlos was old enough to make his own decisions, but Kara couldn't conscience subjecting either to that kind of dreary life. Even changing locations every few months would be better, although in some ways it would be worse.

"That's right," she told Chidi. "I'm still concerned that the people who murdered my brother will come after her and the baby. I need forms from Sumati before I can petition for a protection detail."

Chidi grimaced. It was a harsh sight on his normally sunny face. "Whatever your brother got into, Miss Greims, I can't say I think much of it. I never met him, but I can't imagine his apple fell all too far from yours. Surely, he was on the straight and narrow. Why did someone want to kill him?"

Kara shrugged. *Wish I could tell you.* "My brother was a software engineer. You know how vindictive those techie types can be. He could have turned tail and run for the rest of his life, and they wouldn't have stopped chasing him."

Chidi clicked his tongue. "You have a point there. If there's one thing I know about folks who choose the hard way, it's that they *keep* pickin' the hard way until they're six feet underground."

They entered one of the building's many waiting rooms. It was silent apart from the soft hum of the vending machine against the wall cooling its wares. Kara walked past it to the small sideboard, where a coffee machine waited with its soft blue LED light glowing in the semi-transparent casing.

Kara selected a single-use cup from the basket and popped it into the machine's dispensing station. While she waited for the water to heat, she turned and leaned back on the edge of the sideboard. "You'd know the answer to this question, Chidi."

"Fire away, Miss Greims."

"Call me Kara, seriously." She smiled, then sobered. "How good is the NLAPD's protective detail program? Will my sister-in-law and my nephew be safe?"

Despite Chidi's sunny disposition, the man was far too familiar with the ins and outs of the correctional system not to give someone he respected the honest truth. It was one of the things Kara liked most about him. Chidi gave Kara's question due consideration, then sighed.

"It's good, but it's not the best. Some squads are better than others, just like any other department. The problem with protective details in NLA is that there's just too much going on in most neighborhoods to be thorough. You can have one of the boys in blue staring at a door twenty-four-seven, and things will still slip through the cracks. *People* do.

"I'm not saying *don't* argue for the protective custody. If anyone external can get the ruling, it'll be you. And having six armed guards watching for danger *will* catch a lot of the threats. But they can't be everywhere at once any more than you can. It isn't perfect. Don't rely on it."

Kara pressed the button to dispense her coffee and nodded as it filled the ceramic mug under the spout. "Sounds like they're not quite as vigilant as I am. I'll keep that in mind."

Chidi chuckled. "I don't think anyone could ever be as vigilant as you, Kara. You're a force to be reckoned with, make no mistake about that."

Kara remembered the blood in the snow and the gory sound of the wolves making the evidence disappear, and she repressed a shudder. "Thanks, Chidi. I'll keep that in mind."

Sumati Patel was not one of those who took time off between Christmas and New Year's. Partially because she celebrated other holidays, but mostly because she knew better than most that those times of year were among the most taxing for those most vulnerable members of society.

The coffee-colored, curvy woman sat behind neatly stacked mountains of paperwork and adjusted her glasses. She smiled at Kara when she entered the office, but as always, Sumati's smile was a touch sad. She had seen every type of case in her career with Child Protective Services, and that took a toll on a person.

"I'll certainly do what I can to make sure these papers get in front of the right people," she firmly told Kara. "You might want to go down to your local precinct and see about making personal arrangements for the next few days. I know two judges consented to be on call this week and next, but that means their dockets are packed full."

Kara nodded. "I expected as much. That's where I'm heading after this. I've made friends there as much as I have here, so I'm crossing my fingers I can call in a few favors."

"If anyone can, it'll be you. I read the report on your case just before Christmas. Stunning work."

"Thank you."

The case in question had been one of the anti-corruption files Jack Harper had sent Kara's way. Kara's specialty was corporate law, so it wasn't like her day job left grieving widows with renewed hope because she'd gotten a wrongly accused teenager out of a life sentence. On the other hand, sometimes sticking it to the executive boards who did their damnedest to weasel out of paying benefits or admitting to unlawful terminations felt equally good.

Sumati looked at the small clock on her desk and ran her tongue over her teeth. "If I hurry, I can get these filed before the end of the day. I'd ask if you're sure there was nothing else you wanted to add, but I know how you work." She tapped the manila envelope Kara had handed her with a well-manicured, peach-pink nail. "There'll be enough evidence in there to approve any permit."

Kara shrugged. "Nobody likes to do work twice, least of all me. Besides, when I do my job, it means other people can do *their* job, and that tends to make people like me."

Sumati smiled. "Given that six months ago, nobody here knew you from Eve, and now I can't seem to go a day without hearing about you? I'd say people like you."

Kara wished she could count Athemis among that number, but she supposed it would be too much to ask.

CHAPTER SIX

__Thursday, December 28, 2090__

"Uh-huh. I see. And you're certain that… Yes. Okay. I'm extremely disappointed to hear that, but I won't shoot the messenger. Thank you very much, Officer Green. Let your captain know I'll be in touch after I consult with legal counsel."

Kara waited until she'd ended the call before groaning. She wanted to slap the phone down on the table, but Carlos had *just* gone down for a nap before the call from the NLAPD had come through. Since he'd woken multiple times in the night and Maria was exhausted, Kara was on baby duty for a couple of hours while the tired mother got a bit of shut-eye. The last thing Kara wanted was to have to put the infant back to sleep, or worse yet, wake Maria.

Unfortunately, Maria shifted on the living room couch across from Jacob's dining room table, and her eyes cracked open. "That didn't sound good."

Kara grimaced. "No. Sorry I woke you."

Maria slowly sat up and stretched. A few vertebrae popped loudly enough that Kara could hear them across the room. "It's okay. I wake at the slightest sound these days. My mother says that's normal. I just wish I could fall asleep as easily, too."

"Coffee?"

"Water."

Kara filled a glass and brought it over. "That was the police."

"I figured. What happened?"

Kara handed the glass to Maria, then began to pace. "My application for a protective detail has been denied. I don't understand *why*. I had every box checked, and I included every detail they might need. There's a clear, immediate danger to you and the baby, and it's linked to a case on file. There is *no reason* the NLAPD should have denied the application."

Maria sipped her water. "You haven't been getting much more sleep than I have. Don't take this the wrong way, but are you sure you didn't miss something?"

"Positive. If I had, Sumati would have caught it—or Mindy, at the station. I've worked with both of them before, and even though I have a reputation for solid work, they still do *their* job and double-check. Either would have called me to fix the problem before putting the paperwork through. This shouldn't have happened."

"Okay. What now?"

Kara stopped pacing and took a long look at Maria. "You don't seem as bothered by this as I would have thought."

Maria half-smiled and shrugged. "I'm too sleepy to be upset. It is what it is. We'll figure it out. No sense getting worked up. We just have to take it one step at a time."

Kara heard the wisdom in the tired mother's words and made herself draw a deep breath. "You're right. Either something was wrong with the application, or someone is deliberately denying us protection. That might be malicious, or it might not. It's impossible to know without more information."

"Makes sense. Can you find out who denied the application?"

"Maybe." Kara crossed her arms and drummed her fingers on

her forearm. "On second thought, yes. I should be able to request a copy of the finalized paperwork. If they deny *that*, we have a bigger problem."

Maria yawned. "Then it looks like you're heading to the station."

Kara glanced toward the bedroom door, where Carlos was sleeping. "Are you sure you'll be okay while I'm gone?"

"We'll be fine."

Kara worried the edge of her tongue between her teeth as she waited in the lobby of the nearest NLAPD station to Jacob's apartment. Mid-Wilshire wasn't the seediest district in the city, nor was it the safest, which meant the station was usually busy enough to keep everyone on their feet. The officers and detectives who filtered through the lobby all had bags under their eyes, and every calm answer had a core of held-back impatience.

Kara wasn't worried about the folks who worked in the trenches here. None of them had the clout to deny Kara's application, so it wasn't worth unloading her frustration in their direction. Kara had learned early in life that the best way to get the police to listen to you and help you was to treat them like human beings. It didn't *always* work, but it worked for the officers who wore the uniform out of respect, not a thirst for power.

No, Kara was worried because every minute she left Maria and Carlos unguarded was another minute Athemis could strike. They'd killed Jacob in that very apartment. Maria didn't know that, and Kara had no intention of telling her. Maria hadn't asked about the grisly details of Jacob's death. Kara had no problem keeping them from her until she chose to know, if she ever did.

It didn't help that as far as Kara could tell, Athemis had *built* the hidden room in Jacob's apartment. That could have been a coincidence. Luca and Brendan Mercer had owned multiple apartment buildings before the state confiscated their assets, and Jacob's wasn't the only location where they had added panic rooms or other secret compartments.

Jacob *might* have happened upon the apartment and its hidden room, perfect for storing the skull, weapons, armor, and library he'd inherited from Oskar Greims. Kara didn't think it was very *likely*. Athemis had a nasty habit of popping up where you least wanted them to, and Kara couldn't shake the suspicion that someone farther up the chain had been hunting the Greims family for a long time.

All the more reason I need to find a safer place for Maria and Carlos. Kara tapped her foot and let her gaze flick over the officers working the front desk. *And if you wouldn't mind, I'd like to do so* now, *please.*

"Kara Greims?"

Kara shot out of her seat and headed for the officer on the far left of the desk. He was in his late forties, still fit but showing signs of gray at the temples, with a growing number of crow's-feet at the corners of his sharp blue eyes. His badge read Simmons.

"Officer Simmons," Kara greeted him politely. "Thank you for seeing me."

Simmons' expression of serious courtesy didn't waver, although he did not smile. "Of course, Miss Greims. We're here to help. What can I do for you today?"

"I submitted an application for a protection detail via the municipal offices yesterday. I received notice this morning that it had been denied. I need to provide a copy of the final paperwork to my legal counsel."

The corners of Simmons' lips tightened, and his gaze flicked sideways. Then, the micro expression vanished, and he was back to polite and pleasant. "I'm certain we can handle that for you. If you'll give me a moment?"

He motioned toward the phone at his station, and Kara

nodded. He picked up the receiver, dialed a three-digit extension, and tucked the receiver between his shoulder and head. A moment later, Kara heard a faint voice on the other end of the line.

"Simmons here, sir. I have a Miss Greims asking for a copy of the final paperwork on a protection detail request. I believe that would have gone through your office last."

Simmons paused for several seconds, listening to the other person. Eventually, he nodded, although his mouth tightened again.

That's twice now. Someone doesn't like what he's hearing.

"Yes, sir. I'll let Miss Greims know the copy is on its way. Much appreciated."

Another pause, this one much shorter, then Simmons hung up the phone. "If you'll have a seat, the copy will be down in a few minutes," he told Kara.

"Thank you." She hesitated, then decided she might as well take the shot. "Is it just me, or did something about my request bother you, Officer?"

Simmons' gaze flicked away from her again. It wasn't universally true that this meant lying, but in Kara's experience, it meant the person was uncomfortable.

"For what it's worth, Miss Greims, I'm sorry to hear your request was denied," Simmons finally answered. "We all know how hard you've been working these last few months to help clean up the city. We appreciate that work. Sometimes, lawyers and law enforcement end up at loggerheads. It's been nice to know that someone's committed to doing the right thing."

Kara carefully kept her expression neutral. Simmons wasn't among the officers she had gotten to know personally since she'd arrived in NLA. Nothing grew like a grapevine, but she hadn't realized her reputation was so widespread.

"I'm glad to hear that. Any chance I can ask, off the record, if you know *why* the application was denied?"

Simmons grimaced and looked over Kara's shoulder, then to the right, where the administrative offices were located past a heavy glass door. "Sorry, miss. Beyond my pay grade."

Kara nodded. "Of course. Forget I asked. I'll be over here when the papers come down. Thank you again."

"Any time."

True to his word, Simmons called Kara up again ten minutes later, after another uniformed officer arrived from the offices beyond the door and delivered a manila envelope to him. Simmons passed it to Kara, who flipped the envelope open to check that the paperwork was what she expected. Satisfied, she closed it again and tucked it in her messenger bag.

"Come by again if you need anything," Simmons told her. "And…stay safe."

"Doing my best," she promised. "Have a good day, Officer."

Back in her car, Kara removed the papers from the envelope and flipped through them with a practiced eye. Everything appeared to be in order. Nothing was missing, and nothing had been removed from the application. That was somewhat of a relief. Kara had been concerned that the application might have been tampered with.

The only thing that had changed was the grayscale rubber-stamped DENIED on the final page, next to a signature Kara couldn't quite decipher. Luckily, the signatory's name was printed on the next line over. James Torres.

Kara pursed her lips. The name rang a bell.

She slid the papers back into their envelope and headed home. She could figure out who James Torres was from there and stop worrying about whether Athemis was climbing in the windows while she was away.

Relief washed over Kara as she turned her key in the lock and opened Jacob's apartment door. No signs of damage, no broken door or bloody disaster. Best of all, she'd been able to hear Carlos yelling from halfway up the stairs.

Kara locked the door behind her, set her bag on the dining room table, and located Maria and Carlos in the bedroom. She held out her arms for the squalling infant, and Maria gratefully handed him over for a break.

Unfortunately, the change of scenery didn't placate Carlos.

"He's colicky." Maria made a face.

Kara winced. "Poor little guy. It's okay, buddy. Rumor has it Auntie Kara has some gripe water somewhere, because she heard this might be an issue."

Half an hour and two spluttering attempts at medicating later, Carlos finally quieted down and settled on Maria's shoulder. Both women sank onto the couch with heavy exhales and rested for a moment before doing anything else.

"What did you find out?" Maria asked.

Kara started. "A name! I got a name. I was so relieved to hear Carlos crying when I got home that it went clear out of my head. Hang on."

Maria chuckled while Kara went to fetch the envelope from her bag. "You were *relieved* to hear him crying? Tell me your secrets."

Kara smiled wryly as she retook her seat on the couch. "If he's crying, and I *don't* hear a struggle, it means you're both here and okay. Unhappy, maybe, but you're not being attacked by Athemis…or worse."

Maria acknowledged this with a slight nod. "Fair point. So, you got a name. Who is it?"

"James Torres." Kara pulled out the stamped photocopy of the application and set it on the coffee table, then located her cell phone. "I've heard his name before, but I don't remember where. I'll look it up now."

A moment later, Kara pursed her lips as she read the screen. "He's one of the NLAPD's commissioners, based in Internal Affairs. I'm not sure why he'd be signing off on protection detail requests."

"Maybe he's filling in for someone on leave," Maria suggested.

"Stranger things have happened, but Internal Affairs employees are somewhat legendary for their avoidance of anything that doesn't fall within their departmental purview. It makes a certain amount of sense, given their mandate."

"Fair enough. Can you find anything out about him? Online presence, newspaper articles?"

"Already looking." Kara ran her tongue over her teeth as she scanned the search results. "He's not much of a public face. Takes his job seriously. He spoke to state committees a couple of times about cleaning out corrupt cops a few years back, but otherwise, he keeps a low profile. But I *swear* I've heard his name before..."

A thought struck Kara, and her frown deepened. "Hang on. I'll be right back."

She left her phone on the coffee table, on top of the denied application, and went to the hidden room beyond her bedroom closet. She didn't light Grimm's candle. If her hunch was correct, she would need to talk to him right away, but she didn't need him awake to check that hunch in the first place.

Kara opened the *Book of Deeds* and picked up the pen she kept beside the matchbox. In her neat, tidy cursive, she wrote *James Torres* on the next blank space.

The ink faded, then disappeared. Kara held her breath while she waited for the book to work its magic. Her usual discomfited suspicions about how the Vehmic Court obtained the evidence it documented in the *Book of Deeds* resurfaced. She gently pushed them aside, focusing on her breath to keep her patient.

After sixty seconds, lines of writing began to appear on the otherwise blank page. The first line was the name *James Torres*, now written in Gothic script rather than Kara's handwriting.

Underneath, a litany of misdeeds faded into existence. They dated back nearly forty years, and covered his career as a beat cop, sergeant, and training officer, and continued into his career with the Internal Affairs department.

Kara's shoulders sagged as she scanned the information. "So much for speaking out against corrupt cops," she muttered. "You were blowing so much smoke you could have floated a zeppelin. Not that zeppelins run on smoke…"

The entry in the *Book of Deeds* ended with an injunction to the reader that James Torres could also be found in the *Book of the Guilty*. Kara flipped that book open too, and found the commissioner among the lengthy list of names that had appeared after Kara's successful judgment of Willie Marrow.

That's where I saw it before. You were already on the Big List.

Anger sparked in Kara's chest, and she clenched her jaw. "You're a son of a bitch," she told the magically illustrated image of James Torres. "Was it not enough for you to build a career out of making the lives of hundreds—probably *thousands*—of people miserable? You had to come after a newborn baby, too?"

"What's this, now?"

Grimm's voice emanating from atop the racks of armor suits startled Kara. She looked up and met the reflective gaze of Grimm-the-cat, who stretched leisurely on the high shelf before jumping down to the table.

Kara glared at him. "Was the cat there before, or did you manifest?" She'd been trying to figure out where the cat came from for months, with no luck.

"That is hardly important right now," Grimm admonished her. "You have the *Book of Deeds* and the *Book of the Guilty* out, and you're angry. This is exactly the job I opted *not* to shuffle off this mortal coil for. What's happening?"

Kara firmly tapped the books in question. "This exact man denied my application for a protective detail for the apartment."

Grimm-the-cat wound around Kara's arms, sinuously stepping between the tomes and peering at the pages. "James Torres. He was on the list of Athemis sympathizers and operatives provided to you by the Court after the death of William Marrow."

"That's right. He's a dirty police commissioner. I recognized the name on the paperwork, but couldn't remember the details, so I asked the book. His rap sheet's longer than all the charges he's either increased or let slide, put together. His career is a disaster area of corruption, and he works in *Internal Affairs*."

"He enables others' misdeeds," Grimm concluded.

"Bingo. And apparently, he's decided Maria and Carlos don't deserve protection."

Grimm sat and licked his paw. "From the sounds of it, you might not *want* protection from anyone he'd send."

"He shouldn't be in charge of picking the officers who'd be sent," Kara argued. "This is an overreach of authority. Based on the reaction of the officer I spoke to less than an hour ago, the rank-and-file who *aren't* rotten know the score, and they're no happier about it than I am."

"But no one's done anything to unseat him?"

Kara leaned back in the chair and blew out a long breath. "From the looks of it, James Torres has been honing the art of corruption for longer than I've been alive. He probably has a power base more solid than the Rockies and a better network than the subway system. He'll have fingers in every pie, and he'll hold strings you won't even know exist until he pulls them and unravels the rug under your feet. He's the kind of guy who is just about *impossible* to root out without taking down an entire organization. He's a fungus."

"And you believe he has you in his sights."

Kara grimaced. "How could I think otherwise? My name is on that application as Maria's *and* Carlos' legal guardian, thanks to the Vehmic Court's requirements. I've also been making a name for myself as a lawyer provisionally friendly to the NLAPD with a serious bent for anti-corruption cases.

"Meanwhile, someone the Court *knows* to be either an Athemis sympathizer, supporter, or operative has been listening to all that scuttlebutt. I'd bet you a hundred dollars that he had someone keeping an eye out for anything relating to Maria. He shouldn't be the one to approve or deny this request—it has nothing to do with NLAPD Internal Affairs—but it's his name on the paper. I can't take that any way *but* a threat."

"So, you're considering serving judgment," Grimm stated.

"I am," Kara confirmed.

"Personal vendettas don't justify a terminal judgment," Grimm reminded her. "You can't prove he's discriminating against you because he knows you're a Free Judge, or because you're Jacob's sister, or any other reason. This *could* be a coincidence."

Kara sighed. "I know. Right now, I have nothing but a suspicion that's not the case. Granted, there's more than enough evidence here to merit serving judgment *anyway*. He *was* on the list already. Does it matter, in that case, if I have personal reasons for wanting him out of the picture?"

"Absolutely." Grimm-the-cat ceased grooming himself and fixed Kara with his gaze. "Your task as a Free Judge is to ensure that *justice* is served, not revenge. Your personal feelings or struggles cannot come into play. If you cannot render judgment unto James Torres without remaining impartial, then he is not the target you should select on this day."

Kara held the cat's gaze for several seconds, then broke it to look at the books again. "I'm scared, Grimm."

"I have known few Judges who were not. Those who feel no fear are unlikely to feel compassion, and compassion is vital to the careful judgments required by the Court. What frightens you?"

Kara gestured at the books, then at the wall. Beyond that wall was the living room, where Maria sat with Carlos. "It was different when I was only responsible for Maria. She's a grown woman. She understands what's happening, especially now, and she can take care of herself. But Carlos…

"I am responsible for a life which is barely three days old. In those three days, his life has already been threatened once. Maria hasn't even healed fully and I'm having to consider asking them to go on the run. And this man—*this man*—" Kara slapped the open book. "Is actively endangering their lives for no other reason than a difference of belief."

"Such conflicts have arisen through the entirety of human existence."

"That doesn't make this one any more *right*."

Grimm-the-cat cocked his head, regarded Kara for a moment, then stood and stretched. "You are correct. This is not a personal vendetta. This is another entry in James Torres' long list of cruelties and crimes. Are you ready to render judgment unto him?"

"I am."

As Kara replied, the wick on Grimm's candle flared alight, and the marks on Kara's arms seared with invisible fire. The cat leapt off the table, slipped between the boots carefully paired on the floor, and disappeared.

"Then you have work to do," Grimm told her from the skull.

CHAPTER SEVEN

<u>**Tuesday, January 2, 2091**</u>

Kara rubbed her eyes, then covered her face with her hands. She propped her elbows on the table and sighed deeply.

"You know, I hear sleep is good for you."

Grimm's voice coming from the skull was quiet. Not because it was three in the morning, but because it was three in the morning and the baby was asleep. Everyone living in the small, one-bedroom apartment had become accustomed to keeping their voice down any time Carlos slept. He was more colicky by the day, and neither Maria nor Kara was sleeping well as a result.

"I know," Kara murmured. "I know. I'd love to pass out on the couch. I am *so close* to having the first notices ready, and this is the longest stretch of uninterrupted time I've had in two days."

"You could take a break. Free Judges aren't required to pursue a judgment at all times."

"How long would I have before I started losing my powers?"

"A few months, most likely."

Kara gave this serious consideration. Then she peeked between her fingers with bloodshot eyes and caught a glimpse of the papers she was leaning on. James Torres' face smirked up at her, smug in his presumed inviolability.

Kara grumbled. "I can't take a break. Not now. I have to get Maria and Carlos somewhere safe, and the easiest way I can figure to do that is to get this guy off our tail."

"It might mean a much harder six weeks," Grimm warned her. "He strikes me as the vindictive type."

"No doubt about that." Kara grimaced and flicked through a few papers that detailed Torres' involvement in witness intimidation cases and several disappeared whistleblowers. "However, six really bad weeks with a light at the end of the tunnel is better than an indefinite period of indeterminate security. That's more stressful in the long run. I'd rather Carlos not have to grow up in a bubble."

"Understandable. But, Kara…"

"Yeah?"

The candle flame atop Grimm's skull flickered. "I worry about you."

Kara arched an eyebrow. "Really? That's new."

"It most certainly is not. Your well-being is of paramount importance to me. Without you, I would lose awareness and return to dormancy."

Kara yawned. "Sounds nice."

"I *also* have a vested interest in the continued existence and functioning of the Vehmic Court," Grimm added, somewhat testily. "Need I remind you that you are the last remaining Free Judge? If you are killed, the Vehmic Court dies as well. You are all that stands between this world and lasting darkness."

Kara's heart sank, and her eyes threatened to close even as she did her best to muster up a glare. "Gee, thanks. No pressure."

"It is only the truth. You need sleep. You cannot function at your best on cat naps and caffeine. It puts you, and those for whom you are responsible, at risk."

"Yeah. Yeah, you're right. I gotta get this done—*then* I'll sleep."

Grimm did not respond. Kara squeezed her eyes shut, then forced them open and tried to focus on the pages spread before her. The text wobbled and ran together, and her head dipped of its own accord.

"Goddammit," she whispered. "*Fine.* I'll sleep."

She tiptoed from the hidden room to the living room, where she endeavored to flop onto the couch as quietly as possible. She was asleep before her head hit the cushion.

Anemic sunlight, filtered through thin clouds and NLA's air pollution, woke Kara several hours later. She blinked blearily, dislodging crusty bits from her eyelashes, and stretched. The couch springs creaked as much as her joints. She felt like she'd aged two decades in a week.

She gulped down a bowl of cereal while the coffeemaker hissed and sputtered. Then, cup in hand, she snuck past Maria and Carlos in the bedroom back into the closet. Mama and baby remained asleep, although Kara wasn't so naïve as to think they hadn't been up at least once in the time Kara had been passed out.

Kara didn't light Grimm's candle. She needed to focus. The sooner she delivered these notices, the sooner Maria and Carlos would be one step closer to safety.

An hour later, Kara put the final touches on her documents as she heard Carlos waking in the room behind her. Maria woke with him, shifting in the bed covers and greeting the little boy in murmured Spanish.

Kara sorted and gathered the papers covering the table, then turned off the lights and slipped back into the bedroom with the folders tucked under her arm.

"Good morning," she whispered. "Want coffee?"

"Yes, please," Maria whispered. Her eyes were still closed.

"I'll bring it in a minute."

"Thank you."

When Kara returned with two fresh cups, Maria had sat up in bed and had Carlos in one arm, nursing. She accepted the mug, gratefully sipped it, then set it on the bedside table and relaxed against the headboard.

Maria nodded toward the closet. "You were up late."

"Yeah. Getting ready to serve notice to James Torres. I'll be headed to do just that after I have a quick shower. How are you? Get much sleep?"

Maria shrugged. "I'm getting better at passing out whenever he does. Still feeling like I've been run over by a train, but maybe only by the locomotive and a few cars instead of the entire string. I am *hungry*, too."

"That's a good sign. I can pick something up while I'm out, if you're craving anything specific. My cupboards are pretty bare."

Maria smiled. "That's right. Jacob always said you couldn't cook. I honestly thought he was exaggerating, but I went hunting yesterday while you were working and..."

Kara scratched her nape awkwardly. "It wasn't an exaggeration. Well, no, that's not *quite* true. I can make a few things without burning the house down. I've just gotten very used to not having *time* to cook, so I eat a *ton* of takeout. Law school, then law practice, don't give you much spare time—but they do give you enough disposable income to make up for it."

"Fair enough." Maria chuckled a touch wistfully. "I wish my mom were here. I'm pretty good in the kitchen, but she's *incredible*."

She looked down at Carlos, who had decided he was finished with his breakfast and was now contentedly snuggling against Maria's chest. "She's also fantastic with babies. She was never formally trained, but she assisted with many home births. When she found out I would be her only child, I think she decided to adopt every baby in the neighborhood to make up for it."

Kara tilted her head and sucked her lower lip between her teeth. "How is she with secrets?"

"She's an iron trap, actually, but why?" Maria's brows drew together in a confused frown, then shot up when she realized Kara's implication. "Oh! Do you think we could—"

"I think it's worth asking. We need help. These aren't normal post-natal circumstances."

"Amen to that." Maria thought about the possibility for several more seconds, then nodded. "Let's call her. Ever since Papa died, she's been busier than a whole hive of bees, but she'd do anything for me. It's been killing me not to see her these past few months, and I know it killed her not to be there for Carlos' birth. She's been worried about us since Jacob died. Before that, even."

Maria suddenly chuckled. "Get ready for a *chancleta* to the side of the head, just to warn you. There's gonna be a tidal wave of Latina exasperation coming your way."

Kara snickered. "Any would-be kidnappers won't stand a chance."

"Damn straight."

Maria called her mother Ana while Kara was in the shower. Ana was only too thrilled to come and help out for as long as they needed. She would arrive later that day after driving in from farther up the coast. She also promised to bring groceries.

While they awaited Ana's arrival, Kara dressed and headed out to serve the first of three notices to James Torres. These formal notices of impending judgment were the backbone of the Vehmic Court's traditions. Each notice warned the recipient that they had been found guilty of injustices "according to ancient law" and would be judged accordingly if they refused to surrender to the proper authorities.

The Vehmic Court required that each of these notices be delivered in a manner that ensured receipt and understanding. Dropping a letter in the mail wasn't sufficient since it could be lost. The Court didn't require multiple copies of each notice, but Kara had taken to delivering each one in triplicate as an extra level of insurance. Therefore, she delivered the first notice by certified mail, by publication in a paper her target was known to read, and by a single hand-delivered copy.

Kara sent the certified mail and confirmed that the copy she'd sent to the paper had been correctly published. On the way to Torres' office, she considered the temptation to skip the hand-delivered copy this time around. She already felt as though James Torres was on to her, and she didn't like the idea of putting herself within his sphere of influence.

On the flip side, her hunch that he already suspected her of being connected to the Vehmic Court meant that remaining anonymous to him no longer carried quite as much weight. If he already knew who she was, he couldn't know *more* who she was.

Plus, it sounds like my name's gone around the NLAPD water cooler gossip line a few times already. And James Torres didn't get where he is by being reckless.

It struck her as she pulled into a parking spot outside the gleaming skyscraper of NLAPD headquarters that James Torres showed remarkable restraint in his illegal actions. His attacks were surgical, precise and devastating blows without great amounts of collateral damage. He was a smart man.

He probably relies on blackmail and intimidation more than violence, which makes sense. The longer your trail of bodies, the harder they are to sweep under the rug. On the other hand, the longer your list of contacts, the easier it is to make shit happen the way you like it.

Kara brushed her hair over her shoulder and adjusted the strap on her messenger bag. This wasn't the first time she'd been to NLAPD headquarters. She hadn't spent as much time here as she had in precinct offices, but she'd dropped off a few evidence packets.

The NLAPD headquarters was a high-ceilinged, glass-and-steel affair that made Kara think of towering office buildings in New York. The front desk sat midway in the spacious, planter-strewn lobby. The woman behind it was perfectly manicured and did not look like a police officer despite the uniform.

Kara smiled politely as she approached the desk. "Good morning."

"Good morning!" The receptionist had a chirpy soprano voice that made Kara want to pull out her own teeth. She wasn't wearing a nametag. "How can I help you, miss?"

Kara pulled the envelope out of her messenger bag. "I have a delivery for Commissioner Torres. Which floor is his office on?"

The receptionist offered to take the envelope. Her pearly nails, each easily as long as her first knuckle, gleamed. "Oh, hon, I can take that. I can send it right up to him."

Kara didn't budge. "I appreciate it, but these are legal papers. Gotta be face-to-face, you know how it goes."

Something harder glinted in the receptionist's eyes, but she didn't argue. "All right, miss, if you insist. Mister Torres is up on the twenty-seventh floor. Shall I call ahead for you?"

Kara gave her an ingratiating smile. "No, no, that's fine. I won't take more than a minute. No need to interrupt him twice. Thank you so much for your help."

"Any time, darling." The smile she returned to Kara could have skinned a cat.

Kara skirted the unpleasant woman's desk and headed for the bank of elevators. While she wasn't familiar with the staff at NLAPD headquarters, she *had* encountered that particular receptionist before. Kara's impression of her had been somewhat shallow. She'd never received that level of silent vitriol from the woman.

You don't have to know about Athemis to support someone's dirty work, Kara mused while stepping into one of the elevator cars. *Anyone can choose injustice. I wonder how many other people on the NLAPD payroll either agree with Torres' views or support him out of fear.*

Kara hid a sigh from the other occupants of the elevator car, one of whom was in uniform and one of whom wore a navy suit. If all she'd had to do over the last few days had been drafting the formal notice of judgment, she would have slept much better. Unfortunately for Kara's circadian rhythm, she never did anything by halves.

Waiting in her car, in a box labeled with a different case name, was a file folder. In that file folder sat hundreds of copies of records, all publicly available, that pointed incontrovertibly to James Torres as the spider at the center of a web of corruption.

Kara had five separate copies of everything in that folder. She had deposited one in her secure vault downtown before coming here. The other three were at home in the hidden room, waiting for their moment.

James Torres wouldn't go down without a fight. Kara had little doubt that when he realized his options for avoiding death were to come fully clean and face the music, he would do everything in his power to declaw Kara's threats. The people he could blackmail wouldn't be limited to law enforcement. There would be lawyers, prosecutors, judges, even members of the media.

If Kara picked the wrong target for the evidence bomb, it would be swept under the rug like everything else. If that happened, even if Torres was dead, the network of willingly corrupt officials and authorities would continue unchecked. It might flounder for a time without its king, but someone would pick up where Torres had left off.

While Kara wanted Torres out of the picture for her safety and that of Maria and Carlos, the fact remained that the man's reach and power threatened a great many more. Kara's mandate was to pursue and serve justice. Picking off one man when she had the opportunity to uncover decades of rot would be selfish.

Kara would give Torres the option of turning himself in first. If he did so, Kara would quietly funnel documents to the prosecutors in charge. *Hoping they aren't his cronies, of course.*

That point was a flaw in her plan, and she knew it, but she didn't think it would come to pass. James Torres had been running his network of not-quite-crime for a very long time. She couldn't discount his intelligence and savvy, but she could almost certainly rely on his being an arrogant asshole. The chances of his surrendering were minuscule. He would sooner live in a cardboard box.

In that case, Kara would drop off one hard copy of the evidence packet at the offices of Nestor Palmer Law, a local firm specializing in police brutality and government overreach cases. Kara had already had some dealings with them recently, in conjunction with her anti-corruption work through Jack Harper. She'd met Sarra Palmer, one of the senior partners, and been impressed with her no-nonsense approach. Kara wouldn't have been surprised to find out that James Torres was already on Palmer's radar, albeit on the down low.

Kara's silent reiteration of her plan was interrupted by the *ding* of the elevator doors opening on the twenty-seventh floor. She exited the car without acknowledging the suited man still headed up. The uniformed officer had gotten out ten floors down.

Office buildings all shared certain similarities unless you counted the open-concept, playground-like campuses of the technology start-ups Jacob had occasionally worked for. Most office buildings were quiet, orderly, and decorated in varying neutral tones broken by artfully placed plants. Whether the plants were plastic depended on how much the company cared.

The NLAPD had bigger things to worry about than watering

the plants. The fronds of the ferns scattered among the cubicles and along the walls were glossy, dark green, and entirely fake. The pots didn't even have dirt in them, only coiled raffia.

Kara's arrival did not go unnoticed by those employees closest to the elevators, but it caused no alarm. The handful of workers who bothered to raise their heads from their desks looked her over briefly, noted the messenger bag under her arm, and returned to their work. Kara had opted for a crisp pantsuit in an unassuming hue, hoping to blend into her surroundings. It seemed to be working, but she added a layer of *ausklammern* just in case.

Kara located James Torres' office in the back corner of the floor, down two corridors. A door led to a smaller antechamber set up like a waiting room, where Torres' secretary sat at a tidy desk and tapped away on a keyboard.

The middle-aged woman wore her hair in an austere bun, and her glasses sat on the end of her nose. Her blouse and slacks were immaculate and modern, but the rings that choked her fingers were vintage gold with large gems and settings. She didn't wear a nametag, but the plaque on her desk read Cheryl Hammond.

Cheryl glanced over her glasses at Kara. "Commissioner Torres has no appointments for another hour. May I ask what this is about?"

The secretary had evidently honed her intimidation tactics, but Kara wasn't falling for them. Kara met Cheryl's gaze evenly, betraying no hint of nerves. "I'm here to deliver a legal notice to Commissioner Torres."

Cheryl didn't blink. "I assume that since you didn't give it to the front desk downstairs, you're required by law to hand it to him directly."

"That's correct."

"Very well." She reached for an intercom button on her desk. "I can't promise he'll see you immediately. You might have to wait."

"That's fine." Kara hoped Torres would want to get the nuisance over with rather than make her wait. She wanted to pick up Ana and get on with her day, and truth be told, the unfriendly vibe at NLAPD headquarters was grating on her.

Cheryl pressed the intercom button, released it, and waited. Only a moment passed before Torres' voice emanated from the speaker beside it.

"Yes, Cheryl?"

"Legal notice for you, sir."

No further reply came from the intercom. Instead, the door to the inner office opened, revealing Commissioner James Torres looking extraordinarily bored.

James Torres was attractive, if silver foxes just past the peak of their prime were your thing. He was on the shorter side, with a strong, clean-shaven jawline. He kept his thick, silver-streaked hair short, and Kara could smell the gel and aftershave from across the room. He wore pressed dark brown slacks and a white polo shirt, and a tan that said he hadn't gotten it from a booth in a strip mall. A glint of gold peeked out of his collar.

He looked effortlessly suave and utterly unremarkable. He could have been from any city in any state, and he would fit in at any country club. He would pay with a black card and wouldn't consider it showing off.

He spotted Kara and smiled. It was an easy smile, one that welcomed you at the door and told you Torres was trustworthy— but it didn't reach his eyes, which were chips of brown ice. "You must be the messenger."

He didn't hold out a hand for the envelope, but he didn't move from the door. Kara debated standing her ground to see if she could get him to come to her, but decided that was a tactic for another day. She wasn't here to antagonize him, only to give him the notice.

She crossed the office and offered him the envelope. "That's me. Here you are, Commissioner."

Torres took it but didn't open it or put it under his arm. "Thank you, miss. You have a good day."

Kara nodded. "Much appreciated."

She turned and left.

Six weeks and a day, Mr. Torres. Justice has come to call.

CHAPTER EIGHT

<u>**Tuesday, January 2, 2091**</u>

Ana Reyes swept Kara into a full-body bear hug the moment Kara walked through the apartment door, despite being a head shorter. The stout, solid woman reminded Kara of a boulder, except much squishier and better at hugging. "Ah, Kara, *¡qué bueno verte!* Sometimes I wish I did not spend so much time south of the border. I miss so much!"

"But you're doing important work, *Mami*," Maria called from the living room. "How many times do we have to have this conversation?"

"It will never stop as long as I live," Ana promised, and winked at Kara. "Come, come. I am just making lunch. You two must be *starving*."

Kara smiled. Ana's positivity and verve were contagious, and it buoyed her spirits in a way she hadn't felt in months.

She closed and locked the door behind her, then finally noticed the redolent aroma of rice, beans, and onions cooking in the small galley kitchen. "Oh, my God, that smells so good."

"Smells like home," Maria agreed. She came around the corner to meet Kara in the tiny entrance hall with Carlos in her arms.

She still looked tired, but much happier than she had when Kara had left. "How did it go?"

Kara hesitated out of habit, then replied without going into detail. "Success, as far as I know. He didn't read the notice in front of me. I didn't expect him to."

Maria nodded. "Then I guess we'll have to see how it pans out."

"Yeah. We might be in for an uncomfortable six weeks if he doesn't back down and let us have the protective detail."

"Or if he assigns crooked cops."

Ana appeared on the threshold of the kitchen. Her eyes narrowed, and she gestured at them with her wooden spoon. "Maria would not tell me what was going on, but I am very familiar with *las cerdas.* I also heard about what happened to poor Jacob. So. No secrets. Spill the beans."

Kara and Maria exchanged long looks. Maria tilted her head toward the wall, behind which lay the hidden room, and raised her eyebrows. Then she flinched as her mother smacked her shoulder lightly with the wooden spoon.

"*¡Ay, Mami!*"

"Do not hide things from your mother! Am I here to help or not?"

Kara interrupted, "You are, but there's a lot of danger involved. I know Maria just wants to protect you—*ow!*"

Kara rubbed her forearm, where Ana had delivered a second smack.

Ana pointed the spoon at Kara's nose and glared. "I am no stranger to the threats of men. You know the work I do. I help innocents every day, then I come up here, and I wring money out of rich people's pockets to go back down and do the same thing again. I am not scared. I can keep secrets. These are my *daughters* and my *grandson* who are in trouble. *Tell me everything.*"

Kara drew a deep breath, then nodded. "Okay. But you're

gonna have to promise not to, like, run me out of the apartment with a crucifix."

Ana frowned. "*¿Qué?* You're not a *bruja.*" She narrowed her eyes. "Or *are* you?"

"I'm not a witch. At least, I don't *think* I'm a witch. On second thought, under certain definitions, I suppose I *might* be a witch…"

Ana threw up her hands and rolled her eyes to the ceiling. "*Dios ayúdame.*"

Forty-five minutes and three scraped-clean plates of beans and rice later, Ana nursed a small cup of coffee while Maria nursed Carlos. The Latina matriarch regarded Kara calmly over the rim of her cup, betraying no sign of emotion.

She'd been that way since Kara began the explanation. Kara *still* didn't know what Ana thought or felt about the situation. She supposed it was a good sign that Ana hadn't thrown her coffee in Kara's face.

"This *Athemis.*" Ana spat the word like a curse. "They killed Jacob."

"Yes."

"They want to take my grandson."

"Yes."

"They want to make powerful people more powerful, and poor people more miserable."

"Basically."

Ana set her cup on the table with a *thunk.* "Take me to this spirit skull. I will take whatever vow is needed. You *gringos,* always thinking you have to do everything yourselves. *Qué mierda.*"

Relief rose in Kara as though she were sinking into a hot tub. As she rose and turned to lead Ana to where Grimm sat, she hid a smile at the thought of the impending meeting.

Then she stopped in her tracks. A white cat stood in the door to the bedroom, its tail flicking calmly as it groomed a paw.

"It wasn't always that way, *Frau* Reyes." Grimm's voice came from the cat as it ceased its ministrations and walked toward them. "Once upon a time, the lineage of Free Judges spread around the world. We have lost much diversity, and we suffer for it."

Ana put her hands on her hips and glared at the cat. "You are the spirit in the skull. Grimm. The fairytale writer."

"Correct."

Kara cautiously took her seat. "I didn't expect you to come out before Ana swore the oath of silence, Grimm."

Grimm hopped up onto the dining room table. "I was listening in. The oath will come in due course. You are one Friend of the Court away from creating a Circle, Kara."

Kara frowned. "I don't remember reading about Circles."

"There has not been a Judge's Circle in over a century," Grimm informed her. "The Vehmic Court began to work in cells of two—guide and Judge—not long after the Wolf Court broke away. It was considered too dangerous to do otherwise. Too many opportunities for knowledge to make its way into the wrong hands.

"But in this, as in so many things, you are reforging old paths. It is no wonder the Court expects so much of you."

Before Kara could reply, Grimm refocused his attention on Ana. "Madam. It is a great pleasure to meet you. The Vehmic Court is grateful for the assistance you are rendering to its esteemed Judge, and you will be granted protection under the same wards as your daughter."

"Daughters," Ana corrected. "Jacob was already my son, so Kara is my daughter. It is of no matter that we do not share blood. That is not our way."

The cat slowly blinked. "Understood. The magic acknowledges this as well. You have a formidable will, *Frau* Reyes."

Ana smirked. "My *abuelita* always swore she had the sight. *Mami* didn't believe her, but I did."

"You never told me that!" Maria challenged.

Ana shrugged. "Never thought it would be important. Now it is."

She sat and picked up her cup of coffee. "So, *señor*. How can I help to keep my daughters safe?"

"Right now, by doing exactly what you're doing. Feed them and make sure they sleep," Grimm replied. "Kara has just served a notice of terminal judgment to a man who wields impressive power in this city, and who is connected to Athemis. I deem it very likely that he will retaliate and try to intimidate us. Therefore, Kara needs to be at her best to fight back.

"The Vehmic Court grants some small magic to the members of a Circle, but not the same gifts as it does to the Free Judge. When you become four, you will each gain abilities that will assist you in protecting one another and protecting Kara in her pursuit of justice. Until then, we are limited to mundane assistance."

"Cedric," Kara suggested. "I can ask Cedric."

"Your coach?" Grimm-the-cat did a lap around the table and sniffed the empty plates. "Perhaps. He is trustworthy?"

"He helped me with the daycare intimidation incident, and defended me on the street against Athemis, and he's never pried for more information. I'd say he's trustworthy." Kara paused. "Is a Circle limited to four people?"

"No, although traditionally they have been limited to six for safety's sake. Did you think of someone else?"

Several names flashed through Kara's mind, each with potential, none standing out as a definite. "Not yet. Just wanted to make sure I knew the rules." She leaned back in her chair and drummed her fingers on the table. "My priority is still ensuring Maria's and Carlos' safety. Until we're no longer living with the

active threat of Athemis dropping on our doorstep, it'll be difficult to focus on anything else.

"The wheels are in motion for James Torres' judgment, so I
can't do much more with that until he makes a move. I think it
would be best for us to continue under the assumption that he
won't cave, and we won't get any extra protection from the city."

"Never trust the police." The steely glint in Ana's eyes spoke of
a conviction born from ample personal experience.

"Then we need to find somewhere else to be," Maria
suggested. "Somewhere to live that isn't attached to the Vehmic
Court *or* Athemis, but close enough so travel won't be noticed."

Kara made a face. "Real estate costs a pretty penny out here.
My job gives me enough disposable income to keep this place
and keep us fed. Factoring in travel and expenses for the actual
job, and you know, being a vigilante… I might be able to put a
down payment on something small with my savings, but then
we'd be locked into a mortgage. Also, I definitely wouldn't have
enough to get us something *safe.*"

Maria added, "I'll be on leave for months yet, so I can
contribute to the day-to-day budget but not much else."

"And I send all my money south," Ana concluded. "I could sell
my house, but that would take time."

"And raise questions," Kara mused. "We have the money Jacob
left you, Maria, but even that wouldn't be enough for what I'm
thinking."

"What *are* you thinking?"

Kara blew out a breath and let her head fall onto the wooden
chair's tall back. "That I basically need to become independently
wealthy to have any chance of making this work. I need a private
estate that's isolated enough from the city to make perimeter
security easy, but still *close* enough to get supplies. I need to be
able to make you completely disappear.

"I've been trying to invest with the funds the Court's received over the years from absorbing certain targets' assets, but it's a slow process. The Vehmic Court has had a long run of Free Judges who've been more concerned with staying hidden than with making money."

"What about Jacob's crypto investments?" Maria suggested.

Kara lifted her head and blinked at Maria. "His what?"

"His crypto wallet," Maria reiterated. "Didn't you get that when he died?"

"I have absolutely no idea what you're talking about. Crypto-*what*? Cryptography? Decoded information? Was he selling secrets?"

"Crypto*currency*," Maria interrupted. "The blockchain. Bitcoin. Have you seriously never heard of it?"

Kara rolled her eyes. "Oh, yeah. Right. Yeah, I've heard of it. Seemed like an excellent way to scam people into leaving money in uninsured, non-federally regulated accounts. I'd forgotten about it, frankly. Kind of assumed the craze had died down."

Maria shrugged. "I wouldn't know. Never followed it myself. But when it was all the rage, Jacob hopped on the bandwagon with some coworkers. He didn't sink a *ton* of cash into it—said it was more of an experiment. It might be worth something now, you never know."

"Worth looking, I suppose," Kara admitted. "So, would there have been a card in his wallet, or what?"

"I think it was a key on his phone or computer."

Kara clicked her tongue. "Great. Excuse me while I attempt to divine my brother's file organization system."

She crossed to the gaming desk, which still occupied a significant part of the living room. Kara had packed away many of the personal touches, but she'd left the hardware. She'd had a sneaking suspicion that at some point in the near future, she would need to learn a lot more about technology. Jacob's rig was powerful enough to make a good starting point.

Kara booted up the computer and waited for the login screen.

Jacob had provided his passwords to Kara in the files she'd inherited after his death, so access was a non-issue. It took some time and a few keyword searches to figure out what she was looking *for*, but Kara eventually located the file where Jacob had stored the information to access his cryptocurrency wallet.

"Moment of truth," she announced to the room.

Maria had been dozing on the couch while Ana walked with Carlos. She sat up and paid attention. "Crossing my fingers."

Kara waited until the screen finished spitting numbers at her. She frowned and refreshed the information. "That can't be right."

"What can't?" Maria asked.

"The numbers. I told it to convert Jacob's balance into dollars, but I must have screwed it up somewhere. The decimal point has to be in the wrong place."

"Why, what does it say?"

The total flashed on the screen again, identical to what it had read before. Kara stared at it, hardly daring to believe her eyes.

"It says we have over seventy-five million dollars."

Maria whooped in excitement and leapt off the couch. Ana yelped, covered Carlos' ears, and admonished her daughter for the sudden noise, but she was smiling.

Maria came over to the desk and put her hands on Kara's shoulders. "Sounds like somebody just became independently wealthy," she teased. "So, big spender, where are we moving to?"

Kara couldn't tear her eyes away from the number on the screen. Her chest felt light, as though she were filling with helium. "That's a really good question. Why don't you start house-hunting?"

"You don't want to look?"

"Oh, I'll help, for sure. I just realized something I need to do."

"What's that?"

"I need to quit my job and sell my condo in NorMetro. And maybe I'll buy a Porsche while I'm at it."

Maria laughed with abandon. "We're gonna be okay!" she cried. "We're gonna be okay—I just *know* it!"

For the first time in many months, Kara believed she was right.

CHAPTER NINE

<u>Friday, January 5, 2091</u>

"You know I hate to see you go, Kara, but I never kidded myself it was anything but a matter of time. Are you sure you won't take a bottle with you?"

"Oh, twist my arm, old man."

Kara shifted the folders in her banker's box to make room for the bottle of whiskey Jack was none-too-subtly nudging into her arms. After he tucked the tall glass bottle filled with pricy dark amber spirits into the abundance of files, he leaned back on his heels and crossed his arms.

"So, you still haven't told me your plans out in NLA. You signing on with a new firm?"

Kara shook her head. "I know how long my non-compete lasts."

Jack clicked his tongue. "Come on, Kara. *You* know we'd waive it…unless you told me you were working for Chapman. Then I'd have to sue you myself."

Kara snorted. "God. I'd help you do it. Hell, I'd file the motion to have myself committed. The day I work for Gordon Chapman is three weeks past my soul's best-before date. That slimeball's worse than rotten seaweed salad."

Jack grimaced. "Very evocative."

"I had sushi last night." Kara grinned. "Anyway—I know you'd waive the non-compete if I asked you to, which is why I'm not asking. I might open my own practice at some point down the line, but I don't have anything lined up at the moment."

Jack's grimace turned into a frown. "Forgive an 'old man' his concerns, but how do you plan to support yourself? Our severance package is nothing to sneeze at, I'll admit, but NLA's almost as pricy as New York, depending on your neighborhood."

"I have enough socked away to keep me solvent for a year," she reassured him. "By then, I hope my sister-in-law will be set up on her own with the baby, and I'll have been able to set Jacob's affairs to rest. Some loose ends are proving...*persistent*."

Jack narrowed his eyes. Kara hadn't shared many details with him about Jacob's death, and he'd responded by not prying. Nevertheless, Kara knew full well that Jack had his finger on the pulse of legal work across the country, and *he* knew her signature better than anyone. He'd never voiced a suspicion that Kara had been the anonymous evidence provider for the massive, far-reaching cases against LBM Holdings and their associated companies. Still, if he wasn't *nurturing* that suspicion, Kara would eat her hat for dinner and her scarf for dessert.

"Grief can't be rushed." His tone was sympathetic, but his eyes were hooded. "I'm glad to hear you can take the time you need. If you're ever back this way and need something to do, my door will always be open."

"Thanks, Jack. I appreciate that. And thank you again for how supportive you've been since Jacob's death. Not many bosses would have given me anywhere near the leeway you have. I wouldn't be where I am without you, and I know it."

Jack winked. "Just means you owe me one."

"Any time."

"When are you headed back west?"

"As soon as I close the deal on the condo and see the moving trucks off. So…should be six hours from now. I'll be in NLA by morning."

"Are you driving?"

"No, taking the red-eye zeppelin. I'll sleep on the way. I sold my car this morning before coming here to finish the paperwork, and my new car will be waiting for me when I land in California."

Jack nodded. "Sounds like you've thought of everything, as usual."

"Any undotted i is a loophole," she recited, to his responding laughter. "I've never forgotten that, not even when I realized you said it to every incoming intern."

"It's an invaluable lesson, and one no lawyer worth their letters can afford to miss." Jack's fatherly smile made his craggy face crinkle. "You learned it well. Whenever you open shop in NLA, let me know, and I'll start sending clients your way."

"You're a gem, you know that? That's incredibly kind of you."

He shrugged. "Every business is about who you know. You know me, and I know you. It just makes sense. Now go on, get out of here before you make me cry."

Kara laughed, then hugged him before hefting the cardboard box and heading out.

She had spent years of her life doing good work in these offices. Now it was time to continue that work in a very different way, with no distractions.

Saturday, January 6, 2091

Kara's eyes cracked open when the overhead fans in the passenger compartment kicked in. That meant the air exchangers had been turned on, and the zeppelin was no longer functioning as a sealed unit. They had arrived over Neo Los Angeles, and if they hadn't docked with the elevator tower yet, they would soon.

Kara stretched, popped a few vertebrae, and yawned. Her watch read 4:42 AM. They had made good time. She hadn't expected to arrive in NLA for another hour. *Must have had a good tailwind.*

She turned her phone back on and waited for the network to connect. A few emails rolled in, but nothing urgent. No messages from Maria or Ana since she'd left. Hopefully that meant they were all sleeping soundly.

Kara waited patiently until her row was signaled to depart the craft. She filed along with the other passengers, rode the elevator down to the ground, and zoned out to the low hum of the baggage carousel in the terminal until she spotted and snagged her suitcase.

She stopped at the rental car kiosk to pick up a day rental. She would drop it off later today, after she picked up her new SUV at the dealership. For now, she wanted to get home to the apartment and grab another hour or two of sleep.

The drive home was uneventful. Like every megametropolis, NLA never slept. Traffic continued through the night, and while the sun had set, the city's lights blazed on. Kara threaded through the teeming maze until she pulled into the small parking lot behind Jacob's apartment building.

Kara locked the car behind her and rolled her suitcase through the chilly mud to the back door. One key let her in, then she did her best to stomp the mud from her boots and kick it off the wheels of her suitcase. Then it was up the stairs to Jacob's apartment. The couch was so close, she could almost feel its scratchy upholstery on her cheek.

She was so tired that for a few seconds, she was confused why the key to the apartment didn't unlock the door.

Then she realized it was already unlocked.

Kara's heart rate rose precipitously. Her eyes snapped open. Her breathing sped up.

They might have accidentally left it unlocked. It was a poor attempt at a comforting lie. Ana triple-checked every lock.

Kara thumbed the catch of her hidden wrist-knife to remind herself it was there. Then she set her suitcase beside the door, put her back to the door, and levered it open.

Silence greeted her, the kind that was left after far too much noise. Something fluttered to the floor, brushed by the slight breeze from the door. Kara whirled around the door and pulled a throwing knife from her boot at the same time, but froze when she saw the sound was only a feather.

Kara's heart sank from her shoes into the floor. The apartment was a disaster zone. Books, pillows, furniture—everything was upended and thrown from one end of the apartment to the other. The feather that had floated to the floor was from a destroyed pillow, the remains of which were spread over the living room floor.

Kara hardly dared to breathe as she crept through the mess. She spied no blood, which was a small mercy. She had worried that if push came to shove, Athemis would consider Ana expendable. Kara also had no illusions that Ana wouldn't have fought back, most likely with a kitchen knife.

The apartment was empty. Ana, Maria, and Carlos were nowhere to be found. Interestingly, their attackers had allowed Carlos to be transported in his car seat, and his diaper bag was also missing. *They* really *want him alive.*

This wasn't the most reassuring thought. Rather, it confirmed one of Kara's suspicions, which was that they wanted Carlos for an *active* reason. It wasn't enough to kill the last line of the Free Judges.

"He's a *baby,*" Kara muttered. "You sons of bitches are the worst this fucking planet has to offer."

She had one place left to check. The hidden room. Ana and Maria wouldn't have been able to access the room while she was gone since Kara kept the key on her at all times. Grimm might have been able to come out in his cat form, but Kara honestly didn't know.

However, Luca and Brendan Mercer had been responsible for the hidden room's construction in the first place. Jacob had installed the Vehmic Court's locking system, but it was feasible that Athemis might have access to a back door.

Kara's heart surged from the story below into her throat when she turned the key in the lock in the back of her closet. What lay beyond? Another disaster? Her armory pillaged and Grimm's skull caved in?

The panel slid aside to reveal the hidden room undamaged. Everything was precisely as Kara had left it, down to the papers she'd left on the table.

Kara swallowed against the tightness in her throat. She had left boxes of documents in the bedroom. They were all deliberately mislabeled, but in her fear for Ana, Maria, and Carlos, she hadn't looked to see if the boxes were still there.

With fingers trembling from adrenaline, Kara fumbled with the matchbox until she retrieved and lit a match, then Grimm's candle. For a couple of seconds, the flame flared much brighter than usual—bright enough that Kara had to shield her eyes.

When the light returned to normal, Grimm spoke. "I could do nothing, Kara. I am sorry."

Kara sank into the chair, put her elbows on the table, and propped her head in her hands, bringing herself eye-to-eye with him. "You're a skull, Grimm. I'd have been surprised if you *could* do anything. I suppose you could have scratched their eyes out as the cat."

"They would have shot me, and destroying that vessel would have alerted them to the existence of this room. If acting could have changed the outcome, I would have taken that risk, but I deemed it more advantageous to survive to tell you what happened."

She nodded wearily. "I hate that you're right, but you're still right. Tell me. When did it happen? How much of a head start do they have?"

"Five hours. I presume they waited until you were in the air."

Kara dropped her face into her hands. "Goddammit. That means someone was watching me that I didn't pick up on, even with the *ausklammern* in effect."

"That is likely. Based on what I sensed and saw in their attack, their technology continues to improve. They incapacitated Ana quickly using a device that stunned her, but they refused to do the same to Maria."

"Because Maria was holding Carlos?"

"I assume so."

"Then all the struggle—that was all Maria."

"Correct. The folk wisdom of not putting oneself between a mother bear and safety for her cub has more truth than most would allow. *Fräulein* Maria fought viciously. If she had obtained anything sharper than the edge of a book, she would have done great damage, but I believe she was attempting to shield the babe as well."

"Probably." Kara sighed. "Did they say anything about where they were going?"

"They were professionals. None of them spoke."

"How many?"

"Four. Two took Ana out while the other two tried to subdue Maria. It was only after one returned to help that they were able to overpower her."

A grim smile twisted Kara's face. "Sounds like Maria's a natural. Maybe I should get her to do a few sessions with Cedric."

"It could not hurt, as you say."

Kara didn't reply. She pressed the heels of her hands into her closed eyes until they hurt, and sparks of color flashed across her vision. "NLA is *huge*, and they have a five-hour head start. God, now I wish I'd installed security cameras *inside* the apartment...

except they were probably all wearing masks, so it wouldn't do any good."

"As I said, they were professionals. All black, and yes, with face masks."

"Did they *have* weapons?"

"Only the stun devices and methods of binding their captives."

"So this was fully intended to be non-lethal. They'll keep Maria so she can nurse Carlos, but Ana *will* end up being expendable unless they plan to use her as a hostage to get me to come out."

Kara groaned again. "I'll have to go. I don't have any other way of tracking them. The police are still a no-go until Commissioner Torres is handled. Hell, it's possible he *sent* them, or knows they were here. I'll be stonewalled, and I don't have *time* to break down walls."

Grimm interrupted her. "There is a way."

She lifted her head enough to meet his empty gaze. "Say more."

His reply was hesitant. "It is magic beyond your current practiced ability. It will be difficult, and it will drain you. When you find them, you might not have the capacity to fight back."

Kara shook her head. "I can handle that. No one in their right mind will want to move a newborn more often than is *absolutely* necessary, so unless I tip my hand, I can scout out the location and come back to spring them."

"I hope you are correct."

"It's our only shot so far. Tell me what to do."

Grimm hadn't been kidding. This newest ability, *absuchen*, required her entire focus. The trail of magic linking her and Carlos felt thinner than a thread, and it didn't conveniently wind through Neo Los Angeles' alleys and streets. Kara had to wend through the labyrinthine cityscape while the tiny anchor pulled her toward her destination.

Kara couldn't spare an iota of energy for any *ausklammern* camouflage or any *ablenken* distractions. The *stählen* ability would kick in automatically if she were attacked, but Kara had her doubts about how effective it would be. Therefore, she crept from one shadow to the next, never daring to set a foot into the light for fear she would be sighted.

According to Grimm, Kara had picked up *absuchen* faster than any Free Judge he'd known. Kara had compared the sensation to finding a needle in a haystack, or a single line of reference in a thick book of case law. In other words, exactly the type of precision work she was good at.

Luckily, this natural talent meant it had only taken her six hours to reliably hold onto the magic trace that linked her to her nephew. *Un*luckily, that meant the kidnappers were the better part of twelve hours ahead by the time Kara hit the streets to hunt them down.

It also meant she was doing this in broad daylight, hardly ideal conditions for remaining as invisible as possible without assistance.

It's gonna be okay. Kara had been repeating the words like a mantra since leaving the apartment. She mostly believed them.

Kara slipped around the corner of a building into a back alley. The early afternoon sun was still high in the sky, although its arc would bring it back to the horizon in only a few hours. Only a few steps ahead, even the alley was lit by daylight.

"I'm either gonna have to take to the rooftops or the sewers," Kara muttered. "Staying on ground level isn't an option, and the rooftops are open to zeppelin surveillance. I guess it's the sewers. Ugh."

The nearest utility hole cover was a scant few yards away. Kara levered it open, grimaced, and lowered herself to the ladder.

"The things you do for family," she murmured as she slid the cover back into place. "God, it reeks down here."

The ladder deposited her on a stonework platform beside the slow current of stinking refuse. She tucked her face into her collar, focused anew on the pull in her gut, and followed it north.

Minutes passed in relative peace and quiet. The noise of the city filtered down through grates, but Kara encountered neither maintenance crews nor anyone else desperate enough to hide in the sewer. Kara would be able to cover a great deal of ground as long as the tunnels allowed her to travel roughly in the direction she wanted.

After an hour of walking, when she thought she'd become entirely inured to the stench, she happened upon a taped-off tunnel mouth. The yellow caution tape was old. One strip had snapped or been cut, and its two halves hung limp against the masonry. The dim lights set into iron grills every thirty yards, powered by offshoots of the conduits that carried electricity to the rest of the city, had been disabled in this tunnel. Only darkness stretched ahead.

Kara's curiosity was piqued. In all likelihood, it would be nothing more than a cave-in or an outdated and decommissioned treatment facility. On the off chance it was something *else*…

It was only too convenient that the tug of her connection to Carlos led in precisely the same direction.

Kara dug in her pocket and came up with a pair of night vision goggles. She'd found these among the many gadgets Jacob had amassed, carefully catalogued in the hidden room with the weapons. She donned and activated the goggles, and the tunnel flickered to green-outlined life. She saw no sign of danger, only an unused tunnel. Kara stepped over the tape and into the darkness.

The tunnel curved fifteen yards ahead, then again another fifteen yards beyond that. Then it dead-ended with no indication of why the tunnel had been closed off.

Kara examined the end of the tunnel. It looked as though there ought to have been a door there, or as though there *had* been a door once, and it had been bricked in. She ran her hands over the stonework, and her hand caught on a loose brick.

She pulled the brick free. A stale breeze blew through the hole.

Kara tugged on the next brick over. It came loose with very little convincing. The mortar crumbled under her fingers. Soon, Kara had cleared a hole large enough for her to crawl through.

The room beyond was sufficiently large that her night vision goggles couldn't pick anything up. Going through the hole would require a leap of faith, but the hook in her stomach told her she was on the right track. Carlos, his mother, and grandmother were somewhere out there, straight ahead.

Kara climbed through the hole in the brickwork and cautiously reached for something to steady herself. She found the floor at the same level as the floor she'd left, and it was dry and cold.

Kara straightened, then decided she could risk turning on a light. Rather than attempting to summon light magically, since she was still focusing on the *absuchen* spell, she pulled out her phone and turned on its flashlight.

"The old subway," she whispered. "It's a way into the old subway."

During the Reconciliation War, Neo Los Angeles' subway system had taken extreme damage. The remaining lines served a much smaller, central part of the city. Only a few branch lines delivered commuters to hubs in the outer neighborhoods, where they would have to take aboveground transport to their end destinations. Most people used the overland monorail built by the Imperial Japanese Navy in the immediate post-war years. Kara preferred to drive.

The subway tunnel was much wider than the sewer and stank

considerably less. The tracks sat empty, curving away into the distance.

Kara felt oddly vindicated. Depending on how many of the old tunnels had been filled in or had caved in, this old network might serve her *very* well for clandestine travel.

"And depending on who else thinks the same as me," she murmured. "I'm sure I'm not the only one who's discovered these still exist."

Still, she wasn't about to look a gift horse in the mouth. She set off in pursuit of her quarry, feeling much more confident than she had on street level. These tunnels were silent. She would hear anyone coming before they heard or saw her, which meant she could make excellent time.

"I'm coming, Maria," Kara whispered. "Hang on."

The sensation of the *absuchen* spell strengthened with every step, until Kara would swear someone had caught her hook, line, and sinker and was reeling her in. By her estimate, she had walked almost twelve miles in the old subway tunnels. She'd eaten a protein bar an hour ago, and her water was over half gone.

The rock over her head blocked cell service, so she couldn't figure out where precisely she was without heading up to the street. If she didn't find Athemis' hidey-hole underground, she would have to. Based on the gentle pull *up*, that eventuality was coming to pass sooner than she'd hoped.

At least it's evening now. And I can probably turn off the absuchen *and investigate likely hiding places on the surface*, she thought as she hunted for a way up.

Kara found an access ladder bolted to a wall. Several of the bolts were rusty, and one rung creaked and snapped under her foot, but Kara made it to the top unscathed. The hatch was locked, but Kara had just enough juice left in the tank to pop the old padlock with an inverted *verschliessen* spell.

She levered the hatch up by an inch, then two, enough to peek above ground level. No one was waiting for her with gunfire or magic, so she gingerly pushed the hatch up and over until she could gently place it on the ground. Its hinges grated once, setting Kara's teeth on edge and making the hair on the back of her neck stand up, but no one came to investigate.

Kara was in the back of a parking lot behind what looked like an abandoned warehouse or factory. The sunset painted the disused buildings, fences, and smokestacks in a dusky purple ill-suited to their industrial harshness.

Nothing moved. It wasn't a windy night, and there hadn't been enough snow to stick in NLA. Winter was dust and chill here. The traffic was far enough away that all Kara could hear was a faint hum that ebbed and flowed. It reminded her of being on the outskirts of the city back in Minnesota.

Kara checked in with the *absuchen* in her gut. Carlos wasn't in the building in front of her, but he was close by. Another abandoned building, Kara figured. Maybe Athemis had used the subway tunnels to move them. She hadn't noticed any footprints in the dirt floor of the tunnel beside the tracks, but they might have used a different line.

Kara shut the hatch behind her, but she wedged a pebble into the frame to keep it from closing all the way. Then she followed the magic into this dead section of the industrial district. Her nephew was nearby. She would find him, case the joint, and come back to get them out.

When Kara turned the corner and saw the single lit window in the huge factory at the end of the road, her gut twinged. The line of magic ran straight to the bright yellow opening and stayed, seeming to pulse with electricity.

Found you.

She allowed the *absuchen* to evanesce. Her eyes felt sandy, as though she'd been working for hours on end without a break. She wanted to sit for five minutes, but the work wasn't done. Instead, she took a swig from the canteen slung under her jacket and slipped down the twilit street.

As she walked, the *absuchen*'s tunnel-vision effects lessened, and the enhanced senses Kara was accustomed to came back into focus. Kara scanned the exterior of the large building and found no bombs or trap triggers. She *did* spy security cameras, but determined they were inert after watching them for several minutes.

Kara snuck up to the wall with the lit window. She carefully picked her way up, using tiny finger- and toeholds in the old brickwork to crawl up like a spider. At length, she gripped the metal windowsill and dragged herself up until she could get her toes into a groove underneath it, far enough up so she could see through.

Kara grimaced at the sight through the dusty glass. *Well, at least they're comfortable.*

CHAPTER TEN

Saturday, January 6, 2091

Kara squinted through the grime covering the window. She made out the outlines of a comfortable couch and armchair, lit by a torch lamp set off to the side. Maria sat on the couch with Carlos in her arms, and Ana paced the length of the rug that lay in front of them.

Thanks to the dirty window, even Kara's enhanced sight couldn't make much out beyond the lamplight. Based on Ana's regular glances to her right, Kara guessed someone was guarding them.

Probably more than one. I don't see anything else keeping them there, though. They're not restrained. This window isn't locked, only rusted shut. Opening it would make a ton of noise.

Kara bit her lip, deep in thought. She had to be missing something. Athemis didn't do anything by halves, and they weren't fools.

No one wants to hurt the baby, and they saw Maria fight like a caged tiger when Carlos was threatened. Maybe they think if they hurt Ana, Maria might hurt Carlos. That's ridiculous, but I'm not sure how savvy Athemis would be about moms and kids.

Ana abruptly turned. She paused, facing Kara.

Kara froze. She couldn't tell if Ana had seen her because the window was too dirty to pick out the details of her facial expression. Kara had chosen a black, hooded suit for the night, ideal for sneaking, and the lighting outside was dim at best. She didn't *think* anyone would be able to see her through the window, but Ana's eyes were keen.

Ana headed for the wall. Kara ducked her head under the sill, chancing the movement, but Ana crossed to the window *beside* Kara's. A godawful screech made Kara flinch.

"Not *trying* to jump out the window, *estúpido.*" Ana's voice came through, clear as day. "*El niño* needs fresh air. Did you idiots even bother to sweep before you dragged us in here? There is so much dust I can hardly breathe."

Kara didn't dare move until she heard Ana's footsteps leave the window. She didn't hear anyone else moving, but she still waited a full minute before gauging whether she could swing to the next window without falling.

She grimaced. It would be a tough jump, but there was nothing in between she could use as a stepping stone.

So much for coming back. I can't lose this opportunity. I only hope I can scrape enough from the bottom of the barrel to make this happen.

Kara closed her eyes and drew several deep breaths in a row. Traveling through the subway had saved her some time and stress, so she wasn't as exhausted as she might have been. Still, if she didn't sleep for a day after this was done, she'd be stunned.

The low hum of a zeppelin grew amid the city's background noise. Kara glanced over her shoulder and saw the craft's lights approaching, high in the sky. *I can use that.*

She waited thirty more seconds, then layered a mild *ausklammern* field over herself. Normally, she would use a much stronger field, but she was counting on the familiar noise of the zeppelin to make up the difference.

Another deep breath. Then she pushed off the wall with her

right foot, leaping to the left and reaching for the next window over with both hands.

Her fingertips caught the sill. One snagged on a sharp piece of metal and sliced through the pad of her glove, nicking her fingertip. She winced but held tight. Her toes found purchase on the wall a moment later, and she exhaled in relief. *Step one, complete.*

Now that she was below the open window, Kara could hear those within breathing and moving thanks to her magically enhanced hearing. Based on the familiar sounds of rustling fabric, Maria had finished nursing Carlos and was burping him. Ana was still pacing. Kara couldn't get a bead on anyone else. She would need a visual, however brief, to get more info.

She pulled herself up until her eyes cleared the sill. The details of the room jumped into sharp focus. Ana, pacing, saw her but didn't react. Maria followed her mother's gaze, and her eyebrows rose a fraction. Ana flicked a glance to her right again, and this time Kara followed it and spotted the single guard in the dim periphery, lurking by a railing that might have been at the top of a staircase.

Kara ducked back under the sill and grimaced. The disused warehouse was spacious. The guard was twenty-five yards away at minimum. She would have to knock him out or kill him silently, but there had to be more guards downstairs. Athemis wouldn't have left their most valuable targets under a single lookout.

A sound below her made Kara look down. Her eyebrows rose sharply as she spotted someone strolling nonchalantly around the perimeter with a cigarette dangling from their lips.

A plan formed in her head. A risky one, but no more ridiculous than trying to singlehandedly break her family out of the warehouse.

Kara let go of the windowsill and dropped like a rock. She landed on the strolling guard's back, slamming him into the ground. His head hit sharply, and his eyes unfocused as he passed out.

Kara stubbed the cigarette in the gravel and hauled the man across the road into the ditch. *Thank God there aren't many streetlights around...or any snow.* From a distance, the faint trail of gravel wouldn't show.

She found a ring of keys on his belt and pocketed them, then stripped off his uniform jacket and hat. They were nondescript black, obviously meant to resemble security guard attire without being overtly branded. She put the hat on, then pulled the jacket over her suit, tucking her hood under the back. It would look strange if you examined the bulge, but Kara hoped no one would have enough time to do so.

Kara layered on the *ausklammern* effect as she continued the guard's perimeter check. She spied security cameras and carefully tilted her head away. She also spotted a black van that was too clean to be anything but the vehicle they had arrived in.

Kara checked the keys she'd nicked and grinned when she found a key that matched the insignia on the hood. *About time I got lucky.*

She walked past the main entrance when she spotted another guard inside the door. On her way by, she flicked a lazy wave in their direction. *Just passing by, checking the outside, ignore me... I should have kept that smoke handy.*

The guard didn't call out or follow her. Kara continued around the building until she found another door. It was locked, but a quick application of *verschliessen* solved that problem. Her head was beginning to hurt from the magical exertion, but she was that much closer to freeing her family.

Inside, the building was dark. Kara melted into the shadows, slipping between abandoned crates and stacks of pallets until she could see the light from the main entrance. She examined her surroundings while hiding behind a forklift covered in a thick layer of dust.

The building's interior was simple. Most of the main floor was cramped with huge shelving units, all of which were bare. The back area, where Kara was now, was filled with the crates and pallets she'd been using to hide. A metal staircase led up to the balcony where Ana, Maria, and Carlos were being held. The guard Kara had noticed before stood at the top of that staircase.

Kara eyed the fire alarm panel on the wall and wondered whether it was still connected. The building had power, but if they checked for a nonexistent fire and turned the alarm off, they would be far more attentive after that. She might have to set a real fire.

Or you could just use ablenken, *you idiot. Then you're not giving Carlos smoke inhalation, either.*

Kara dug deep into her last reserves of energy. As soon as they took the bait, she would have to run for the front doors.

She focused on both guards and on a spot under the balcony. *You hear fire. You smell it. Something's burning, and this place is full of old wood and God knows what else. You have precious hostages. You need to get them out.*

Several seconds passed and nothing happened. Kara was about to give up and find something to *actually* set a fire with, when the upstairs guard leaned over the railing and yelled, "Chris! Did you leave your butt inside, you idiot? What is that smell!"

Panic shot through Kara. Chris was outside in the ditch, no doubt, but if he didn't answer...

The guard at the door left his post and walked out onto the factory floor. "He's on perimeter duty, Jeff, that's not him! Something must have started smoldering when we turned the power back on!"

"Shit," Jeff replied, but he was interrupted by a very angry Latina mother.

"Fire? You have to get us out right now!" Ana admonished

him. "You said your boss needed this baby safe and sound—that means no fire and no smoke! *¡Vamos!*"

"I don't see anything," the downstairs guard called. "It's probably just dust on the heaters or something."

Kara redoubled her efforts on the *ablenken.* She'd never done visual distractions before, but if she could manage to get him to see a single flame, the plan would work.

In the middle of his deflection, the guard on the floor flinched and stepped back. "Flames! I see fire! Jeff, deactivate the shield and get them down here now! I'll get Chris and start the van!"

A shield? Kara grimaced. *Good thing I didn't go charging up there. God knows what that's all about.*

The third guard hightailed it for the main entrance. He and Jeff were making enough noise that Kara chanced running across the factory floor after him. She caught him in a full tackle as they went through the door, and they skidded across the gravel.

The guard yelped with pain as his face scraped over the gravel. "What? Who—"

Kara didn't say anything. She snagged the baton out of his belt and cracked him over the head with it. Then she threw his unconscious body over her shoulder, jogged a few steps to a concrete planter that hadn't seen greenery in a long time, and dumped him onto the bare dirt.

She scrambled to the outside wall beside the entrance with the baton ready to strike. One more to go.

Ana came out of the door first, with Carlos' diaper bag slung over her shoulder. Maria was right behind her, holding Carlos tight. "Your friend must already be in the van," Ana called. "I see exhaust and the lights are on. Hurry!"

Jeff was two steps behind them. His brows drew together in puzzlement as he stepped outside. "What? I don't see any lights—"

Kara swung the baton full force against the side of his head. Jeff crumpled like a ragdoll.

Ana had turned at the sharp sound. She laughed and punched the air. "Well *done, mi hija!* They never saw you coming!"

Maria's face was wet with tears. "Thank God you came. We were so scared."

"Speak for yourself," Ana replied. "These guys are nothing compared to back home. We got off easy."

"Because they didn't want to hurt Carlos," Maria reminded her.

Ana's face darkened. "*Si.*"

Kara finished heaving the unconscious Jeff into the planter beside his colleague, then dusted off her hands. "We gotta go. We're taking their van at least part of the way, because I don't want to take Carlos back the way I came."

Maria made a face. "Based on how you smell, I don't want to go that way, either."

"Yeah, it wasn't fun. Come on, let's go."

They ditched the van at a park-and-ride for the monorail and cruised over the NLA skyline in the last car in the train. Kara slumped back in the seat and tried to keep her eyes open.

"How did they get in?" she asked.

Ana's reply was flat and angry. "With a key."

Kara blinked. "What? But that..." She slowly shook her head. "I had the locks changed when I moved in. They shouldn't have had a key."

Maria sighed. "It's my fault."

"How do you figure that?"

"I was pickpocketed while out grocery shopping. I needed to stretch my legs, so *Mami* stayed with Carlos while I went to the corner store. Some kid bumped into me when I was leaving. He was just a kid on a skateboard, and he apologized until he was blue in the face, so I didn't even think twice. I thought I'd just dropped the key."

Kara groaned. "Goddammit. We can't trust *anyone*. We need a place to stay, and we need it *now*."

"Put it under the name Alvarez," Kara told the clerk. "I'm paying in cash. Do not ask questions if you know what's good for you."

The acne-scarred young man's eyebrows had taken up residence in his hairline two words into Kara's greeting, and they weren't coming down any time soon. "You got it, ma'am. One room, two nights up front, name of Alvarez. Do I need to call the—"

"Absolutely not."

"Yes, ma'am."

Kara snatched the key from his hand and headed down the dingy corridor. The Travel Motel only held its one-star rating by sheer charity. Its walls, ceilings, and carpets bore the stains of decades of nicotine hidden by ample use of industrial deodorizer. The furniture was scuffed and threadbare, and Kara didn't want to look under the mattress in their tiny room.

It was the kind of place where no one asked questions as a matter of course, and Kara knew from her trustworthy friends at the NLAPD that the owners kept their own code of honor. They could be trusted to keep their mouths shut about anyone strange renting a room...*until* someone paid them more, or threatened them.

It wasn't *safe*, but it was a known variable. Kara hadn't stopped the clock, only bought them a day or two.

Not that I want to stay here any longer than that. She grimaced at their surroundings. *I don't want to live here, and I certainly don't want Carlos to live here.*

"I'm ordering food under the alias," she told Ana and Maria.

"Don't open the door for anyone who doesn't have the password, and keep a chair under the knob at all times. Don't open the windows. You don't exist.

"I'm sneaking back to the apartment next. I'll get us all a few things, and I'll talk to Grimm. My hope is that we won't be here more than twenty-four hours. I know *I* don't want to sleep on that bed."

Ana shrugged. "I've slept on worse."

Maria grimaced. "*Ay, Mami.*"

"I'm serious. Bed bugs are survivable. Bullets are not." Ana put her hands on her hips and turned to Kara. "You need to rest, *mija.*"

Kara shook her head. "I can't. Not yet."

"You are going to pass out in the street."

Kara wiggled her phone. "I ordered coffee."

Ana's jaw set in a way that reminded Kara uncomfortably of her own mother, but she said nothing more. Instead, she took Carlos from Maria and began walking with him, singing under her breath in Spanish.

Kara winced. She knew she needed to rest, but she also *desperately* needed to get a step ahead of Athemis. Not to mention she still had a case of terminal judgment ticking along in the background, which she hadn't paid any attention to in the last forty-eight hours. She hadn't even checked the headlines today, much less the legal papers.

She brought her phone out to do that, then sighed. It was Saturday. The legal notices wouldn't publish again until Monday.

God, I'm so tired I don't even know what day it is anymore. Using magic this much without sleeping well is exhausting. At this rate, I might do myself in before Athemis has the chance.

She yawned and sank into the uncomfortable wooden chair in the corner. She had to wait until the food came. She might as well close her eyes until then.

The smell of greasy fries and gas station coffee woke her. Her stomach growled, then her brain caught up, and her eyes snapped open.

"You weren't supposed to open the door!" she protested.

Ana fixed Kara with a glare that could have melted steel. "Do you trust your Circle or not?"

Kara wilted but rallied. "Yes, but Athemis is still out there looking for us! If that hadn't been—"

"If the young woman who delivered this food works for Athemis, we will find out soon. If she does not, they will still find us eventually. There is no point in paranoia, only vigilance. *Ay, niña,* stop borrowing trouble. Have a hamburger and go talk to your skull."

Kara ate the hamburger.

"I like her," Grimm observed. "Perhaps I shall suggest she volunteer to become a guide."

Kara glared at the skull. "I thought you were on my side."

"I am on the *Court's* side," he corrected. "That means I am in favor of whatever means you can do your job. Exhausting yourself means you cannot."

Kara growled under her breath. "*Grimm.* Athemis is onto us."

"I am perfectly aware."

"We need a place to go. We can't keep moving every few days."

"I am also aware of this."

"Then *help me.*"

"I am doing my best," he fired back. "In case you haven't noticed, I am rather limited in my mobility, and my long-distance missives rely on the attention of others to be seen at all. *However,* it just so happens that while you were out, I received a reply to one such missive."

Kara's heart leapt. She grabbed the edge of the table and

eagerly leaned forward. "A good response? Please say it was a good response."

"It is a door ajar," Grimm replied. "Neither good nor bad. A possible opportunity. It will require you to put your absolute best foot forward, make no mistake. There is no margin for error in your first impression here."

The solemn tone of his admonition broke through Kara's haze of fatigue. "Who the hell did you hear back from?"

"The Court of Fog and Grove."

Kara blinked. "I have no idea what that is."

"It is the descended line of the faery court that made the first contract with the Westphalian Vehmic Court nearly a thousand years ago. It holds the contract with the True Vehmic Court today."

Kara's eyebrows gradually rose until she felt her eyelids stretching. "So…they're essentially my boss."

"Correct. Part of the contract is that they do not meddle in the affairs of mortals, just as they ensure that other members of the fae realm do the same. For them to agree to see you at all is an immense gesture of goodwill."

"In other words, do not fuck this up," Kara murmured.

"*Quite so.*"

CHAPTER ELEVEN

<u>Sunday, January 7, 2091</u>

Kara's stomach was a ball of nerves from the moment the zeppelin left the ground at 8:00 PM the next night.

After a fitful several hours of rest at the motel, she'd spent the day inducting Cedric into her Circle, then moving Ana, Maria, and Carlos to his place before passing out for a few hours.

Luckily, Cedric had taken the news of magic being real with only a few minutes of wide-eyed incredulity, and he and Ana were kindred spirits when it came to protecting others. He'd sworn to protect them with his life, and Kara didn't doubt him for a second.

She felt much better about Ana's and Maria's safety with him standing guard, but her nerves had not abated—only shifted. Now she was silently freaking out about meeting her first fairy.

Grimm had directed her to several history books in the Court books on her shelves. Kara had skimmed them over breakfast but hadn't retained much. They now sat on her tray table, waiting for her to pore over them during the long transatlantic flight.

The Court of Fog and Grove was in the Black Forest in

Germany…sort of. Kara would travel to Germany by zeppelin, then rent a car and drive most of the rest of the way.

Eventually, she would have to park the car and walk into the trees until she happened upon a black horse with a white mane. She would have to ride it bareback farther in until she reached the Court grounds.

"How will I know when I've arrived?" she'd asked Grimm. "Is there a port of entry? Customs? Border control?"

"You'll know," he'd told her. This hadn't reassured her.

The second book detailed etiquette in the fairy courts. Normally, Kara could absorb this type of ultra-detailed information in short order, but her mind was still sluggish after the last two weeks' whirlwind.

At this point, all she could do was cross her fingers and hope she had retained enough not to make a fool of herself.

The third book was essentially a travel guide. Kara had scanned this one in the least detail, mainly because she didn't want to spoil the sense of wonder she expected upon her arrival. The etiquette guide said fey creatures tended to appreciate when mortals were awed by their world.

Any advantage Kara could get, she would take.

Kara settled in for the long ride and tried not to think too hard about what awaited her. She couldn't guess, so it was pointless to try. Better to organize her thoughts and be ready to present her case.

The way Grimm had talked, it sounded like Kara would only get one shot at convincing the Court of Fog and Grove to protect Maria and Carlos.

And if I fail, there's nowhere else to turn.

She grimaced and chastised herself. *You'll find something. There's always a way. That's what you told Jenny Rodriguez less than a year ago. Don't make Athemis' job easier.*

A flash of lightning snaked through the clouds beneath the

zeppelin. Kara couldn't hear the thunder, but she would swear she felt it in her chest. She hoped it wasn't a bad omen.

Monday, January 8, 2091

Kara stood with both feet on the asphalt and stared at the thick forest that stretched across her entire field of vision. She had left Baden-Baden half an hour ago, driving the compact European car along the edge of the Schwarzwald until she caught sight of a flash of white in the trees.

When she'd pulled over and gotten out of the car, the black horse had taken a few steps beyond the tree line. It tossed its mane and watched her. Kara got the sense it was much smarter than your average horse.

Her feet didn't want to leave the hard, familiar surface. Part of her wanted to remain on solid, human-made ground. She had no idea what awaited her beyond its edge. Surely, she could manage Athemis on her own. She could protect Maria and Carlos.

Her mother's voice floated through her head. *Don't be proud. Be smart.* The gentle admonition had been a frequent refrain through Kara's high school years, when Kara had been hell-bent on proving herself to no one in particular.

Even though Linda Greims was long gone from the world, her words still rang true. Better to be smart and ask for help than to be proud and dead.

Kara stepped off the road into the grass.

As she approached the horse, it remained still, watching her calmly. Kara also realized that it was much taller than she'd thought. She wasn't certain how she would get on its back without a stirrup to step into.

Luckily, an old, gray stump protruded from the ground beside it. As Kara used the stump to propel her up and onto the horse, she wondered if the horse had known to stand beside it, or if the stump had appeared in response to her need.

"Either way, thanks," she whispered to the horse. "I appreciate not having to make a fool of myself just yet."

The horse nickered faintly, then turned and trotted into the trees.

Kara hunkered down over the horse's neck and tried not to squeeze its sides too hard with her legs. She'd ridden horses before, but not often, and never bareback. If she weren't careful, she'd humiliate herself by falling off before she reached the Court.

Kara's first clue that she was passing from the mundane into the faerie was subtle. She frowned as she realized her surroundings were becoming brighter—not in light, but in hue. It was midday in Germany, so sunlight peeked through the thick canopy, but the greens were gradually shifting to brighter, more vibrant hues.

Next, Kara noticed flora and fauna that didn't look quite right. Flowers with unnatural shades of blue and purple hung from the underside of branches covered in thick, glittering moss. A deer ran past them, and Kara glimpsed a smaller critter riding on its antlers that she would swear was a rodent with two tails.

When the horse came alongside a stream that flashed with light from within, and the tiny pinpricks of light that rose on its mist resolved into butterfly-winged humanoids that glowed like fireflies, Kara knew without a doubt that she was no longer in the human world. The pulsing mushrooms growing on the edge of the stream only confirmed it further, and the nail in the coffin was the tree that waved as they went by.

Kara grinned. She felt like a kid again, except better, because the worlds she'd only ever explored in her imagination now surrounded her. If she dismounted, she could touch the mushrooms. A butterfly fairy considered landing on her outstretched hand, then darted away behind a fern.

The horse followed the stream to a large pool ringed by weeping willows and tall pines. Its surface hid beneath a thick layer of swirling blue-gray mist, but the water at the edge of the pond was clear as crystal, allowing Kara to see the jewel-like rocks at the water's edge. Sparse reeds speared up through the mist. The sunlight had disappeared entirely. While it was day in the mundane world, here it was twilight. The delicate purple sky was speckled with stars Kara did not recognize.

Small creatures skittered and chittered within the trees, darting between and up the trunks and along the limbs. The butterfly fairies swarmed to the long, trailing leaves of the willows, creating stalactites of light that swayed within the moving mists over the pond.

The horse scraped its hoof in the dirt and tossed its head. Kara took the hint, murmured another thanks in its ear, then did her best to dismount gracefully. Her physical training kicked in, and she landed on her feet.

She faced the pool and bowed deeply. She remembered this part of the etiquette guide well because she had repeated it until she'd memorized it word for word.

"I am Kara Greims, daughter of Oskar and Linda, Free Judge of the True Vehmic Court. I seek audience with the most grand Court of Fog and Grove," Kara announced.

She did not move from the bow until she heard water in front of her. Then she slowly straightened, and as she did, she gasped.

A woman had risen from the depths of the pond. She appeared to be made entirely of water apart from her hair, which was made of reeds and fallen willow branches. Her face was smooth as glass, and her hands dripped as she held them out to Kara. Her legs disappeared at the calf into the pool, and as Kara watched, a tiny silver fish darted up her right leg and into her torso.

"Greetings, Kara Greims. The Court of Fog and Grove bids you welcome in the name of our ancient contract." If Kara hadn't been listening for words, she would only have heard a babbling brook. "Hollow Tree will grant you audience. Come forth."

Kara glanced at the water lapping at her feet. "Um…"

The atmosphere in the grove shifted in an instant, as though everyone present was holding their breath.

When you're at someone's house, you follow their rules, Linda Greims whispered in her daughter's ear.

Kara would have to trust that these otherworldly creatures had her best interests at heart.

For the second time that day, Kara stepped forward into the unknown. Her boot broke the water's surface. The colored stones rolled beneath its sole.

Kara took the nymph's proffered hands and inhaled sharply at the shock of cold. This was no Caribbean lagoon, but a glacier-fed lake. The chill spread up the inside of Kara's arms, traced the lines of her Vehmic Court tattoos, then sped into her back and chest and up her throat.

On Kara's next step, the ground dropped out from under her and she plunged into the deep. She gasped again, then reflexively snapped her mouth shut, only to discover that she had no urge to cough or choke on the water filling her lungs.

Beside her swam a woman of uncanny beauty—the nymph in her natural form. Her pale blue skin was flecked with glimmering scales, and her eyes iridesced like opals. She had no nose, but gills fluttered along her neck.

Still holding Kara by the hands, the nymph shot forward, pulling Kara through the water so fast she barely caught a quarter of the wonders in the pond. Arrays of ancient driftwood housed more glowing fairy denizens, and far below them, Kara glimpsed a faint pulsing of something very large and very alive.

A moment later, they broke the surface again. The nymph encircled Kara from behind, drawing her legs up into a lotus position underneath her. Kara crossed her own legs in response, automatically sitting in the nymph's lap. She floated in the center of the pond, effortlessly held up by the nymph. It felt as though Kara was sitting on ice that wasn't cold.

"Thank you," she murmured. She thought she heard a quiet laugh in the nymph's watery bubbles.

In front of her bobbed a log at least the size of a school bus. Unlike most logs that ended up at watery rest, this one floated vertically. Ten feet of it protruded from the water, covered in moss. Kara couldn't tell how far the other end of the log stretched under the surface.

A mushroom perched on a small ledge carved into the log's left side stretched and stood at attention. "His Majesty, the Lord Hollow Tree, Caretaker of the Court of Fog and Grove," it declared in a surprisingly resonant tenor.

Kara blinked, and the mushroom was a mushroom again—but the lines of bark shifted and squirmed until they made the face of an old man with bushy eyebrows of moss and a beard that disappeared into the water.

"The Court of Fog and Grove bids welcome to the Vehmic Court." Hollow Tree's voice was the crack and creak of wind in branches. "To what do we owe this particular and uncommon honor, so many years awaited?"

Direct, but polite, Kara remembered. *Don't hide what you want, but don't demand it.*

"On this day of meeting, recognizing the long bonds of alliance between our courts, the Vehmic Court would beg a boon of the Court of Fog and Grove," she replied.

"A boon?" Hollow Tree repeated, his eyebrows rising in slow surprise. "To hear so little from our ally for so long, only to have them beg our aid at the door—be this not impudence? We freely provide magic beyond mundane ken by the terms of our ancient contract. What more could be needed?"

Kara's stomach flip-flopped. *Too direct. Shit.*

"I beg the Court's patience," she quickly added. "Please, Your Majesty, hear me."

"Oh, let her talk," a new speaker interjected from behind the giant hollow log. The voice was a light alto with an edge, and it sounded closer to human than anything Kara had heard since getting out of her car.

Hollow Tree grumbled with a sound like shaking leaves. "So little respect for our ways, Ivonne. You would do well to hold fast to our traditions."

"Sure, Dad. We'll have this argument for the thousandth time when the human's gone." The source of the voice paddled around from the back of the log, emerging from the mist to reveal a curvy woman with green skin and waist-length wavy brown hair that trailed in the water behind her. Her emerald eyes twinkled with interior light, and she winked at Kara as she treaded water.

"Ivonne of the Hollow Tree," she greeted Kara. "This guy's youngest daughter. Hi. Nice to meet you."

"Nice to meet you," Kara weakly echoed.

Ivonne slid up out of the water and sat cross-legged on its surface without any support. "So! What're you here to ask for? The last time we had a human in the Court was, like, two centuries ago, and he stumbled in by accident. Dad's forgotten how to talk to humans, so maybe just talk to me."

Kara realized her mouth was hanging open. She snapped it shut and hoped her blush was somehow invisible in the dim light. "Uh… Well, okay. I'm a Free Judge of the True Vehmic Court. You're familiar?"

"Oh, yeah. I know all about the contract my great-grandfather made with the humans. Rendering justice tempered with mercy, six weeks and a day before they kick the bucket, special powers, yada yada."

"Right." Despite the "solid" surface of the nymph supporting her, Kara felt more at sea with every passing moment. This, beyond everything else she had seen, felt the most surreal. "Do you also know about Athemis? The Wolf Court?"

Hollow Tree rumbled so deeply that a group of passing tadpoles hastily squiggled away. "The *poachers*." Several strands of moss hanging from his left eyebrow curled and turned brown with disdain.

Ivonne scowled. "We know them. They've been trying to usurp the contract for centuries. If they gain control of the Court's authority in the mundane world, we'd have no choice but to honor them as the last remaining scion of the contracted party. We'd hate to have to do that."

"Then I need your help. *Badly.*"

Ivonne rested her chin in her hands and eyed Kara intensely. "Go on."

"I don't know how much news you get in the fey realm, but I'm the last Free Judge," Kara explained. "Athemis killed my brother six months ago, and they've been doing their best to off me ever since. If it were just *me* in danger, that would be one thing—Grimm is teaching me magic, I'm training, I can protect myself—but it's *not* just me.

"When my brother was murdered, he left behind a pregnant fiancée. She gave birth to a son two weeks ago. Athemis tried to kidnap him within days. They managed it earlier this week. I got them back, but I can't do my job as a Free Judge and protect them at the same time. I have a small Circle of the Court, and they're helping, but we're in a *really* tough position because Athemis has infiltrated everywhere in the city we're living…the city that is my jurisdiction as a Free Judge."

Ivonne's eyes gradually narrowed through Kara's recounting. "So, what are you asking for? More power?"

Kara shook her head. "I'm asking if you can keep them safe. Here, somewhere else, it doesn't matter. Maria will go *anywhere* as long as it means she can protect Carlos."

Ivonne's eyebrows rose, and Hollow Tree rumbled again. "You want to bring them *here.*"

"Anywhere," Kara repeated. "Anywhere Athemis can't find them. Somewhere Carlos can grow up safely, so he and Maria aren't constantly looking over their shoulders. Somewhere *I* know they're safe, so I can fulfill my end of the contract as a Free Judge."

The two fey beings were silent, although Ivonne turned her gaze on her father and the knots that represented his eyes turned to her as well. A long moment passed as the two either communicated silently or considered Kara's request.

At last, they returned their attention to her—or Hollow Tree did. Ivonne looked beyond Kara, over her shoulder, with a thoughtful frown turning down the corners of her lips.

"This cannot come to pass," Hollow Tree intoned.

Kara's heart sank, and her throat tightened with anger. "What? Why not?" she demanded. Her voice cracked. "Please! We're desperate—if you don't help, Athemis will control the last of the Free Judges! I can't hold them off forever!"

"Mundane mortals cannot live in the fey realms." The tree's pronouncement thudded like a club the size of a telephone pole. "The longer you are exposed to raw magic, the less human you become. Our contract is with the human Vehmic Court. If this babe were to be raised in the wild fey, he would lose his eligibility as a Free Judge. The outcome would be the same. This is not acceptable per the terms of the contract."

Tears pricked Kara's eyes, and she blinked them away furiously. "Then what am I supposed to do? If I go back without help, Athemis wins anyway! There *must* be some exigent clauses in the contract! Contingency plans for if something went this awry— surely, someone had to have planned for something like this!"

"The contract has been unaltered for many years," Hollow Tree replied. "You are the first in many generations to speak the language of the lawmakers. Perhaps you will be the one to amend what has lain untouched for so long."

Kara's hands curled into fists. "Not if I'm dead, I won't!"

"Father, I have an idea." Ivonne broke into the heated discussion with a softer tone.

"What is it, little leaf?"

"I will go."

Kara blinked. Tears brimmed in her eyes, and she swiped them away with the back of her hand. "What?"

"I'll go," Ivonne repeated. This time, she grinned, and her solemnity evaporated into the mist. "I'll come with you, and I'll help. A full-grown fey is worth at least half a dozen fighters. Athemis won't know what hit them."

Hollow Tree grumbled wordlessly, but the tenor was thoughtful rather than discontented. Eventually, he muttered, "There is no clause prohibiting a fey creature from joining a Judge's Circle. It has simply not been done in over seven hundred years."

"High time we got back into practice, then." Ivonne dusted her hands off—figuratively, Kara supposed, since they were still dripping—and stood on the water's surface. "Come on, then! Bring me home!"

Kara stared at her. "I don't want to sound ungrateful, but… you're gonna stand out. You're green."

Ivonne laughed. "Oh, that's easy to change. Humans see what we want them to see. Don't worry about that. It'll be fine!"

"If you say so," Kara murmured.

"I do say so," Ivonne firmly stated. "Now, you'd best thank Father properly or else the magic will get antsy, and nobody likes antsy magic."

"Definitely not," Kara agreed. She had no idea what "antsy magic" entailed, but she suspected she wouldn't like it.

She tore her eyes off the voluptuous green beauty still standing on the surface of the pool and focused on the giant floating log who was apparently her boss. "The Vehmic Court extends its deepest gratitude to the Court of Fog and Grove for its hospitality and its generous offer of assistance in the Vehmic Court's time of need. We honor this gift, and we will…protect her to the best of our ability." The line was supposed to be, "and we will use it wisely," but Kara thought she'd better not call Ivonne an *it.*

"The Court of Fog and Grove renews its vow of alliance and support to the Vehmic Court," Hollow Tree replied. "May your justice be swift and true. Until we meet again."

"Until we meet again," Kara echoed, but the grove was already gone. She stood at the edge of the forest, fifty yards from her rental car.

Kara stared. "Did I just dream all of that?"

A laugh to Kara's right brought her attention over. Ivonne, now olive-skinned and wearing a tight T-shirt and jeans that left nothing to the imagination, grinned and winked. "You're definitely awake."

Beside the nymph, the black horse nickered, ate a mouthful of grass, and disappeared into the trees.

CHAPTER TWELVE

<u>**Tuesday, January 9, 2091**</u>

"I find it hard to believe you've never flown before," Kara told Ivonne, who was glued to the zeppelin's window. "Don't you do this, like, all the time?"

Ivonne waved dismissively. "Never in a *machine.* This is *completely* new. It's so weird not to feel the wind! It's so *quiet.*"

Kara shook her head. She'd been in a perpetual state of mild bemusement since leaving the Black Forest with Ivonne in tow. Somehow, Ivonne had produced a passport at the airfield, allowing her to purchase a ticket with a credit card that had appeared in a wallet that Kara would have sworn hadn't been in Ivonne's purse two minutes earlier—mainly because she hadn't *had* a purse two minutes earlier.

She can make whatever she needs appear, Kara marveled. *Fey magic is insanely powerful. And she's coming to help protect us. My God, I might just have done it.*

The flight back to North America seemed to pass much faster with Ivonne beside her. Kara was kept busy explaining any number of human customs and items, all of which Ivonne had some small knowledge of, but nothing specific.

"So you *have* to eat? You can't just stand out in the sun with your feet in the water?"

Kara glanced at the gentleman across the aisle, who was obviously trying not to eavesdrop and failing miserably. She couldn't blame him. She'd have done the same in his shoes.

"Yes, that's how it works," she told Ivonne. "Although I gotta say, people will start looking at you funny if you keep talking like that."

Ivonne's eyebrows rose, and she looked around the cabin. "Oh, you never let me have any fun. Can't a girl pretend?"

Kara awkwardly chuckled. "I mean, I guess so…"

Ivonne winked. "Just getting into character. It'll be so much easier to play a fairy on TV if I really *nail* the 'fish out of water' angle. Or should that be nymph out of water?"

Kara blinked, then genuinely laughed. She'd been kicking herself for not setting up a cover story, and Ivonne had plucked one out of thin air. "Either way works."

The man across the aisle visibly relaxed. A hint of an amused smile played over his features, and he went back to his newspaper.

Dodged a bullet. Thank goodness. Now, we just have to hope Ivonne doesn't accidentally cast any flashy magic.

"I wouldn't have thought it possible, but humans have become even *more* paranoid since the last time I was out here," Ivonne commented when they were safely enclosed in Kara's car, back on the ground in Neo Los Angeles.

Kara started the car, put it in reverse, and backed out of her parking spot. "What do you mean?"

"On the zeppelin. You freaked out about the guy listening to us. I know you're anxious about Athemis, but I didn't feel any of their signatures on board. What was he gonna do?

Out me as a fairy, which he probably doesn't even believe in?"

Kara frowned. "He might have thought you were crazy."

"So? What's the harm?"

"Well…" Kara paused and thought about it. "I guess not much, in the middle of a zeppelin. You could get involuntarily committed to a psych ward if someone thought you were a danger to yourself or others. In some places, you might get shot —either by your average Joe or by law enforcement."

Ivonne shrugged. "So I make them forget me, and I slip out the door. Last I checked, bullets aren't made of cold iron. I'd be fine."

Kara looked skeptical. "Rumors spread, you know. That has to be equally true in the fey realms as it is here."

"Oh, definitely. Stories spread like wildfire back home."

"Okay, so, think about it, Ivonne. We're trying to *hide*."

Ivonne made a face. "And here I was thinking we could just lure all of Athemis out and be done with them."

Kara didn't reply. She pulled off the highway at the next exit, found an empty spot in a gas station parking lot well away from any streetlights, and put the car in park but left it running. Then she turned in her seat to face Ivonne head-on.

"Why are you here?"

Ivonne cocked her head. "To do my part, as a representative of the Court of Fog and Grove, to uphold the contract between my people and the mundane world. Meaning, I help you beat Athemis."

"How do you plan on doing that?"

The glamoured fairy raised an eyebrow. "Like I said. I was thinking we lure them out and be done with them. How hard can it be?"

Kara drew a deep breath and let it out very slowly. "When was the last time you were in the mundane world?"

"A century ago, give or take a few decades, I think. There was a lot of fighting going on."

"Almost exactly a century ago, then," Kara clarified. "That was probably the Reconciliation War."

"Sounds familiar."

"How long were you here?"

"Not long. Couple of days. A friend of mine said the humans were putting on a hell of a show, so we went to watch."

Kara stared at her, speechless, for several heartbeats. Then she managed, "Are fey beings immortal?"

"Not in the way you're thinking. Different kinds of fairies have different lifespans. Nymphs are more or less immortal because they can go through the water cycle infinitely. Dryads like me, well—we live as long as trees live. You saw how old my dad was. But the little floating fairies, they live and die in weeks."

"Can you be killed?"

"Like I said, cold iron. Which no one seems to keep on them anymore since nobody believes in fairies. But our spirits go back to our home courts, and we can take physical form again. Happens all the time."

"*There* we go. Okay. Now I understand. You do realize that *doesn't happen* for humans, right? We weren't just...*putting on a show* when you were last here, and if we tried to take on all of Athemis at once, those of us who *can* die *would* die. This isn't a game, Ivonne."

Ivonne frowned and drew back, offended. "I never said it was. And of course I know humans can die. That's the whole point of taking out Athemis, isn't it? Kill them before they can kill you?"

Kara blinked. "I feel like I'm beginning to understand why the Vehmic Court has this agreement with the fey to handle justice down here among the mortals. Did more fairies visit our parts of the world before the Vehmic Court was established?"

"Sure. Humans were always asking their favorite fairies to do them a favor and kill this guy or that guy. Some folks made real careers out of it."

Kara slowly nodded. "And the agreement with the Vehmic Court means you can't do that now, right?"

"Yep. Humans handle humans, fey handle fey. That's why no fairy has been a member of a Judge's Circle in such a long time. We're supposed to support from the background. This is exciting!"

"And very serious," someone interjected from the back seat.

Kara jumped a foot. "*Grimm!* Since when can you appear in my *car?*"

The white cat hopped onto the center console, flicked its tail, and sniffed Ivonne. "Since the presence of a dryad is augmenting your magical reserves. Well met, *Fräulein.*"

Ivonne let the cat sniff her hand, then scratched under its chin. "I thought I felt magic growing in here. I figured Kara was getting pissed off at me. You're the spirit guide, then?"

Grimm-the-cat rubbed the side of his face along her hand, then remembered himself. He drew back and sat regally between Ivonne and Kara. "That is correct. I am Jakob Wilhelm Grimm, spirit guide to the Free Judges of the True Vehmic Court. I am the last remaining interpreter of the contract between the fey and the mundane. Upon that point, I must inform you that you are mistaken as to the extent of your powers as a member of Kara's Circle."

"How so? I'm still a dryad. I still have all my magic."

"That is true. However, when you swear your oath to join the Circle, you will become bound by the terms of the contract *on the human side.*"

Ivonne's eyes gradually widened. "Oh, shit. I never thought of that."

"I suspected as much. I believed it prudent to inform you before *Fräulein* Greims became any more frustrated."

"Appreciated," Kara put in. "I knew I was missing *something*, but couldn't figure out what."

"So, what am I allowed to do while I'm here?" Ivonne asked. "Since apparently it *doesn't* include calling down a meteor swarm on Athemis' stupid heads?"

Kara's jaw dropped. "You could *do that?*"

Ivonne snickered. "Well, no. That's not really my department. I can do earthquakes and tsunamis though, and if push came to shove, I could summon a *really* nasty thunderstorm."

Grimm interrupted. "*While you are here,* you may use your powers to protect the Judge to whom you have sworn your service, as well as the other members of your Circle. You may not directly harm another human unless it is specifically in defense of yourself, your Judge, or your Circle, and lethal force will be judged according to the terms of the Vehmic Court's contract."

"So, she *could* kill Athemis operatives," Kara observed.

"Only if they are attacking, and only if they have already been judged guilty and given at least one notice, or are in the service of one who has. The terms that bind her are far stricter than yours, Kara."

Ivonne sighed. "Any limits on defensive work?"

"Far fewer, which brings me to another topic." Grimm-the-cat stretched and turned to Kara. "Maria has found an excellent candidate for our new domicile. There is enough time left in the day that she can meet you there, if you wish."

Kara narrowed her eyes. "She's not driving herself, is she?"

"No. *Herr* Cedric would accompany them."

"In that case, tell me where I'm going."

Kara stopped outside the massive iron gates. The pillars on either side of the wide entrance towered over them by at least ten feet, and trees of equal and greater height crowded behind the wall that stretched away.

"Welcoming," she commented with one eyebrow raised.

"Looks cozy," Ivonne opined.

Kara side-eyed her. "I guess it would look like home to you."

"Yup. I could enchant those gates, too, easy-peasy."

"How do fairies learn human slang?"

"We get HBO."

Kara opened her mouth, then closed it again and shook her head.

The gate was ajar, wide enough for them to drive through. Kara noted the weathered foreclosure sign zip-tied to the bars. "Must have belonged to some millionaire who lost it all in the crash in the '70s. Did Maria say it was in decent shape, Grimm?"

The cat, who had decided car rides were not its preferred mode of transportation, peeked out from where it was curled in Ivonne's lap. "She did not."

Ivonne clicked her tongue and petted Grimm-the-cat comfortingly. "Aw, kitty, you're gonna be fine."

Kara bit back a snort of laughter as Grimm grumbled under his breath, and the cat's ears flicked. Then she eased her car through the gate. On the other side, she parked and got out, leaving the engine running.

She swung the gate shut. A rusty padlock hung from the latch, and as a precaution, she locked it, too. Even if Maria didn't have the key, she could always magic it back open. Kara wasn't taking any chances.

This gated estate was half an hour outside of NLA's city limits. In the mid-twentieth century, NLA had been rapidly expanding into these neighborhoods, but the Reconciliation War put a sudden end to those plans. A number of self-made or war-made millionaires had built mansions out here in the post-war years, but when the economy took its nasty downturn a couple of decades earlier with the dotcom bust, many had gone bankrupt.

As a result, this place wasn't exactly on the beaten path. Kara hadn't seen another car since leaving NLA. This area of the state was largely uninhabited, and last she had heard, the district was considering turning it into a nature reserve.

Depending on the state of the house, Kara thought she might be able to work with this. Half an hour was a fair way to go, but it wasn't insurmountable, and the grounds seemed defensible. The biggest problem she foresaw was that there was only one way in and out, so any comings and goings would be easy to track.

Kara returned to the car and headed up the heavily treed drive. The sun hadn't quite set yet, but the trees were thick and tall enough that it already seemed like the dead of night. Kara's headlights flashed along the trunks, glinting off the eyes of wildlife hiding within, and she slowed further.

The tree line arrived abruptly, opening into a wide stretch of unkempt lawn with overgrown hedges and a disused fountain. The driveway circled the fountain, which stood in front of a mansion that had seen better days. Its white façade was cracked and weathered, the windows were shuttered, and some were boarded over. Dead leaves piled in drifts on the porch and steps. Faint light broke through the dirty glass over the front doors, which looked about as heavy as the main gates. Cedric's beater of a red Corolla sat farther along the drive.

"Charming," Kara murmured.

"Isolated," Grimm remarked. Now that they'd stopped moving, he jumped off Ivonne's lap and back onto the center console. "Shall we?"

Kara led them from the car, up the steps. She knocked three times, then twice more, then waited ten seconds before opening the door. "It's Kara and Grimm," she called. "Plus a new friend."

The entrance hall stretched the full two stories. A dusty chandelier hung in the center, providing the light they'd seen from outside. A grand staircase, equally dust-covered, curved up to the second floor, where a corridor disappeared to the left and right.

The banister, railings, and floors were all made of the same dark, red-tinted hardwood, while everything else was white—or had been white, at one point.

Cedric emerged from the right-side corridor upstairs and came to the railing. "Glad you could make it. This place is *nuts*. Come on up. We're still finding more rooms. Also, hi, I'm Cedric. Who are you?"

"Ivonne of the Grove," Ivonne replied. "I am a dryad and the newest member of Kara's Circle."

"Dryads. Those are tree spirits, right?"

"Yep."

"Wow."

An hour later, the troupe gathered in the entrance hall and sat on the stairs, leaning on the banisters to face one another. Maria had Carlos in a sling on her front and was rocking him gently. He'd fallen asleep several minutes before.

"So, what do you think?" she asked Kara. "Pretty cool, right?"

"It's huge," Kara replied. "That's my first thought. Like, absolutely huge. Did you count the rooms?"

"Seventy-two, not counting hallways."

"We can knock some walls out, though," Cedric put in. "On the main floor, if we took out the wall between that one living room and the study—"

"Because we totally have time for that," Kara interrupted. "Look. I can't argue that it's isolated and secure, and it has more than enough room for Maria and Ana to live here. But it's still half an hour away from town, which means it'll be easy for Athemis to follow us, and did I mention it's huge? It'll be a *bear* to do maintenance on. I might be able to buy it, but I don't know if I can afford the upkeep."

Ivonne lifted a finger. "Don't worry about that. I can call in a few favors. This place will be spick and span in no time."

"Can you also call magical movers?" Kara deadpanned.

Ivonne thought about it, then shrugged. "Probably. I was

thinking about asking some buddies to *make* you new furniture. Not like you don't have enough trees out there."

Kara frowned. "I mean, that'd be cool, but we were kind of hoping to get Ana and Maria out of Jacob's apartment as soon as possible."

"Oh, sure! That's no problem. Give me a day, and I'll have a couple of rooms set up for them. Maria, you said you liked the north side rooms, yeah?"

"Yes..."

"Cool. Consider it done." Ivonne put her hands behind her head and chuckled at Kara's disbelieving look. "Come on. I'm not allowed to hunt down and slaughter your enemies, so at least let me turn my powers loose on making these digs livable."

Kara drew a deep breath, then let it out. "Okay. Sure. Go nuts."

"*Fantastic.*" Ivonne rubbed her hands together. "There is an oak tree outside that I am *dying* to get my hands on."

Cedric cocked his head. "Is it just me, or does this seem vaguely cannibalistic?"

"It's not just you," Kara confirmed. "Ivonne is apparently solving our maintenance and furniture crisis, after which I assume she'll be working on setting up defenses."

"Judging by that nasty grin, that's a yes," Maria muttered.

"But we still don't have a way to avoid being followed," Kara continued. "Anyone have any ideas?"

Ana spoke up. "*Si.* There is a walled-off section in the basement that I want to look at again."

Kara's eyebrows shot up. "That sounds like the opening to a horror movie. Now I don't want to spend the seven-figure sum that this place costs. What do you think is down there?"

"I believe it is an access to the tunnels that run under the city," Ana explained. "I have worked in the houses of many rich people. When they build their own homes, especially when they build them after a big conflict, they always build escape routes and places to hide."

"Could just be a bunker," Cedric suggested.

Ana shook her head. "Then it would not have been walled off, only shut. They would only have walled it off if it went somewhere off the property."

"That makes sense," Kara admitted. "And after using the old subway tunnels the other day, I have to say it's currently my preferred way of getting around the city incognito. I'll need to put in something a little faster than *walking*. Maybe I could fit a Smart Car in there."

"Bicycle?" Cedric mused.

"Oh, sure, vigilante on a bicycle." Kara rolled her eyes. "No one would *ever* take me seriously."

Cedric smiled innocently. "What about an e-bike? Those are all the rage."

Maria hooted with laughter. "You could get one of those e-scooters!"

Kara glared at them. "You guys are *not helping*."

Ana patted Kara on the shoulder. "*Mi niña*, laughter is good for the soul. Relax. We will find a way."

Kara sighed, then admitted, "Batman on a bicycle *is* pretty funny." The thought made her laugh. "Like, really funny."

Ana pulled her in for a side hug. "See? And now you feel less heavy. Today, we sleep on the floor. Tomorrow, we live in a mansion!"

Kara chuckled again. "Sure, but I'm putting a vote in for *air mattresses*, at least."

CHAPTER THIRTEEN

<u>Thursday, January 11, 2091</u>

Kara woke up on a very different surface than the one on which she'd fallen asleep. It was much squishier and at least two feet higher off the floor. Sunlight sliced across her face, but not at such an angle that it hurt her eyes. From the corridor outside her room, she heard vague noises of people moving. She also smelled frying onions and warm Mexican spices.

She stretched and rolled over, and realized she wasn't in a sleeping bag but under real sheets and blankets. The mattress was memory foam, not inflatable. She was in a real bed. To her left sat a nightstand with a lamp, both hand-carved from wood. Her phone lay on top of the nightstand.

"How long was I *out?*" she muttered.

Kara sat up and stretched again. Her muscles were sore, and her joints creaked. She felt like she'd slept for a week, but she could have sworn she'd only just closed her eyes.

She grabbed her phone. It was charged, which meant someone had plugged it in. *Just like someone put me in bed. I usually sleep pretty lightly. I must have been seriously out cold.*

The screen read 9:33 AM…on Thursday.

Kara laughed in disbelief. "I slept for a day and a half? Holy shit."

"You were damn tired."

Kara looked up to see Cedric halfway in her door. "You're still here?"

Cedric chuckled. "Is that a problem?"

Kara blushed. "No, not at all. I didn't expect you to stick around. You have your own life to live."

He waved dismissively. "The gym will survive for a few days without me. Rolando has it under control. You guys need a hand more than he does. And…" His eyes twinkled.

"Yes?"

"Watching Ivonne work has been *fascinating*."

Kara swung her legs out of bed and stood. She was in the same clothes she'd fallen asleep in two days before, and she very much wanted to change. "Oh? I'm almost afraid to ask."

"Well, I was always partial to the story of the shoemaker and the elves as a kid. My dad ran a little auto shop, and there was always too much to do. I used to fantasize about those same elves showing up and helping him out overnight."

He gestured at the room as Kara approached. "Now, I get to see that happen in reality. It has been *impressive*, to say the least."

Kara took a look around, as prompted. The bed was of the same construction as the nightstand and the lamp, as were the matching dresser and wardrobe. The dresser included a large mirror, which reflected the gorgeous drapes pulled back on either side of the window.

She had fallen asleep in a dusty, disused, empty room, lying on an air mattress. She'd woken up in a fully furnished room that could have come out of a magazine.

"They *made* all this? Including the mattress?"

"No, I think they got the mattress from IKEA."

"Seriously?"

"Yeah."

"How'd they pay for it? Or move it?"

"Apparently IKEA also has elves."

Kara covered her face with her hands. "I cannot even. What the hell. I need coffee and food so badly right now."

"Right this way, then, and if I were you, I'd avoid looking anywhere but the floor if you want to avoid any more surprises."

"Oh, God."

Kara kept her gaze glued to the floor all the way to the kitchen, but the trip took longer than expected, and she kept getting glimpses of things she desperately wanted to look at. Her resolve held firm, and she made it to the gorgeous butcher-block-covered kitchen island without her jaw dragging on the floor.

Ana passed her a cup of coffee and a plate of eggs, rice, and beans, then leaned on the island across from her. Cedric took his leave, saying he would help Ivonne, and Ana sipped her coffee and waited for Kara to speak.

Kara shoveled several forkfuls of food into her mouth and drank half the cup of coffee before she said anything. At length, she looked up, although she still hid behind the mug. "Is the whole house done?"

Ana shrugged. "Not the whole house, but more than enough to be livable. Ivonne's workers are tireless. They've asked if you want a garden."

"If I want a *garden*?"

"If not, they'll replant the trees they cut down."

Kara blinked. "I have no idea if I want a garden."

"Good thing to have, if you ask me."

"Okay, then I guess I…want a garden." She ate a few more bites. "So, my house has been full of fairies since I fell asleep."

"*Si.*"

"Has Athemis shown up yet?"

"No, but Ivonne set up wards right after she got the most important rooms done. Oh, we also moved all of our things from Jacob's apartment. Your clothes are in your dresser."

Kara's hand immediately went to the chain around her neck, where she kept the key for the hidden room. "You didn't—"

"No, we did not move *Señor* Grimm or any of those things."

Kara's heart was still racing. "You moved everything, but Athemis *hasn't* come? I thought for sure they'd be watching the apartment."

Ana smiled a nasty smile. "Ivonne called in a few favors. We went in and out without using the doors. I *like* her."

Kara processed this, then drank the other half of the coffee and slid the mug across the island. "More, please. I don't think I can quite wrap my head around the idea of teleportation being possible without more caffeine."

Ana took the cup and refilled it. "She said you'd be curious about that. She also said to tell you that it takes a long time to set up, doesn't last forever, and according to Grimm, definitely falls in the 'can't use it to help you directly' category."

Kara sighed as she accepted the full mug. "Damn. I guess I should be grateful I didn't have to vet and hire movers."

"*Si.* Cedric said he will help you move everything from the hidden room today. For now, eat." Ana lifted a hand to stop Kara's reply. "You have been running yourself into the ground, Kara. You need to do one thing at a time, and you need to recognize that it is time to focus on your work. Ivonne is strong and powerful, but she cannot do your job. Maria and Carlos are safe here. Your Circle is complete. You can relax."

Kara bit her lip. "I've always had a hard time believing things like that until I prove them to myself."

"Then today, you go pack up all your books and knives, and you leave us to our own devices. By the time you come back, we will have been without your active protection for two days. Will that be enough proof?"

"Maybe. I've worked hard to develop a strong sense of skepticism."

Ana chuckled. "It serves you well. Now hush and eat."

"Yes, ma'am."

"That's *Mami* to you."

Kara's heart ached. She'd always gotten along well with Ana, but she hadn't had much opportunity to build a relationship with her while living in NorMetro. "You're serious, aren't you?"

"Entirely. You've lost too many people already in your life, and you're set to lose more in this job. The least I can do is take you in."

Kara smiled. "Thanks, Ana—I mean, *Mami*."

"Don't mention it. Now eat your eggs."

***

Kara wiped sweat off her brow and stood back. The hidden room was cleaned out, apart from the table and Grimm's skull on top of it.

"You're about to lose your wax," she told Grimm. "Any last words?"

"Bring it with you," the skull replied. "Athemis could trace our magical signature by remelting it."

Kara gave him an unimpressed look. "You know, if you'd told me *that* when we first talked about moving you, I would have been much more understanding. I'll make sure we keep all the bits and pieces. Ready?"

The white cat slithered through the closet door behind her. "Ready."

Kara looked between the skull and the cat, then shook her head and blew out the candle. While waiting for the pool of melted wax to harden, she brought the box she'd packed out to the living room. "Almost ready," she told Cedric.

"Good." He adjusted his work gloves and checked out the window. "I still don't see anyone like the guys you've described. We might have pulled this off."

"Not if you say things like that," she chided. "But it's good to know that my *ausklammern* field is working."

The full day and a half of rest, plus Ana's excellent cooking, had made a huge difference in Kara's magical ability. She didn't like to admit it, but eating three square meals a day was good for her. Using her magic hadn't given her a headache all day, and she had turned the *ausklammern* field up to max the moment she'd left the new house.

According to Grimm, living in proximity to a fey creature was also likely to amplify her abilities. Kara wouldn't complain, but she had decided not to take that for granted. Ivonne might not always be around, and she wouldn't be able to accompany Kara on outings.

Twenty minutes later, she and Cedric had loaded everything from the hidden room into the moving truck they'd rented for the day. Kara dropped the keys off with the superintendent, whom she thanked kindly for her understanding over the last couple of weeks.

"Oh, it's no problem, Miss Greims." The older lady smiled and scratched her pen over the lease-cancelation paperwork. "Your brother was such a sweet man. I was sorry to hear he ran into trouble. Do come by and bring your nephew for a visit sometimes, won't you?"

"Absolutely." Kara had no intention of doing so. As far as she could tell, Agnes had no connection to Athemis, but that didn't mean she wasn't unknowingly giving them information. Better to let the empty pleasantry stand. It wasn't like Agnes would come looking, and Kara had left a post office box as a forwarding address.

As Cedric wheeled the big van away from the curb, Kara felt as though she'd tied off a cord and let it drop. She had left her job and sold her condo in NorMetro. She'd ended the lease on Jacob's apartment. Maria had sold the house left to her by Jacob.

Neither woman had any ties left to the city itself, only the people in it.

In a way, Kara felt as though she were going into hiding. She had no formal employment, and her mailing address was now a P.O. box in Cedric's neighborhood, which he would check on her behalf. There was almost no reason for Kara to come into the city except to do her job. Unlike Jacob, who had tried to balance his day job with his responsibilities as a Free Judge, Kara could focus entirely on her oath to the Vehmic Court.

With that realization, the marks on Kara's arms flared under her jacket. Tension sloughed off her shoulders, and she lifted her chin. Her jaw set. Her vision focused on the road ahead, then flicked over the riot of billboard-covered buildings. Sunlight flashed off a monorail train car in the distance, its track winding between the skyscrapers. Zeppelins floated serenely through the skies above the city, which hummed with activity.

Somehow, Neo Los Angeles had come to feel more like home than anywhere Kara had lived. She'd always longed to leave Minnesota. School had felt like a stopover point. NorMetro had been frustratingly *not quite right*.

Kara never would have pegged herself as a Neo Los Angeles girl, but as they wound through the streets, she realized she already knew them like the back of her hand. She noticed the mom-and-pop store on the corner and smiled when she saw it was doing good business. Her gaze hardened when it caught on two people roughing each other up in an alley.

This was *her* city. She cared about it, and its life ran in her blood. She had a responsibility to it. It needed her help and her protection.

Athemis had a stranglehold on her city. She had to root it out.

"From the look on your face, whoever you're thinking about should duck and cover," Cedric observed. "I hope it's not me."

Kara exhaled and laughed. "No. Athemis."

"Ah, of course. Your nemesis."

The word made Kara pause. "No," she repeated. "They're not my nemesis."

"Oh?"

"I'm *theirs*."

Kara settled into the passenger's seat. A small, self-satisfied smile lurked around the corners of her mouth. She'd been looking for a vigilante alias for months. She'd finally found one.

Nemesis.

Kara hung the last blade on the wall in her new study, then turned in a slow circle. She nodded, satisfied, and struck a match to light Grimm's candle for the first time in the new space.

The wick flared to life. It wavered a couple of times, then burned steadily. "Very nice," Grimm commented. "It does still lock, *ja?*"

Kara held the key up, still attached to the chain around her neck. "Oh, yes. It's not just in my closet this time, either. There's a secret door in the wall in my bedroom, *and* a second door that leads to a corridor going down to the tunnels. Whoever built this house was paranoid as *hell*, but it works well for our purposes."

"Good. Have you solved the issue of clandestine transportation yet?"

"No, but Ivonne's going to talk to a friend about it. For now, my *ausklammern* will have to do when we need to drive somewhere."

"In that case, it sounds like it's high time you got back to work."

"Agreed." She pulled the chair out from the table, sat, and scooted it back in. Ivonne had outdone herself with the new table for this room. It had drawers underneath that would hold documents and supplies, and it was big enough for her to spread out all the necessary files for a case. Grimm's skull was at the head of the table, not in the center, getting in the way.

Even better, the skull nestled in a purpose-built pedestal with channels carved into it to funnel the melting wax into pools for easy retrieval. The pedestal also had a spot to hold the matchbox, and runes were scorched into the wood under the glossy finish. The three ancient Vehmic Court tomes had a shelf of their own at the base of the pedestal, which locked with Kara's key.

"How do you like your new lodgings?" Kara asked while she flicked through a folder of papers in the drawer beside her. "Ivonne said the runes should amplify your power even more."

"They do." Grimm's flame burned brighter. "She has etched similar runes into all the furniture in the house, as well as all the window and doorframes…and the moldings along the ceilings. And—and the banisters, and the perimeter trees, and the defenses she's built… *Gott in Himmel.*"

Kara looked up from her perusal of the documents. "You sound surprised."

"I am. These runes allow me to see and hear everywhere in the house with perfect clarity. They also allow me to operate the defensive systems. I had read accounts of guides with these far-reaching abilities, but I believed they were extensions of my power that would come as my Free Judge's powers grew. I despaired of ever reaching them, since it is so rare that a Free Judge lives more than a few years."

"Don't remind me," Kara muttered.

Grimm continued as though he hadn't heard her. "Now I see I was mistaken, or that this is not the only way to obtain these capacities. Kara, this renewed alliance with the Court of Fog and Grove might have been the best thing you've ever done."

"As long as it helps me take out Athemis. What are the defenses like?"

"Most create distractions, illusions, or suggestions. A select few will cause damage. None seem intended to be lethal."

"No surprise there, since she's not supposed to kill humans if she can help it."

"Yes." Grimm sounded distracted, like he was too busy playing with his new toy to pay full attention to Kara. She couldn't blame him. If she woke up with a CCTV system in her head, she would explore it too.

Kara left him to it. She got her laptop out and pulled up her preferred news sites, checking for any indication that James Torres had taken her up on her offer. So far, she saw no sign.

More than likely, he ignored it. He probably gets threats, even legal ones, multiple times a day.

She crossed her arms and drummed her fingers on her forearm. *If he's keeping an eye on me and Maria on Athemis' behalf, he'll soon figure out that we've dropped off the map. A few days could be a vacation, even with a newborn. Longer than that, and people ask questions. Especially if one of the people who disappeared is NLA's anti-corruption rising star lawyer.*

A thought struck her. *I don't want to hide until he finds me. I'd rather take the fight to him, try to get him on the back foot. Also, he might not realize I'm serious. He might think I'm trying to cause trouble for Athemis, but not for him. He probably thinks he's untouchable after so many years of screwing everyone else over.*

Kara's gaze strayed to the secure vaults installed on the far wall. Her "treasure troves" of evidence were stored within. One anonymous drop to the right law firm, another one two days later to a reputable journalist, and James Torres would be facing some very uncomfortable questions.

With the second notice due next Tuesday, the timing was perfect. Kara chuckled, opened a word processor on her laptop, and started drafting the cover letters for her anonymous drops.

CHAPTER FOURTEEN

<u>**Friday, January 12, 2091**</u>

Kara strolled up to the skyscraper housing Nestor Palmer Law, feeling more relaxed than she had since before Christmas. Her *ausklammern* field kept most bystanders' eyes from landing on her for more than a few seconds, but even those who looked more closely would only see a confident, well-dressed woman walking with purpose.

The legal profession had its rumor mills, just like any other vocation. Kara wasn't privy to many of them anymore since lawyers tended to keep their grapevine speech-only. Nobody wanted to put anything in text that didn't absolutely have to be... at least, in public. Private emails were fair game for gossip-mongering.

This was the first time Kara wished she had less of a moral code. She would have *loved* to know what the legal community of Neo Los Angeles thought of her. She especially wished she knew better what they thought of the anonymous tipster who had given the Feds scads of information to take down the Mercer empire. Unfortunately, without a connection to a firm, Kara was locked out of those grapevine loops unless she wanted to hack into email servers.

This was on Kara's mind as she walked into Nestor Palmer because she *wasn't* here on official business. She had picked an outfit completely divorced from her typical business formalwear, opting for a looser and more casual appearance rather than the extra sophisticated look. She wanted people to see her and think she was a secretary or a paralegal, not a lawyer. This was how she intended to build her vigilante alter ego. This was *Nemesis.*

Nemesis was stealthy. Nemesis didn't stand out. Nemesis blended in wherever she went, the least objectionable, most unassuming person in the room. At a law firm, that meant appearing as an underling, not a peer.

Kara rode the elevator up to the forty-third floor in silence, politely ignoring the two other occupants. They paid her no mind, just like she wanted, and they didn't even nod when they debarked on the floor before hers.

Kara brushed the long, red locks of her wig out of her face as she approached Sarra Palmer's receptionist. Louise had met Kara on several occasions, so this would be the hardest test of Kara's new disguise abilities yet.

Louise's gaze slid over Kara easily and without recognition, only the polite courtesy of a professional. "Can I help you?"

Kara slipped a small oblong box, no bigger than her palm, out of her handbag. She offered it to Louise and smiled faintly. "Delivery for Ms. Palmer. She's expecting it."

Louise took the box and set it in the tray beside her. "I'll let her know."

"Thank you. If you wouldn't mind, I'd appreciate it if you let her know as soon as you could. My senior partner says she'll want to see them right away."

"Of course. Have a good day."

Kara nodded politely and retreated. She remained nearby long enough to make sure Louise picked up the phone, then headed for the elevators. If she was playing the part of a paralegal, she couldn't press the privilege of a lawyer. She would have to trust that Sarra would get the documents in time, and that she would act on them as quickly as Kara suspected she would.

She had arranged the press package drop-off for Sunday afternoon. If all went as planned, James Torres would feel the heat the moment he got into the office on Monday, and the arrival of his four-week notice the day after would throw fuel on the fire. Best-case scenario, he turned himself in. Worst-case scenario, he doubled down and made more people's lives hell.

The worst-case scenario is more likely than the best-case, Kara admitted to herself as she watched the LCD numbers in the elevator car tick down. *But if he's truly Athemis, not just a supporter, he'll know a Free Judge being involved means serious business. He* might *start panicking, which would mean mistakes. Mistakes mean the snowball rolls down the hill faster, and if I'm very lucky, that snowball causes an avalanche that clears out a ton of Athemis' network in NLA.*

The elevator *dinged,* and the door opened on the ground floor. Kara stepped out.

Then again, I'm rarely lucky. Not that lucky, anyway.

She adjusted the strap of her shoulder bag, reinforced her *ausklammern* field until the nearby security guard's eyes slid over her, and left.

Saturday, January 13, 2091

Kara ducked Cedric's blow, pivoted, and drove a fist into his stomach. He tensed against the punch, absorbing most of the impact, but he grunted.

"You're getting faster," he commented as he danced a couple of steps away.

"Thanks." She matched his footwork and kept her gaze glued to his. Then she threw an *ablenken* bolt at the corner of the newly finished dojo, where a crate of wooden practice weapons stood.

Nothing happened, but the sound of the weapons clattering together as though they had fallen filled the air.

Cedric's head turned involuntarily. He wrenched it back a split second later, but not quickly enough to dodge Kara's powerful right hook. He staggered, then doubled over as she landed a knee between his legs. The kick to the back of his knees brought him to the floor.

Three heartbeats later, she had his arms pinned behind his back with one hand and the trigger of her wrist-knife poised at his throat. He panted several times, then tapped his toe on the hardwood floor.

Kara let go, hopped off, and offered him a hand up. He accepted it, then dusted himself off while catching his breath. When he stopped panting, he nodded. "Well done. That was the loudest one yet. I'm used to your distractions, and that still surprised me."

She cracked her knuckles. "Thanks. It helps when I use sounds that make sense in context. If I made a horse whinny, you'd know it was me."

Cedric acknowledged this with an eyebrow. "You could still use that against people who *don't* know you have magic. If I was beating someone up in an alley and I heard an elephant, I'd be confused as hell."

"Point. Police sirens are usually a good bet, though."

He chuckled in agreement, then motioned at the benches on the side of the room. They crossed and grabbed their respective water bottles, and he sat and shook out his left hand before cracking his open and taking a long drink.

"Your *stählen*'s gotten an upgrade too, I think. I'm gonna need to start wearing knuckle guards to spar with you." Kara scratched the back of her neck sheepishly, and he chuckled. "I wonder how other Free Judges handled that little problem."

"They often fought with swords," Grimm answered, slinking around the open door in his cat form. "And they often wore practice armor for anything more impactful than drills. *Stählen* will turn away a dull blade, but no more than that. Also, they typically focused on magical defenses and stealth until they could deliver a single, decisive strike against their target. There was much less of this…gang warfare."

Kara leaned on the wall and raised an eyebrow. "You're telling me targets didn't make a habit of sending their lackeys after us?"

"Not with near such frequency. It was a waste of resources."

Kara made a face. "Lucky me, living in the modern world."

The cat hopped onto the bench beside Cedric and delicately walked between the small towels and water bottles. "It is good to be well-rounded, but it has always been in a Free Judge's best interests to play to their strengths. One Judge might favor sword-play, another might favor ranged attacks. Ultimately, all that matters is that the Judge in question be able to deliver justice swiftly and without fail. How they do so is their choice."

"You seem to favor a killer right hook," Cedric commented.

"And a killer subpoena," Kara joked, then sobered. "Am I going too hard on you, Cedric?"

Her trainer shook his head. "No, I just have to adjust. What Grimm mentioned about drills is probably wise. Sparring is great for practicing *watching* your opponent, but when it comes to learning different fighting methods, drills are the way to go. Make it muscle memory, like we talked about when you first started coming to me."

He tapped his fingers on his water bottle. "Did you say you had a sword instructor?"

"Yeah."

"Might be worth vetting her for the Circle. My specialties are all in hand-to-hand. If I could work with her, we might be able to put something together that's uniquely you. Then *no one* could see you coming."

Kara considered this, then nodded. "I'll see what I can dig up."

"It would be advisable also for you to seek out *Fräulein* Ivonne and ask her to teach you better control of your magic," Grimm suggested. "Her mastery of her craft is evident in her work here. No doubt she would have much to pass on."

Kara nodded again. "Every advantage counts. I don't imagine many Free Judges have had the opportunity to learn directly from a fae."

"You are correct."

Kara stretched and cracked her neck. "I'd better go shower. Ana will eat us all if we're late for supper, and I need to double-check my media packet for tomorrow's drop-off."

Sunday, January 14, 2091

Kara flipped the page of her newspaper, then adjusted her sunglasses lower on the bridge of her nose and crossed her ankles under the café table. It was a sunny day in Neo Los Angeles, which meant that even though it was mid-January, she could sit on the coffee shop's sidewalk patio without freezing. That made using *ausklammern* fields to make people ignore her much easier, because she only had to make passers-by ignore a sentence or two, not a protracted conversation.

Not that she expected this to be a long meeting. Renée Carter had a well-earned reputation for being direct. Kara expected that Ms. Carter would scan the document Kara offered, make a snap judgment on whether she wanted the story, and leave before her coffee would be drinkable temperature.

Kara shifted again, sliding the hem of her long coat a few inches farther down her leg. She had opted for a skirt and heels today, playing up the "legal assistant" image. The sun was nice, but it didn't keep the wind off her nylon-clad legs.

She also didn't relish the thought of fighting in heels, but she would do it if she had to. She intended to do some footwork and sparring drills in varying heights and styles of heels moving forward. She couldn't believe she had overlooked that until now.

A woman exited the coffee shop, bearing the aromas of cinnamon and coffee with her. She set her paper cup on the table, where steam blew away from the spout in the light breeze, and pulled out the chair across from Kara.

You could be forgiven for assuming Renée Carter was nonthreatening, from a distance. She was short and waifish, with mousy brown hair tied back in a bun with plenty of flyaways. Her clothing was immaculate and tailored, so she looked every inch the professional she was, but her stature and build made her fade into the background in any press pool.

The moment she caught your eye, however, you would be thoroughly disabused of this idea. Her eyes were too big for her thin face, and they notionally hid behind harsh square glasses, but their astonishing, piercing blue-green pinned you to the spot instantly and betrayed the intensity of the intellect behind them.

Kara also didn't think the woman was capable of smiling. Her pale lips were already pursed when Renée sat, and the creases in her cheeks said they had kept that expression for a very long time.

The famous—or perhaps infamous—reporter gave Kara a practiced once-over. Her nostrils flared with a slight exhalation when she'd finished, giving no indication whether she had found Kara satisfactory or wanting.

Renée Carter ignored her coffee and folded her hands on top of the table. They were dry and a little chapped, with graphite and ink stains on her right index finger. "What do you have for me?"

Kara pulled the envelope from her bag and slid it across the table without comment.

Carter accepted it, slit it open with a brittle nail, and pulled the single paper out. She scanned it, careful to keep it at an angle that shielded it from anyone else's view.

Her left eyebrow rose a fraction of an inch, and she glanced at Kara over the edge of the paper. "You can back this up?"

Kara tapped the paper. "Everything's on the encrypted server. You can download the files at your leisure and confirm them yourself."

Carter held her gaze for a moment, then reread Kara's letter. Without looking up again, she added, "He's been untouchable for decades. How did you get any of this?"

"Legally, if that's what you're asking." That much was true. Just like with the Mercers and their patsies, Kara had dug up the tiny anomalies that added up to a hell of a lot more than circumstantial evidence.

On their own, each instance of James Torres' overreach could be dismissed. Put together, it was damning. Enough to tarnish his reputation, at the very least. More likely, if made public, it would be enough to prompt rumors, then the reality of a grand jury. Whether it went anywhere from there was a gamble at best, but Kara didn't think tipping the scales would hurt. After all, in this instance, doing so would bring the scales back to even.

"Have you reached out to anyone else?" Carter asked.

"No other media outlets. You have the exclusive coverage at this point."

"But you *have* offered it to someone else who *isn't* in the media."

"Nestor Palmer."

Carter's eyes narrowed thoughtfully. "Palmer does good work, for a lawyer. They gonna move on it?"

Kara shrugged. "You'd have to ask."

"Mm."

The journalist folded the letter and slipped it back into its envelope, then slid the envelope into the inside pocket of her beige peacoat. She picked up her coffee and stood. "See you around."

Kara nodded, then watched her go. She finished her coffee and left, pulling the *ausklammern* fields along with her. They felt like an extension of herself now, like a bubble that floated around her at all times. It didn't stop people from running into her on the street, but it meant they didn't give her a second glance.

Kara stuck her hands in her pockets. Tomorrow would be an interesting day. She could feel it in her knees.

Monday, January 15, 2091

Much to Ana's displeasure, Kara kept refreshing her phone at the breakfast table that morning. "*Ay, niña,* put that thing away! It is impossible to truly enjoy one's morning coffee if you are chained to that thing! It is worse than a pair of concrete shoes. *Dios mío...*"

Kara pulled the screen down to refresh the headline feed again. "Sorry, Ana. If anything's gonna happen, it's happening in the next ten minutes. I don't want to miss a second of it."

Ana kept grumbling in Spanish, making Maria chuckle under her breath while she ate her breakfast beside Kara, but Kara wasn't paying attention. Her last refresh had borne fruit, and she was reading the just-published article while wearing an ear-to-ear grin.

NLAPD Commissioner Complicit in City-Wide Corruption. Torres Tops NLAPD Statistics for Dirty Policing.

Naturally, the byline was Renée Carter's.

The article had pride of place on the *Post*'s coverage. If Kara picked up a paper edition, she had no doubt it would cover the top half of the front page. It went on to list dozens of Torres' indiscretions, irregularities, and illegalities. Carter finished the article by decrying the NLAPD not only for *allowing*, but for aiding and abetting this dirty commissioner in his favoritism-laden, reactionary policies.

In short, it was the type of bombshell few people's careers would survive. Time would tell at this point whether the career that would go up in flames was Torres', or whether it would rebound and erase Renée Carter from the *Post*'s eminent ranks.

Kara hoped desperately for the former, and not only because it would take James Torres out of the position of authority he'd been abusing for decades. Kara also hoped that if she could bring James Torres down publicly, she might be able to limit the collateral damage. Anyone who stuck their neck out to tell the truth might be a target, and Kara couldn't be there to protect them all, as much as she might like to.

Part of her knew it was wishful thinking to even *hope* for a limit to the collateral damage. James Torres had built an impressive, well-entrenched network. It wouldn't only be *him* digging his heels in and fighting back, but everyone he controlled and everyone who held their positions thanks to him.

Even now, the comment section was filling with reactionary crap. Kara sucked a breath in through her teeth as she scanned the vitriol. Some people were calling for Torres' head, but an equal number wanted Renée Carter drawn and quartered for daring to besmirch a valued public official's reputation.

"What's that?" Maria leaned over. "You look bothered."

Kara grimaced. "When you fight someone who fights dirty, everyone gets covered in mud."

Kara set her phone aside and dug into her breakfast. She would check the news again later to see if Torres had commented. Either way, she had a notice to finalize for tomorrow morning, and in the meantime, Ivonne wanted to show her new ways to use her *ausklammern* skills for visual camouflage. The day promised to be busy.

A sly smile crept across her face. *But not as busy as James Torres', I hope.*

CHAPTER FIFTEEN

<u>**Tuesday, January 16, 2091**</u>

Just like with Willie Marrow, Kara layered redundancy into the serving of James Torres' notices of judgment. This time, she had paid to publish a copy of the notice in the newspaper she knew ended up on his desk every morning. She'd also hired a courier to show up with a second copy on his coffee break.

Again like Willie Marrow's set of four-week notices, Kara was taking the third copy personally. She wouldn't run into him face-to-face, not unless his daily movements were extraordinarily out of the norm, but she was taking the opportunity to case his residence. She hadn't yet made a plan for day zero since she'd been so busy keeping Maria and Carlos out of Athemis' grip. She needed to remedy that.

This excursion also afforded her the chance to test a few more things.

One was the stealth suit she had found while packing Jacob's hidden room. It looked like something out of a video game or a movie, all smooth black leather with a million pockets and holsters for weapons. It was also tailor-made for a woman, and the craftsmanship was incredible.

This was puzzling since Grimm had insisted there had never been a female Free Judge for any great length of time. The only two in the line before her had, according to him, "taken their oaths in times of dire distress." She'd looked them up in the *Book of the Dead.* Neither had lived more than three weeks after taking their oaths.

Not enough time to have a suit like this made, that was certain. And the suit couldn't have been more than a couple of decades old, whereas Greta and Aminta had lived in the 1890s and 1930s, respectively.

The suit also fit her like a glove, which was the biggest hint that something about this was strange. Grimm claimed not to know where it had come from. Maria didn't remember Jacob having it made. Kara had a hunch her mother had been in on it somehow, but she had no proof and didn't expect to find any. It would remain a mystery.

The suit fit perfectly under her preferred red-and-black leather jacket. With the wrist-knife hidden under the cuff and her chosen weapons tucked into their various holders, and the leather mask tight over her face, Kara met her reflection's gaze in the mirror and felt her chosen moniker settle over her shoulders like a heavy cape.

Nemesis.

The notice tucked in the inner pocket of her jacket bore the name at the bottom of its dire, weighty words. She had signed it herself, although not in her own handwriting. That was too easily traced, especially by someone with police connections. She had practiced writing the word in Gothic lettering until she could copy it perfectly every time.

Grimm had chided her for the theatrics, but Kara privately thought he was quite pleased.

The leather suit would be extra stealthy at night, where she would blend into the shadows with ease. However, it had proven equally useful in daylight. After handling the garment, Ivonne had informed her that the thread was enchanted. It would amplify Kara's *ausklammern* fields, rendering her the next best thing to invisible.

The second thing Kara was testing today was the new transportation method Ivonne had installed in the tunnels between Kara's estate and NLA proper. Kara had come home after yesterday's outings to see a dozen stocky, diminutive men with rock dust on their clothes and cuticles rimmed in black being fed hearty portions of rice, beans, and fish by Ana Reyes.

These were, unsurprisingly, folkloric dwarves, on loan from the Court of Iron and Diamond. Their king, Dwendal of the Morian Slate, had owed Hollow Tree a favor. Kara had begun to protest the use of such a boon on someone as unimportant as her, and Ivonne had skewered her with a look before she could finish the sentence.

The Morians had cleared the tunnels between Kara's house and the city limits. They'd been careful not to clean anything that would have tipped off city maintenance, but they had made everything passable between Point A and Point B...and they'd installed a lightning-fast train system. The train was enchanted, to boot, which meant that only those Kara deemed trustworthy enough to carry one of the enchanted tokens could even *see* the train, much less ride it.

The train could take passengers and cargo alike between the estate and the city with a transit time of less than ten minutes. From the disembarkation point, one could climb a hidden staircase to reach the city proper, emerging in a hidden corridor in a subway station.

They would have to work out a plan for getting groceries through without people wondering why someone was pushing a shopping cart into a subway station's maintenance corridors, but as long as they could slip away, it would seem like they'd gone through a brick wall.

Kara patted the pocket with the notice safely tucked inside, then plucked the token from atop her dresser. The thin metal coin warmed to her touch. It looked like a dime unless you examined it closely, in which case you would spy the spelling error that marked it as a counterfeit.

Good thing I never buy anything with change. The last thing I need is for these to get lost. Here's hoping Athemis never mugs me for my lunch money.

She slipped the token into another pocket, then headed to the basement. She waved at Ana on her way through the kitchen, then ran into Cedric at the entrance to the tunnels. He was leaning on the wall with feigned nonchalance.

"You're sure you don't want backup?"

Kara smiled. "It's just recon. He won't even be there. Plus, I'm pretty sure I could take him if he were. He's a police commissioner, not a mercenary. He works a desk job. He hires *other* people to do the beating up."

Cedric's lips tightened. "Stranger things have happened."

Kara tapped the side of her hood. "You'll be on the comm the whole time. If I need you, I'll call. Promise."

This didn't reassure him. "You'll still be over half an hour away."

"It will be *fine*, Cedric. And if it's not, I promise you can tell me 'I told you so' when I come back."

"As long as you're alive for me to tell you."

Kara smiled behind the mask. "It's good to know you care. I'll be back. Cross my heart."

She pulled the door open and slipped through into the cool darkness of the tunnels before she could let herself wonder about the strange look on his face, or the butterfly that had fluttered abortively in her stomach.

Kara rolled her shoulders, then jogged down the tunnel. *Recon first. Then consider whether you're developing a crush on your sparring coach.*

She emerged into the "train station," the platform at the end of the tunnel the Morians had built that housed the magical foci necessary to create and maintain the enchanted train. Crystalline structures grew from the concrete and along the steel rails in an odd juxtaposition of fantasy and reality.

When Kara got close enough, an array of green-tinged crystals glittered and the air over the empty rails shimmered, revealing a train car that looked remarkably like a standard NLA subway compartment. Its doors slid open when she stepped up to it, and when she sat on one of the vinyl-covered benches, it silently rolled away from the crystals.

The magical subway picked up speed in utter silence. Kara felt as though she were sitting on a stationary park bench, with the world moving around her. The experience was surreal—another fairytale, like the glade in the Black Forest.

Ivonne's promise bore out. Within ten minutes, the blur of movement outside the windows slowed and stopped, and a matching set of crystals glowed to welcome her and light the debarkation platform.

Kara stepped out and slowly shook her head in wonder. An old line from a book ran through her head: *Any sufficiently advanced technology is indistinguishable from magic.* Part of her preferred to believe that this display couldn't truly be *magic*. Surely, it was more likely that the fairies were an advanced civilization, maybe ancient aliens, who had evolved before humans and chose to live alongside them.

She snorted and headed briskly for the exit to the mundane subway. *Yeah. Because that's any more believable than "fairies are real."*

Kara came to the end of the hidden corridor a minute later. It looked like a solid brick wall, but if Kara had learned anything in the last six months, it was that looks could be deceiving. She tentatively reached out to touch the faded red bricks, and her hand passed through them.

I really hope they were right about the design, and no one's on the other side about to watch me walk through a wall.

Kara drew a deep breath and strode forward. She instinctively closed her eyes, only to snap them open again in case of imminent danger half a heartbeat later. As a result, she caught a flash of the incoming brick wall, and even though her foot and leg were already through, she flinched.

She passed through without incident into an unlit corridor, only feeling mildly ridiculous. The far end of the tunnel was taped off, much like the tunnel she'd snuck into when tailing Maria's and Carlos' kidnappers. *Smart. Not likely that anyone will come down here without a good reason, which means I need to avoid giving anyone a good reason.*

Kara let the *ausklammern* fields slide into position around her. The familiar sensation of warm blankets eased some of the tension in her shoulders, and she stalked forward like a cat. Nemesis was on the prowl.

An hour and forty-five minutes later, Kara couldn't believe she had made it to James Torres' house entirely unnoticed. She'd boarded buses, jaywalked, and on one occasion, danced a grapevine past a pair of beat cops eating mini donuts from a street vendor. Not a single person had glanced in her general direction. This suit truly *was* magic.

To be fair, I'm expending a lot of energy to keep it locked down so tight. I'll have to be a little more actively *stealthy on my way back.*

Still, testing this suit was part of the reason she was out here, so it was worth the effort. It was also deeply reassuring to know that if she wanted to, she could completely disappear.

As long as Athemis doesn't have Torres' place blanketed with ausklammern *cancelers. That could be interesting.*

James Torres lived in a mansion in one of NLA's most affluent neighborhoods. It paled in comparison to Kara's new house out in the hills, but Kara didn't want to think about Torres' property tax bill. *Not that he probably pays it.*

Tall hedges hid the mansion from the street *and* the iron fence posts with sharp tips that kept people out. Two elegant pillars of smooth coral stone flanked a modern gate with an electric lock. Security cameras perched atop each pillar and lurked every couple of dozen feet in the hedges. A long driveway curved away from the gate, allowing passers-by a view of the neatly tended lawn and flowerbeds but no glimpse of the house.

Kara had no intention of going in the front door. She didn't sense any *ausklammern* cancelers, but that didn't mean they weren't there. Instead, she circled the property, hunting for a contractors' or delivery entrance.

It took another fifteen minutes of walking, but she hit paydirt. The hedges continued around the perimeter, thick and thorny, but at the very back of the lot, she found a smaller metal gate all but hidden in the foliage.

Kara thoroughly examined the gate and found only the basic electronic locking keypad attached. That was a simple enough job for her *verschliessen* ability to cut through. She couldn't guess the code, but she could send a pulse of magic through the physical mechanism it kept shut and undo it.

The gate soundlessly swung open. Kara slipped through and locked it behind her. No sense leaving it open for someone to notice.

The back entrance opened into a sprawling, well-kept garden of topiaries. Kara couldn't imagine James Torres as a gardening aficionado, unless he had other, more nefarious uses for the pruning shears. Then again, Kara's imagination had never been her strong suit. She'd always preferred cold, hard facts after her early teens. Maybe James Torres really was an avid gardener. Maybe she would find a smorgasbord of bonsai trees inside the house looming ahead of her.

James Torres' primary residence was a two-story Colonial-style mansion. Big and square main building, whitewashed, with smaller one-story wings on either side. The gardens took up most of the spacious yard, and a large patio obviously meant for entertaining stretched across the back of the house. The patio was a much more modern style, featuring a stonework grill area and a seating area covered with open wood trusses draped in ivy. A covered hot tub sat in the corner closest to the house.

Kara realized as she crept closer that if she had continued around the property, she would have found the delivery entrance. She ducked behind a topiary as a pair of men in coveralls emerged from behind a panel van emblazoned with the logo of the food services company used by the NLAPD. They were toting a large crate between them, which seemed awfully heavy.

Wonder if Torres hires a personal chef, or if he's planning a party. Either way, I didn't consider the possibility that he might have staff. I'll have to be extra careful.

She watched until they reached the French doors on the patio. The guy on the right maneuvered until he could get his hip up to a box beside the door frame. A light flashed green, and the guy turned the lever and swung the doors open.

Card lock. Noted.

Kara stayed low to the ground as she darted between the artfully pruned bushes up to the side of the house. She spied more security cameras at regular intervals on the walls and hidden in the topiaries. She still didn't feel any *ausklammern* cancelers, but she was uncomfortably aware that if there *were* any, she would be visible from multiple angles.

That said, I want him to feel vulnerable. Maybe seeing someone get past his security without issue will make him grow a conscience?

Kara tucked herself between a decorative pillar that stretched to the roof and the west wing of the house. As far as she could tell, this was a blind spot for the camera array, and it gave her a chance to judge entry points.

The spot she liked best was the balcony above her on the back side of the west wall. It didn't extend over the wing, so if she could get on the roof of the single-story section, she could parkour up to the balcony. She had no doubt the sliding doors would be locked, but that was surmountable.

Do all police commissioners have this level of security at their personal homes? Or is Torres paranoid for other reasons?

Impossible to know without a better grip on the man's personality and history. Maybe she would learn more when she was inside.

Kara easily scaled the addition's wall. The house was old enough that it had minor cracks in its brickwork, which were child's play to dig into and use as foot- and handholds. While crouching on the roof, she gave it a once-over for anything odd before gauging the distance to the balcony railing.

It's a big jump, but I think I can do it. If not, it's a soft fall into the grass, and I'll come back with a grappling hook.

Kara stifled a chuckle. Her life had changed so much in six months. This time last year, she never would have dreamed of breaking into someone's house with a grappling hook and magic spells unless she was playing a video game or reading a book.

She bent her knees, drew a deep breath, and took a couple of running steps before leaping up and forward. Her hands caught the edge of the balcony's floor, not the railing, but she held on. Her gloves provided a good grip against the rough concrete.

She slowly pulled herself up, hand over hand on the railing, then over the top. She rested for a moment on the balcony, catching her breath and waiting to hear or see any evidence that she'd been detected.

I need to do more upper-body work. That was harder than it should have been.

No one came to investigate, either from inside or from the yard below. Unless they were lying in wait inside, Kara was good for now.

He relies on his cameras. No patrolling guards, at least not while he's not here.

The sliding door was locked, but not with a cardlock like the back doors. The simple mechanical lock was easily bypassed with an application of *verschliessen*, and Kara took care to ease the door along its track as quietly as possible.

No expectation of people climbing onto the balcony. Maybe not as paranoid as I thought, unless there's a tripwire on the other side of this curtain.

Kara lifted the curtain that hid the interior until its hem was even with her mid-calf. She saw no glint of wire, and a hail of bullets didn't immediately assault her, so she gently pulled the fabric to the side and stepped through the door.

She clapped her hand over her mouth to keep herself from laughing out loud.

She had hit the jackpot without even trying. This was James Torres' bedroom. It couldn't be anything else.

The room was decorated in a modern, minimalist style. The dark blue fabrics matched the hue of the light blue walls, and the furniture was polished dark wood. Nothing was a hair out of place, and there wasn't a speck of dust on any surface. The carpet was plush, and a shade of blue somewhere between the walls and the upholstery.

Thin blue line indeed. Do you bleed blue, Torres? Or is this all for show?

The reason she had pegged it as Torres' bedroom immediately wasn't solely the preponderance of police-uniform blue. The plaques on the walls all had his name engraved on them, and they spanned the gamut from service awards from the NLAPD to honorary degrees from NLA universities, with a few fawning acknowledgment plaques for donations thrown in.

Kara hadn't moved. She had returned the curtain to its place but hadn't closed the door. She wanted a quick getaway and was willing to risk someone keen-eyed noticing the open door if it gave her a few more seconds.

She checked the corners and saw no security cameras. She entertained the notion that one might be hidden in the large mirror on his dresser, which faced the bed. Still, Torres didn't seem the type to record sexual escapades unless they were for blackmail purposes, which put the idea firmly back in the "possible" column. It also made her stomach roil.

He's too clean. Too straightlaced. That never bodes well.

Her gaze caught on the rug at the foot of the bed. At first, she rolled her eyes. Who needed a rug on top of thick carpet? Then her jaw clenched. The design on the rug wasn't glaringly obvious, but if you knew what it was, it was unmistakable.

Woven into the rug were the barbed arrows of Athemis' sigil, the bastardized version of the symbol of the Vehmic Court.

The tattoos on Kara's arms seared hot under her suit in response to Kara's recognition. Kara exhaled slowly and crept across the room, giving the rug a wide berth. She knew where she wanted to leave the notice. If she had any tape, she would have taped it to the mirror, but failing that, she intended to leave it on his pillow.

Before she did so, she wanted to check the other doors in the room, of which there were three.

The first door yielded an ensuite bathroom the size of a small locker room. A Jacuzzi sat in the corner, across from a shower that could easily accommodate two. His and hers sinks were carved from a single block of marble, and mirrors in gilded frames reflected every glitter of mica in the stone tile floor.

No second set of toiletries, though. I knew he wasn't married, at least not openly, but this suggests he doesn't have a paramour living with him. Good to know.

Back in the bedroom, she slipped past the rug to the next door. This one opened into a hall that led to the rest of the house.

Kara briefly considered pressing her luck and investigating further, then decided against it. No need to tempt fate.

Kara was betting on the third door being a walk-in closet. The dresser and wardrobe were large enough to hold plenty of clothes, but this house had the feel of excess in the same way that hers did. Even if its racks were sparse, a walk-in closet would be the most likely candidate for door number three.

Kara frowned when the knob didn't turn. Walk-in closets didn't usually lock. If you kept valuables in it, *those* cabinets might lock, but most people considered it a real pain in the ass to have to unlock their closet in the morning to get their shoes and tie.

Kara stood there, hand on the knob, debating the wisdom of unlocking it. The rug on the floor told her without a shadow of a doubt that James Torres was in deep with Athemis. Neither the knob nor the door showed similar sigils, but the probability that this door was magically sealed, like hers was at home, had skyrocketed. Using a *verschliessen* on the lock might leave a record or set off a trap.

Next time, she promised as she released the brass knob. *Whatever you're hiding in there, I'll see it next time. For now...*

Kara crossed to the bed and withdrew the notice from the inside of her jacket. She laid the folded, sealed paper on the pillow. She considered taking a picture for proof, then shook her head. Documentation for legal purposes only worked in your favor if you weren't documenting your own crimes.

She slipped past the curtain and drew the sliding door closed, then locked it behind her by reversing her *verschliessen* spell. She watched the yard below for sixty seconds, and when she neither heard nor saw any sign of movement, she hopped onto the balcony railing, lowered herself until she hung from the edge, and let go.

Kara landed with a soft *thump* in the grass, crouching to absorb the impact. Then she crept to the edge of the house and surveyed the yard. The food service van was still there, but she heard no talking or the sound of the doors opening.

She took off, sprinting while staying as close to the ground as possible until she vaulted a low hedge. A minute later, she let herself through the back gate the same way she had let herself in and kept running.

After she'd put a couple of blocks between herself and the Torres residence, she relaxed and slipped back to the main road. She stuck her hands in her pockets and strolled toward a bus stop, easing up on the *ausklammern* a touch. She didn't need to be completely invisible now, only unremarkable. Easily overlooked. Somebody wearing their hood up against the wind that was kicking into high gear, blowing dead leaves down the street.

Being a vigilante isn't so bad when you're not fighting for your life. I could get used to this.

CHAPTER SIXTEEN

Tuesday, January 23, 2091

"I had a very interesting chat with Sarra Palmer yesterday."

"Oh?" Kara arched a polite eyebrow in the direction of her phone's camera, but otherwise did not react to Julia Kline's obvious fishing expedition. "I didn't realize you two talked."

Julia chuckled. "Sarra and I graduated the same year, only on different sides of the country. We've been in each other's orbits ever since, especially since we share several areas of interest—areas you share, too."

Kara nodded. "You'd think lawyers specializing in anti-corruption would be *more* numerous, not less. It's a rich field."

"And a dangerous one, if you don't play the game well," Julia reminded her. "Easy to fall afoul of the nastier side of humanity."

"You know, once upon a time, I would have believed that violent crimes would be the field to avoid," Kara commented. "Don't get on the bad side of the folks who like to carve people up in their spare time. But no! The ones you actually have to look out for are the ones in suits in corner offices. Anyone can kill you, but they can *really* make your life hell."

"And walk away scot-free," Julia agreed. "It takes someone

with balls of steel to stand in the way. But you aren't going to distract me that easily, Kara. I'd heard from Jack Harper that you did some consulting for Sarra, and she confirmed it.

"Then, barely two weeks after you disappear from the face of the Earth over the holidays, an anonymous legal assistant drops off a packet of documents tailor-made to take down a huge network of police corruption. And you're saying you have nothing to do with it?"

Kara shrugged. "I appreciate the legal gymnastics Ms. Palmer's going through right now. I've been following the opening salvos of briefings being filed. The NLAPD is scrambling, even though they're doing their best not to look like it."

Julia's eyelids lowered to half-mast, a sure sign she'd noticed Kara's lack of answer. Instead of pressing, she added, "It's very difficult to root out networks of corruption that go so deep. A lot of people's livelihoods ride on the load-bearing structures created by those rotten networks."

"I know. It's not pretty. Things will get a lot worse before they get better."

In the week since Renée Carter's allegations hit the papers, on the heels of Sarra Palmer's legal filings, the ever-present tension in the city of Neo Los Angeles had bubbled up to a boil. Chaos hadn't erupted yet, but tiny explosions kept cropping up. Officially, the NLAPD neither confirmed nor denied the allegations against James Torres, which was exactly as it ought to be. Kara had no problem with that. Innocent until proven guilty still mattered when you couldn't produce a supernatural book in court to prove that guilt.

What bothered Kara was the uptick in the general crime rate and in police brutality. The number of incidents was rising sharply, and it wasn't always easy to tell who had provoked whom. Meanwhile, behind the glass doors of every precinct, Internal Affairs had turned its hawk's eyes onto every department of the NLAPD. Given that the general public was split down the middle on whether it believed Renée Carter's allegations, this wasn't as reassuring as NLAPD public relations had likely hoped.

Kara still believed taking out James Torres and as much of his network as possible was necessary. Allowing him to continue in his position, especially with the knowledge she suspected he had on *her*, would make it impossible for Kara to protect and serve justice in her adopted home.

She only wished it wasn't resulting in so much collateral damage.

The holding cells were overflowing. The streets were less safe than ever. People were staying home at night and even during the day. Overnight, NLA had become a danger zone. Kara was infinitely grateful she had relocated herself and her chosen family outside city limits.

"I hope it's worth it." Julia's voice broke into Kara's thoughts.

Kara returned her attention to the video feed. "It has to be. If anything, it has to prove that the allegations are true, don't you think?"

Julia pursed her lips. "Or that the criminal elements of the city are pushing that interpretation. No assumptions, Kara. You know better."

Kara did. She had asked the question primarily to gauge Julia's view—whether her former mentor thought as she did. Based on the crinkling around Julia's eyes, she agreed with Kara, even though her words kept to the official neutral line.

Kara nodded and let a beat pass. "Have you ever worked with James Torres?"

Julia made a noncommittal face and tilted her head. "He's Internal Affairs at the NLAPD, so I've never had cause to do business with him. We've always been a few degrees removed from one another."

"But you obviously don't like him, based on that reaction."

Julia laughed. "That obvious, am I? Good to know. I'm due in court tomorrow, so my poker face had better be rock-solid."

She sobered. "No, I don't like him. Even at a distance, he's always given me an uncomfortable feeling, like he's not on the level. That's not what you want in a police commissioner, let alone in Internal Affairs. I dislike it when politics influences law enforcement, and he's always felt like a politician at his core."

Kara hummed with mild interest. "You think he's angling for a political career. Has he ever made noise about doing so?"

"Not to my knowledge. He just feels..." Julia chuckled. "He feels slimy."

"In your professional opinion," Kara teased.

"Oh, of course." Julia grinned. "I've never bothered looking into him, because again, I've never *really* had dealings with the man. But if you're in the middle of it there, and if you're doing any clerking or consulting for Sarra Palmer... Well, maybe you should dig into the man's background. Often, where someone comes from will tell you a lot about where they're trying to go."

"Good advice." Kara chuckled faintly. "Some days, I feel less like a lawyer and more like a detective."

"I know the feeling." Julia paused. Her expression shifted to the concern Kara had seen more than once that summer. "Kara..."

"I'm fine, Julia." Kara did her best to make her smile convincing. "Promise."

Julia held her gaze through the video link for a few seconds, then nodded once. "If you say so. I'm keeping an eye on you, you know."

"I appreciate it. Talk soon?"

"Any time."

Kara ended the call and put her phone on the table. The truth was, things were moving *very* fast in NLA right now. When Kara had set the wheels in motion to uncover the mess of regulatory nose-thumbing LBM Holdings was up to, it had taken weeks and *months* for Julia's efforts to bear fruit.

Sarra Palmer was pushing hard, and the city was responding. It made Kara suspect that unrest over James Torres' actions had been growing for a long time, hidden in the background. Unless people believed speaking up would be effective, most would keep their heads down. Better not to draw attention to yourself.

Which way would this uprising of public outcry tip? Would James Torres and his cronies be unceremoniously uprooted and dumped, or would a few token patsies take the fall, leaving Torres to continue? *It wouldn't surprise me if he resigned his position and kept at it from the shadows. He reminds me of a spider.*

She flicked her phone awake and scrolled through the headlines. A new one caught her eye.

Witness in Federal Regulatory Case Speaks Out.

She tapped into the story and skimmed it.

Luca Mercer, formerly of LBM Holdings, LLC, has issued a statement to the press regarding his family's company's dealings with NLAPD Internal Affairs Commissioner James Torres. According to Mercer, Commissioner Torres was a friend to the family and a support in navigating municipal administration.

"Jimmy's loyal," Mercer said when asked for comment. "You can always count on him to do exactly what he says he'll do."

Mercer declined to speculate on the veracity of the allegations facing Commissioner Torres. "That's not for me to speak on. I have nothing but respect for this country's judicial system, so it's not my place to say one way or the other."

When asked whether the terms of his plea agreement with the

*District Court of California required the disclosure of informa-
tion regarding cooperation between LBM Holdings and
Commissioner Torres, Mercer declined to comment further. "I
can't speak on any cases currently before the courts. All I can
say is that Jimmy Torres knew a lot of people, my family
included, and that he's very good at his job—hunting down
criminals."*

Kara narrowed her eyes at the last sentence. The use of the
word "hunting" could easily be a coincidence. It was hardly the
first time anyone had used the verb to describe the actions of law
enforcement. For Luca Mercer to use it about James Torres,
when both men were—or had been—involved with Athemis, an
organization that used "hunting" like a flag...

"He wanted to talk to me," she muttered. "He didn't know I
was the one he wanted to talk to, but he wanted to talk to me."

At the end of the Willie Marrow case, Luca Mercer had
turned state's evidence. Part of his request was to speak to
whoever had been gathering evidence against him and his
brother. The NLAPD and the lawyers involved had hedged on
promising to honor that request, mainly because most of them
didn't know who the anonymous tipster was.

Julia Kline, who had been Kara's direct line to Greg Hollis, the
USA Assistant District Attorney assigned to the LBM Holdings
case, most definitely knew. It hadn't surprised Kara in the least
when she'd called to ask if this new surge of legal activity had
anything to do with Kara.

Julia had kept her mouth shut, citing whistleblower
anonymity privilege, and Kara had faded into the background. At
the time, Kara hadn't wanted to go anywhere near Luca Mercer.
He and his brother had been responsible for *her* brother's death,
whether they were aware of the fact or not. They'd given Willie
Marrow ample leeway, and the enforcer had run with it.

Kara had also believed that Luca Mercer's heel-face turn had most likely been driven by fear, rather than an awoken conscience. His family's empire was crumbling, his chief enforcer was dead at the hands of a lawyer he'd been stalking, so Luca had nothing to lose and everything to gain by switching sides.

Opportunistic people didn't change their tune even if they changed their colors. Kara hadn't heard much from Luca in the last couple of months, but any time she had, she'd been mildly impressed by the sense of reform she got from the man. This latest article was no exception.

Maybe he did repent. Wouldn't that be something? The Vehmic Court's true purpose coming to fruition.

If that was the case…

Kara drummed her fingers on the tabletop. Luca and Brendan Mercer had been, unquestioningly, members of Athemis' network in NLA. Their construction companies had been responsible for the hidden room in Jacob's apartment, in a weird flash of coincidence that Kara believed was nothing of the sort, and again, *they'd killed Jacob.*

If Luca had truly turned back to the light side, he could be a fountain of information.

The thought struck Kara that she was shocked he was still alive. As far as Grimm had told her, Athemis preferred to keep a clean house. Loose ends were ruthlessly tied off.

"I guess NLA's witness protection resources are better than I thought," she started to say to the empty air of her study, until another thought interrupted her. *Until James Torres decides otherwise.*

Kara sprang from her chair like a jack-in-the-box. Luca Mercer's comments about Torres in the article were milquetoast at best, conciliatory at worst. They said very little, and Kara now had no doubt they were meant to.

He's in danger, and I need to know everything he knows not now, but now.

Kara threw her jacket on and raced from the room.

———

After she had arrested her headlong rush into action with a few seconds of even-keeled thought, Kara had returned to her study with a sheepish blush and dug into research. It hadn't taken her long to determine Luca Mercer wasn't being held in any of the district's correctional facilities.

Now she stood in front of an unassuming apartment building in downtown NLA with her hands on her hips, looking up at the windows stretching into the night sky. To be more precise, she stood in the alley opposite the building's entrance, hidden in a deep shadow cast by a particularly large billboard. Her *ausklammern* fields were turned up to eleven, and her stealth suit hugged her like a second skin.

Kara tugged the sides of her hood, ensuring it was secure on her head. Even if she was seen, she wouldn't be recognized. No one would associate the confident, professional Kara Greims, attorney at law, with this lurking, mysterious shadow figure.

If she stopped to think about it, it both scared and excited her that she was beginning to feel more comfortable, more *empowered*, as Nemesis than she ever had as a lawyer.

I guess that's why Grimm always talks about checks and balances. Can't let a Free Judge go too far. That's how you get folks like Athemis.

Luca Mercer lived behind closed doors on the seventeenth floor of the building in front of her. It was your garden-variety apartment building, except for the single suite rented by the NLAPD under the name of whatever rookie was newest to the force that year. An effective tactic, Kara had to admit. Few would think twice about a rookie cop renting a place in this section of downtown.

Kara waited for the traffic to stop. It wouldn't clear—this was too busy a neighborhood for that—but when the light turned red, she could duck across the street without anyone paying attention.

Within thirty seconds, she was through the two lanes of unmoving cars and into the alley beside the apartment building. Back here, alternately draped in the shadows cast by the ever-present advertising and lit in flashes by their obnoxious projections, she would be nearly impossible to pick out as she climbed the fire escape.

Kara kept an ear out, but the only sounds she heard were traffic and pedestrians. After the number of times Athemis had made appearances on her last case, *not* being jumped by thugs every couple of days seemed like cause for concern.

Willie Marrow specialized in intimidation tactics. James Torres has built a career on restraint. Stay alert.

She reached the seventeenth floor and laid her hand on the exterior handle of the fire door. Locked from the outside. A *verschliessen* spell through the cool metal made it *click*, and she eased the heavy door open and slipped inside.

The scent of mildew and ammonia hit Kara's nostrils like a punch to the gut. She grimaced behind her mask as she eyed the stains on the concrete stairs. This was not a five-star hotel. This place would barely qualify as livable if the rest of it was this bad.

The interior door leading to the hall was unlocked. Kara waited for a moment with her ear to the door, and when she heard no one in the corridor beyond, she entered. The NLAPD's secret safe house was suite number 1782. They kept beat cops in the lobby, masquerading as low-cost security, but they didn't appear to have left any guards outside the apartment.

Normally, I'd call that arrogant, but they probably don't want to blow their cover. That's fine. Works for me.

Kara snuck down the corridor, ignoring the peeling, discolored carpet and dingy wall sconces until she found the door marked 1782. She didn't knock. Instead, she unlocked the door with another *verschliessen* and creaked it open. The sound of muffled TV filtered out, along with muted, flickering light.

She slipped through the door, then closed and locked it behind her. No chain lock, she noticed, only the deadbolt. *Maybe I should put a chair under the door—but then again, no one should have any reason to suspect I'm here.*

"Mr. Mercer?" she called quietly into the dim apartment.

No response. A mild prickling of dread took up residence under her ribcage. What if she was too late? What if James Torres had ordered Luca Mercer killed before she could get there?

She shook the paranoia away. *He has no reason to think you'd go after him. Don't borrow trouble.*

Kara crept forward. The safe house was minimally furnished and certainly wasn't overflowing with Mercer's belongings. A jacket hung by the door, and a pair of boots were crooked on the mat. No art hung on the walls. The stale smell of takeout permeated the air, mixed with ancient nicotine. Judging by the appliances in the tiny kitchen she passed, the décor hadn't been updated in fifty years or more.

A door to a bedroom led off from the short hall from the entrance, directly after the empty closet. It was ajar, but Kara didn't look in. She would check the open areas first and return to the bedroom if she didn't find Luca elsewhere. The door after the bedroom was the bathroom, and a glance inside revealed similarly out-of-date furnishings and no Luca Mercer.

The hall ended in a living room with a sagging couch and an old television. A large window covered most of the wall, allowing a gorgeous view of billboards and not much else. Curtains of an ugly peach paisley were half-drawn to conceal the gaudy cityscape. A nicked and scratched coffee table sat between the worn-out couch and a threadbare armchair, covered in several magazines, newspapers, and empty takeout boxes.

Luca Mercer was asleep on the couch. He'd lost weight since being taken into custody. His press photos at the time of his arrest showed a man with full cheeks and thick hair, somewhat of a baby face. Now, those full cheeks had sagged into jowls, and his hair, while still thick, lay in greasy clumps on his head. Even asleep, there were bags under his eyes.

He wore glasses, which were askew on his face, and he had on a stained T-shirt and ratty jeans. One of his socks had a hole. He was certainly a far cry from the confident, suit-wearing man she had seen on the front cover of the *NLA Times*.

My, how the mighty have fallen.

The TV was playing a rerun of an old soap opera with the volume down. Most of the newspapers on the table were open to the crossword section, and a pencil in dire need of sharpening lay over the latest issue. Judging by those she could see, Luca Mercer was a fair hand at word puzzles.

Kara sat in the armchair. Its springs squeaked, and she winced as Luca's eyes shot open and he bolted upright. His eyes were bloodshot, and he immediately grabbed for something under his head before waking up enough to realize that whatever he was looking for wasn't there. Instead, he scrambled back on the couch and got his hands up in front of him, cowering behind his own shield as he stared, bleary-eyed and terrified, at Kara.

"Please don't kill me," he rasped. "Please, I—"

"I'm not here to kill you," Kara told him. "Sorry I startled you."

The exhausted, frightened man blinked at her several times before his brain caught up to reality. Then he sagged against the back of the couch, dragged a hand over his face, and straightened his glasses. In a much more normal voice, he remarked, "People who sneak into NLAPD safe houses are typically the kind who kill first and don't bother asking questions at all, so you'll pardon me for the assumption."

Kara inclined her head. "I'm sure I'd have made the same one in your shoes."

Luca Mercer laughed. It didn't sound amused. "Who are you?"

"I'm here to talk."

He raised an eyebrow at the lack of answer, then shrugged. "About what?"

"Athemis."

He nodded. "About time."

CHAPTER SEVENTEEN

<u>Tuesday, January 23, 2091</u>

"You know what I am," Kara stated.

Luca lifted a hand, palm up. "I can guess. You don't wear your symbol, though."

"We don't advertise. We prefer to let our actions speak for themselves, rather than putting our brand down everywhere like a power-hungry corporation."

Luca chuckled. "That's truer than you know." He tilted his head. "Why did it take you so long to come, Your Honor?"

Kara grimaced. "Don't call me that."

"Why not? You *are* a Judge."

Kara was about to protest, then paused. Letting on that she wasn't comfortable with a title she hadn't earned could give away clues to her identity. "Call me Nemesis."

His eyebrows rose. "Dramatic." He smiled suddenly. "Then again, we deal with magic on a daily basis. Theatrics come with the territory."

Kara narrowed her eyes, examining him. "You're not what I expected."

Half of Luca's mouth turned up in an ironic, twisted smile.

"I've had a lot of time to think over the past couple of months. I don't go out, you know. In here all day, unless I have an appointment, and those are fewer and farther between now than ever."

Kara tilted her head toward the TV. "And I suppose cable gets boring."

"Like you wouldn't believe. So, yes, I've lost some of the grandstanding, freewheeling attitude my brother and I used to share, but I didn't have as much of it to begin with as he did. I would have preferred to go into academia. Classics, actually. My brother was the businessman. Unfortunately, neither of us had much choice."

"What do you mean?"

"Athemis, like the Vehmic Court, passes its ideals down from generation to generation. Our father, and his father before him, and his father before him—all members of a secret society sworn to pursue 'justice...' Or rather, power and profit."

Kara blinked. To have Athemis' values laid out in such stark, gray words was a shock. "Athemis is a corruption of the Vehmic Court," she slowly replied. "They want to usurp the True Court's mandate to maintain justice in the mundane world, and they think our method of delivering justice is too merciful. Not decisive enough."

Luca shook his head. "That's how it started, but that's not how it is now. I'm glad you finally came to talk to me. It sounds like you need several things cleared up. But truly—why *didn't* you come sooner?"

Kara bit her lip. She'd been hoping to avoid the question. "Because I didn't trust you," she finally admitted.

He shrugged. "Fair enough. In that case, what changed?"

"I realized you were in danger. I still wasn't convinced you had actually reformed, but I knew if I wanted to get any information from you, I had to talk to you soon."

Luca let his head fall to the back of the couch, now staring at the ceiling. "Ah. Torres."

"Mm-hmm."

He rolled his head to the side to pin her with a one-eyed gaze. "Why the hell are you going after *him?* I'm sure you've noticed by now, but you picked a hell of a target."

Kara resisted the urge to avoid eye contact. "No choice."

Luca slowly nodded, eyes dark with recognition. "He caught wind of you. Threatened someone you love or someone you're protecting. Am I close?" When she didn't react, he smiled. "Figures. That's his M. O. all over. Rat bastard."

Kara cocked an eyebrow. "Do all Athemis operatives think so little of each other? I got the impression you were all cronies, like the old boys' club."

Luca chuckled. "They—we—play at it, when appropriate, but you'll never meet a bigger bunch of back-stabbers."

His amusement faded as soon as it arrived. He lifted his head from the couch and met Kara's gaze squarely. "You've picked a very apt name for yourself, Miss Greims."

Kara jolted. "How—"

Luca held up a hand. "There's no point dancing around it. Athemis knows who you are. I know who you are. We've been hunting Free Judges for generations, and your family is the last."

Kara's grip tightened on the arms of her chair. She knew she'd gone pale behind the mask. She felt faint. Of course they knew. "Then why doesn't Torres…"

"Gun you down in the street?"

She nodded.

"Not his style. That was Brendan's style, as you'd know all too well."

For a second, Kara didn't realize what Luca was referring to. Then the image of her brother's face, lifeless like a block of modeling clay, on the slab in the morgue, flashed across her mind's eye. She swallowed against the wave of bile that rose in her throat. They hadn't quite gunned him down in the street, but they'd killed him in cold blood in his own apartment.

"Tell me," she managed. Her voice was hoarse because her throat was tight as a vise.

Luca sighed. "You deserve to know. And you're right—my days are likely numbered. Hard to say, with James. He plays the long game like no one else I know. So, if I don't tell you now, God only knows if I'll get the chance otherwise."

He drew a deep breath, then let it out. "I'd offer you a drink, but all I've got is tap water, and frankly, I don't trust the plumbing."

"Get on with it."

Luca nodded. "The second-last lineage of Free Judges was eliminated forty years ago in London. I won't go into detail or further back into history. Not relevant right now. What's important in your case is that the Greims lineage became the final stand of the True Vehmic Court in the mid-fifties."

"My grandfather?"

"Yes. He was young, and he was good. He kept Athemis on its toes for an impressively long time. He'd been properly trained by your great-grandfather.

"Athemis hadn't established a presence in the Midwest. We were focused on the coasts, in the population centers. Truth be told, we knew *of* your family, but we didn't know where you were. That was thanks to the immigration clerks on the East Coast, in large part."

"Our name changed when we left Germany," Kara guessed.

"Yes. That was the first thing that threw Athemis off your scent. But questionable record-keeping in the civil service wasn't the only reason we lost track of you. The other was the war.

"The Reconciliation War destroyed a great many records. Whole swaths of people lost their documentation, and it wasn't until the middle of the century that it all got sorted out. By then, Athemis was hunting for the Grimm line with everything it had. You were, after all, the last family standing between it and a great deal of magical power.

"It took a long time, but they found your grandfather eventually. It's hard for a Free Judge to remain under the radar if you know what you're looking for. Unless they remain itinerant and constantly change their base of operations, eventually there are too many mysterious deaths to overlook.

"He fought hard, or so I'm told. Almost convinced the operatives sent to kill him that he didn't have a son, too, even though we already knew he did. Charismatic man. Persuasive."

Kara's stomach had turned into a clenched iron fist. She knew what was coming next. She also knew that the story she'd believed all her life, that her grandfather had died of a heart attack, was a lie. She'd suspected it since becoming a Free Judge, but to have it confirmed in stark, uncompromising terms was a blow.

"Your father did just that," Luca continued. "He kept us on a merry chase, taking contracts all over the country. We were so busy following him around that we didn't realize he *had* children until just before we killed him, and the sly bastard managed to die at home in bed anyway."

Kara blinked away tears that slid down her cheeks and into her mask. She'd been at her father's deathbed.

Luca looked up and caught the glimmer of tears in Kara's eyes. He winced. "Oh, God. I'm sorry. That was incredibly insensitive. If you can believe it, I meant that with the utmost respect. Your father was impressively good at avoiding capture."

Kara inclined her head, then brushed more tears away with the back of her gloved hand. "I could hear it in your voice. Otherwise, I probably would have decked you."

"And I'd have deserved it." Luca sighed heavily. "After your father's death, the last person standing between Athemis and full control of the Vehmic Court was your brother. Athemis found him here, which meant he was in our district."

"Athemis has districts?" Kara straightened and squared her shoulders, trying to banish the roiling emotions to a corner of her mind. She had buried her brother. She didn't want to think about it.

"Just like Free Judges have their areas of influence, yes. Only ours still make sense, because we still have enough operatives to have more than one district. Your purview is Neo Los Angeles on paper, but in practice, it's the world. Although I don't imagine your magic books give you contracts outside the city."

Kara opened her mouth to reply, then paused. "I don't know if I should tell you that, seeing as you keep saying *we*."

Luca lifted his hands in acknowledgment. "Fair enough. I can't blame you. All I can say is that… Well, I'd be lying if I told you I'd always had my doubts about the family business. I didn't. I was as gung-ho as the rest of my generation. 'Who do these fairies think they are, telling us humans how to live our lives?' et cetera. I enjoyed *sticking it to the man*, even after I realized that in the grand scheme of things, *we* were more The Man than the Vehmic Court ever was."

He clicked his tongue. "Rich men will bend reality to suit their whims, no matter how far they have to bend it. And unfortunately, reality is resilient. It doesn't always break."

"That's where I come in," Kara muttered. "Anyway, you were saying you didn't always have doubts. Does that mean you do now? I have to admit, I suspected as much, but I wasn't convinced."

Luca nodded. "You're correct. Until Jacob became Athemis' target, my brother and I were several arms' lengths away from the day-to-day operations. Our family had been deeply involved a few generations back, and we were coasting on the inherited money and prestige and kicking back into the pot while enjoying the community that came with it. Repeating dogma that, while we certainly believed it, we didn't really *understand* it."

"Easy to do with any belief system," Kara observed. "Not everyone instinctively asks questions when they're handed a worldview from someone they trust."

"Especially if it comes with comfortable living and a sense of security. But when we were informed that Athemis' final target lived in Neo Los Angeles, that meant the ball was squarely in our court. We were given the task of ending your brother's life.

"My brother's a nasty piece of work," he admitted. "We discussed potential plans for some time, but he was the one who came up with the idea of manipulating things so Jacob would find, then lease, one of our apartments. Then we'd let him get comfortable in his new position as a Free Judge and nudge him toward targets that were convenient for us."

"Making him work for you." Kara's voice felt dull and her heart was heavy. She'd wondered at the string of coincidences that had led to Jacob renting an apartment belonging to Luca and Brendan Mercer—and the Russian nesting doll of shell companies that hid that fact.

"Precisely. Brendan was pleased as punch about the result. Said it proved whoever was running the Vehmic Court was an idiot, if they couldn't figure out that their ancient, sworn enemy was playing them like a piano."

Luca's lips tightened, and his gaze drifted into the middle distance. "I've always been the more bookish of the two of us, so I was starting to research the histories of the Vehmic Court and of Athemis. It didn't take me long to realize that Athemis had a brutal advantage on the playing field, simply because it doesn't require its members to maintain full secrecy. We keep our ranks closed because it suits us, not because we'd die if we didn't.

"That wasn't a fair fight, and it rankled me. After that seed of doubt was planted, I began to realize a whole host of our beliefs were cruel and unusual. I couldn't believe it was acceptable to hunt individual humans like it was a sport—that was the second domino. The third, and the one that broke the dam, was realizing that Athemis' ulterior motive of world domination through power and magic was actually, well, not justice at *all*.

"Athemis claims that the Vehmic Court no longer upholds

justice. That it's too slow, too ponderous, and shows mercy where it is unwarranted. The longer I looked at the actual state of affairs, the less I could convince myself that our way was better. At some point in our history, we'd shifted from executing criminals without due process—which was bad enough—to killing anyone who didn't agree with us."

"Did you figure this out before or after you killed my brother?"

Luca closed his eyes. His face burned with shame. "Before. Not long before, but long enough that if I hadn't been a coward, I might have made a difference."

With visible effort, he forced himself to open his eyes and look at Kara. "If it were just for you to kill me here and now, I accept it. I accepted that possibility a long time ago, before you even sent the first notice to Willie Marrow. I know I've been living on borrowed time. I've been trying my best to do the right thing with that time, but I know I can't make up for what I did *or* for what I allowed to happen."

Kara held his gaze for a long moment. Luca didn't flinch or look away. Eventually, Kara nodded. The sigils on her arms ebbed and flowed with warmth, but did not burn with conviction the way they did when she knew terminal judgment was warranted. This one was in her court.

"I believe your repentance is genuine," she told him. "From what I've seen in the papers, you've been doing everything you can to help the authorities pin your brother down, regardless of what it's cost you. And from what you're telling me now, you're not doing it for personal gain."

Luca cracked a wry smile. "Again, I'd be lying if I claimed there wasn't *any* self-interest involved. It would be the cherry on top if I came out of this with not only my life, but something to live off. So, yes, part of me hopes for that, but I'm not holding my breath."

"You don't expect it," Kara paraphrased, and when he nodded, so did she. "That's the key. This isn't tit-for-tat. You're making amends and hoping for the best, but you recognize you might not get your preferred outcome."

"Yes."

"Then I have no reason to kill you." Her tattoos flared once, but where usually the heat was like fire, this time it reminded Kara of a hot bath. More tension left her shoulders.

Luca sat up a little straighter and blinked as if the sun had just come out. "Really?"

"Really," Kara repeated. "The point of the Vehmic Court—my *job*—is to uphold and fight for justice. Justice isn't always *death*. That's why we send the notices. If someone has a change of heart, a *real* change of heart where they *do* something about it, the Court recognizes that as authentic repentance. Justice is served either way."

Luca let out a breath that Kara would swear he'd been holding for years. "Thank God."

Kara raised an eyebrow. "You do realize that this means you're in at *least* as much danger from Athemis as you ever were from me, right?"

A giddy, slightly loopy chuckle bubbled up from within him. "Oh, yes. I know how they work better than even you do. I'm no less marked for death than I was five minutes ago, but now I feel...relieved. If Athemis kills me, it's a crime. If you killed me, it would have been a just punishment."

Kara let him have his moment of relief while she processed everything he had already told her. When he'd relaxed against the couch again, and his eyes seemed marginally less haunted, she asked, "So what do they want with Maria?"

Luca's brow creased together with recrimination and anger again. "They want the baby, which I assume you already knew."

"Yes. Why?"

"At first I thought they would simply kill him, but apparently infanticide is a step too far even for my former brothers. Instead, they intend to raise him as one of them. Usurp the contract without the murder. Almost like passing the torch."

Kara didn't flinch. This wasn't a new idea for her. "Will it work?"

Luca shrugged. "Your guess is as good as mine. Athemis has no magic of their own. They've been trying to find ways around the Vehmic Court's magic for centuries, whether by clever technological devices or making deals with creatures one shouldn't name in polite conversation."

Kara's eyebrows shot up. "Demons?"

"Essentially."

"Oh, *great.*"

"I wouldn't worry about that too much. The cells that have experimented with such Faustian bargains have never lasted long, and they've gone out with a bang every time. The party line now is technological advancement only. Humans are better than fairies, and so on."

Kara's heart rate slowed incrementally. "I will provisionally believe you on that, but I'm tucking it away for further investigation."

"Wise."

"One more question. James Torres."

Luca released his heaviest sigh yet. "I wondered when we would get around to him."

"Is he head honcho of Athemis in NLA now that you and Brendan are out of the picture?"

"Not quite. He was head honcho all along, but Brendan and I were the front lines. He worked above us and directed us, along with the rest of his network."

Kara's heart rate ticked up again. "Does everyone in his network know about Athemis?"

Alarm passed over Luca's face. "God, I hope not. Not as far as I know. If they do, that would be a massive breach of secrecy. Just because Athemis didn't keep the Circle as tight as the Vehmic

Court did doesn't mean they opened the floodgates wide. We were—it was—it *is* still a secret society."

Kara exhaled in mild relief. "Okay. That's good to hear. I'll take mundane criminals over Athemis any day of the week."

She glanced at the curtained window, then over Luca's shoulder toward the door. "Are you safe here?"

Luca shrugged. "Until James Torres decides I'm no longer worth keeping alive."

"You're a federal witness. Surely, capping you would cause him more problems than it would solve."

"You would think so, yes, and normally I'd agree with you. James is pragmatic. He won't move against me vindictively or out of any sense of personal discontent. But if he thinks I'm endangering Athemis, and if he thinks he can get away with it…"

Luca let his disconsolate gaze drift over the grubby apartment. "If that comes to pass, I'm certain I won't be the only ghost haunting these halls."

CHAPTER EIGHTEEN

<u>Wednesday, January 24, 2091</u>

Kara left Luca's apartment the same way she arrived. She left behind a way to contact her anonymously, and double-checked that she had erased the memory of any security cameras she had passed on the way by. There was only one in the hall, but the last thing she wanted was for her visit to tip James Torres off about how deep Luca's change of heart had gone.

Now his statements in the paper make even more sense, she reflected while skulking through the shadows away from the apartment building. *He was trying to reassure Torres that he wouldn't speak against him while maintaining his commitment to not being a piece of shit anymore. That's a fun line to walk.*

Her mind spun with possibilities and considerations. Could she spring Luca from the apartment building and take him back to her estate? Would he be a valuable asset? Just how much did he know about Athemis, and could he help her?

These questions ran in circles around her brain, creating a whirlwind of thought that meant she almost missed the cry for help that echoed down the alley.

Kara snapped back into focus and sank into a fighting crouch, still ensconced in the deep shadows. It was past midnight, but the streets of downtown NLA never slept. She might have been hearing a mugging in progress, or someone suffering from hallucinations on a bad trip.

"Please, Officer, he can't breathe!"

Dark anger flashed through Kara's heart, and the tattoos on her arms lit up with angry fire. Someone having a bad trip wasn't *technically* her responsibility, but police brutality—especially when the infamous James Torres might have sanctioned it—*very much was.*

Kara sprinted down the alley toward the voice. "Not on my watch," she whispered.

She arrested her momentum a few feet from the alley mouth, just shy of where the streetlight reached. She hardly needed her enhanced senses to hear what was happening outside her field of vision.

"*Please*, Officer!" The begging voice belonged to a woman, its pitch artificially raised with fear and despair.

"No can do, ma'am! He was resisting!" The answer came from a man with a deep voice whose nonchalant, almost *amused* tone curdled Kara's stomach and filled her chest with burning rage.

"Yeah!" "You tell 'em, Sarge!" "Show 'em who's boss!" "Keep these streets safe!" Three more voices, two male and one female, jeered in support, presumably of their fellow officer. In between the shouted comments, they cackled with raucous laughter.

Kara couldn't believe what she heard. If she didn't know better, she'd have said they were drunk. *Maybe they're off-duty and making a plainclothes arrest.*

She debated, for a split second, what tactic suited the situation best. Keep the *ausklammern* on and sneak up on them? Use an *ablenken* to scare them off?

Then Kara's ears picked up the sound of a man struggling to breathe.

She dropped the *ausklammern* fields keeping her invisible in the darkness. Her mask and suit would let her remain incognito, but she didn't want rumors of magic floating around NLA's city streets.

Not yet, anyway.

Kara sprinted out of the alley and skidded to a stop on the sidewalk, facing the tangle of voices with her fists balled and her stance wide. "Hey!"

Thirty yards away, a broad-shouldered man in the dark blue uniform of the NLAPD had a knee on the back of a larger man, who was prone with his arms bent up behind him. Kara couldn't see either man's face. The victim's face was turned away, and the cop's face was bent over and in shadow.

Two of the three other cops stood directly behind and at the aggressor's feet. They were also in uniform, although Kara noted they were of a lower rank than the sergeant pinning the man to the ground. The third cop stood a few feet away, half-turned from the action. Keeping a lookout, if Kara had to guess, although for what, she didn't know.

The woman whose scream had alerted her to the incident stood between Kara and the group. She, like her companion—Kara presumed—wore casual clothes that looked a little worn. Her jeans had a hole in one knee, and the cuffs of her purple sweater were frayed and faded.

She was otherwise clean, however, and neither of them gave off a criminal vibe. If anything, Kara would have guessed that they'd been out for a late-night bite to eat, based on the purse under the woman's arm and the plastic bag with Styrofoam takeout containers dropped on the concrete a couple of feet behind her.

I see no motive. That's backed up by the nasty smiles on the cops' faces. Do they think they can get away with this just because it's the middle of the night? Or is it because they think, since Torres is under scrutiny, no one will pay attention to them letting off a little steam?

At Kara's yell, the woman had whirled. Her face was round

and open with terror. "Please! You have to help him! He can't breathe, he has asthma!"

One of the cops, the woman, laughed. *"He has asthma!"* she mocked. "You gang rats will claim anything!"

The woman in the purple sweater turned back. Her hands curled into shaking fists, and the tension in her throat made her yell come out strangled. "We're not gangsters! We were *buying Chinese!"*

"Yeah, yeah! Everybody knows that dive is an Eastern Front business. Can it, bitch!" This was from the guy standing beside the female bystander cop. He rolled his eyes and scoffed.

The cop pinning the guy to the sidewalk had only looked up long enough to notice that someone had arrived. While the woman had been calling back to Kara, he'd returned his attention to the guy he had pinned. Kara saw the uncaring smile that painted his face and left the other three to trade barbs.

She reactivated her *ausklammern* field, just strong enough to keep them from paying too much attention to her as she moved. It was a gamble. They'd already seen her, and it was always harder to convince someone that the person they'd seen was *no longer* there, instead of convincing someone that no one had been there to begin with.

Still, she suspected they were having too much fun and were too secure in their perceived control of the situation to pay her any mind.

She was right. The only one who reacted to her circuitous rush, arcing toward the pair on the ground by deking around close to the wall of the building beside them, was the one keeping lookout—and he was too slow. The lookout had barely opened his mouth to warn his sergeant of Kara's approach when she cannoned into the aggressor.

The sergeant flew five feet and landed awkwardly on his shoulder. He shouted and tried to roll the rest of the way, but the rough concrete had already arrested his momentum. He *thudded* to the ground, out of breath, his face creased with pain.

Kara got her toe under his ribs and levered the big man over onto his stomach. He yelled as the movement jostled his injured shoulder, then let out a harsh gasp as Kara yanked his wrists together behind his back and cuffed him with a zip tie from his belt.

She did the same to his ankles, then turned sharply to face the two who had been closest. She wanted to render medical aid to the guy on the ground, but she had three more cops to handle. Her attack had only taken a few seconds, but cops were still trained to move quickly. Add to that a dose of indignation, and they would be all over her.

As Kara had expected, when she lifted her gaze from the incapacitated sergeant, she was faced with two very angry officers. The woman's hand had strayed to the handgun on her belt, and the man had taken out his baton. They were advancing very gradually, and if they were intimidated by Kara's quick takedown of their superior, their fury displaced their fear.

"Call 911!" Kara shouted over their shoulder to the woman in the background. "Get help for your friend! And for God's sake, start filming if you can!"

A radio squawked static behind her. "5-Echo-25, this is Officer Franklin. Relay to emergency dispatch that they're about to get a civilian call they can disregard. We have a civilian interfering in an arrest here, but we have it under control."

Kara could have laughed out loud if the outright disrespect for public services and public *decency* wasn't so blatant. "Emergency dispatch can't *ignore a call,* you idiot! They have to come!"

The woman advancing on Kara sneered. "That's what you think. But when you drop the right name, it makes all the difference."

Kara gauged the distance between her and the woman, then shot out with a quick, disabling jab to her wrist. The woman swore, but the handgun she had unholstered skittered across the pavement. Kara followed up with a series of lightning-fast blows designed to incapacitate, not injure, and the female cop went down hard.

Kara reached for the zip ties on her belt, but had to dance away as the male cop's baton swung for her head. He was faster than his partner, and Kara was forced to dodge and pivot. Behind him, the lookout was craning to see farther up the street, and behind Kara, the female cop was struggling to get to her feet.

"I'm filming!" the woman behind them all shouted. "Terry, are you okay? Can you breathe?"

"I can," the guy on the ground managed. "Barely."

"See? He's fine!" The man with the baton laughed in Kara's face, then menaced her again with the baton. "So now you're in *real* trouble, whoever the fuck you are."

Kara gritted her teeth while continuing the dance. She stomped her right foot and was rewarded with a choked-off shriek from the female cop. "You're all about to go on record for brutality against an innocent man. How far do you think James Torres' protection is really gonna go? What do you think you're worth to him? I guarantee it's not this much. He'll let you rot."

Uncertainty flickered in the man's eyes. It was enough for Kara to plunge her fist into his gut, then her knee into his groin, and the follow-up punch to his jaw sent him sprawling.

Kara zip-tied them with deft efficiency, then turned her attention to the lookout. A glare was enough to send him running.

Kara rolled her eyes, then came back to Terry, who was still on the ground. "Hey. You okay?"

"Yeah," he panted. "But if you hadn't shown up, I wouldn't have been."

"The paramedics are on their way," his friend promised.

"Thanks, Violetta."

Kara gently touched Terry's back, then pulled her hand away when he winced. "How's the pain level?"

He breathed shallowly and shook his head. "Hurts bad. Can't get a good breath. I swear I heard something crack."

Kara grimaced. "Okay, then we're even *more* definitely not moving anything until the paramedics get here. The last thing we want is a punctured lung to top off your bad day."

"Better a punctured lung than a body bag," he muttered, then wheezed.

Kara clenched her jaw and threw a nasty look at the three cops on the ground. They stared back at her, stony-faced. She was surprised they weren't firing back with more macho one-liners. Maybe their bravado had run away with their fourth buddy.

"Did you catch the fourth cop's name?" Kara asked Violetta.

"Franklin," the purple-clad woman confirmed. "These guys are regulars in this neighborhood. Nobody likes them much."

"I see. This isn't the first time something like this has happened, in other words."

Violetta shook her head. "Usually, though, there's at least *some* reason. Terry and I were minding our own business. Guess they just wanted to have a little fun."

The wail of sirens approached, cutting through the murmur of NLA's nightlife like a scalpel. Kara considered her options, then bit her lip. "I need to go," she told Violetta.

Violetta's eyebrows rose sharply. "What? But you're our best witness!"

"That means I'll be dragged into the station as soon as any other cop gets here." Another siren with a different sound added its cry to the incoming ambulance. "And while I'm all in favor of accurate statements, that only goes so far when the corruption is systemic. I'm sure I don't need to tell *you* that."

Violetta's lips tightened to a thin line. "No, ma'am. You most certainly do not."

The woman glanced up and down the street. After Kara had subdued the officers, more bystanders had begun to peek out of the hidey-holes they'd slipped into when things had gone south. By now, they were being watched by at least a dozen others, and several held phones in recording position.

Kara nodded with satisfaction. "If any of them were recording the whole time, they'll have more than enough evidence to make tonight very awkward for the NLAPD. I'll be more help if I keep an eye out for retribution. I'm no use to anyone in a holding cell or under house arrest."

Violetta took Terry's hand at the same time as the flashing lights of the ambulance rounded the corner a few blocks away. "I understand. Stay close for a while, if you can? Just in case…"

Her gaze flicked to the cops on the ground, then back up to Kara, and she glanced over her shoulder toward the ambulance.

Kara hummed in understanding. "Just in case," she echoed, then stood and turned to disappear into the alley.

Violetta grabbed her wrist. "Wait."

Kara looked down and met the woman's dark eyes. "What?"

"What's your name?"

Kara hesitated for a split second. Then she decided, *In for a penny, in for a pound.* "Nemesis."

Violetta's brow creased with a mildly confused frown, then understanding dawned in her eyes, and she chuckled. "Well, how do you like that. NLA has a superhero. Godspeed, Nemesis. Don't let them catch you."

"Never," Kara promised. She took off running into the alley a second before the ambulance pulled up beside them.

Once in the shadows, Kara plastered herself to the wall and edged closer until she could see around the corner. She watched until the paramedics exited the ambulance and went to examine and help Terry. When she saw no sign that the EMTs wouldn't treat him, as the cops had implied, she nodded.

The whole system isn't corrupt. Not yet, anyway. Some public servants still take their oaths seriously.

Kara waited a few minutes longer. Violetta stole a couple of glances her way, as did the cops Kara had tied up, but none of them tried to follow her. Kara was surprised that the cops hadn't, but maybe they figured she was long gone.

That, or they didn't want to draw more attention to how thoroughly in the wrong they'd been. In Kara's experience, dirty cops tended to have "technical difficulties" with their bodycams at very convenient times. In this case, any missing bodycam footage would line up with the video Violetta had taken—or that of any other bystander.

Another squad car pulled up to the scene a moment before Kara was going to leave. She chuckled under her breath when the man who got out immediately started tearing a strip off the cops on the ground. It sounded like he meant it, too. It wasn't a performance to cover anyone's ass.

Satisfied that Terry was in good hands and that someone honest was taking care of the perpetrators, Kara disappeared into the noisy, kaleidoscopic, Neo Los Angeles night.

Back at her estate, which she had taken to calling "the Grove" in her head, Kara hung her stealth suit up in the wardrobe in her new study. Then she slumped into her chair, leaned over to grab a match, and lit Grimm's skull.

"How do you fight a war on two fronts?" she asked him outright.

Grimm's candlelight flickered, although there was no breeze in the windowless room. "Carefully and with trusted allies," he cautiously replied. "You seem upset."

Kara cracked her knuckles, then her neck, and let her head drop onto the back of the chair. She recounted the details of her visit with Luca Mercer, then the incident in the street on the way home, before sighing and putting her chin in her palm with her elbow propped on the chair's arm.

"I guess my real question is, how can I support a system that's so corrupt? How can I trust the mundane judicial system to get it right?"

Grimm hadn't said much during Kara's tale, only interrupting a few times to clarify or for further detail. Now, instead of matching Kara's troubled frustration, he sounded sympathetic as he replied, "You can't, but you must."

"Those two verbs are mutually exclusive."

"They only *seem* so," he countered. "No one can ever know with absolute certainty what another person will do. This extends to the systems we build, as well. We cannot know that the courts will serve justice."

"Especially when we know it *isn't*," Kara grimly added. "Not always."

"Indeed. However, the moment we stop supporting it, the moment we take matters into our own hands and throw away any faith or trust we have in the structures we have built... That is the moment when those structures start to rot.

"It is also the moment when we switch sides," Grimm cautioned. "As Luca Mercer reported, Athemis is now driven by the desire for power. But when they split from the True Court, their goal was to deliver what *they* saw as 'true' justice."

Kara scrubbed her hand over her face, then detangled a few stray knots in her hair. "Right. I have to put my faith in the system, or else I'm undermining it just as much. But what if the system genuinely *is* broken?"

"Name one system that is not," Grimm countered. "Nothing we make is perfect."

"There's a big difference between dirty cops mugging and mocking innocent pedestrians, and... I don't know, fast food joints upcharging but not paying their delivery guys." Kara pursed her lips. "Okay, maybe that wasn't a great example. Wage theft is also horrible."

"But you cannot fight every system all the time," Grimm reminded her. "You would exhaust yourself, as would anyone else.

"We are forced to work within the confines of the systems we live in," he continued. "Some of us have more opportunities than others to push back against those systems, if we find they are more oppressive than helpful. That's what you have now. A chance to change things."

"I'm one person."

"One person with allies and a great deal of magic. Do not sell yourself short, Kara. You can make a difference."

Kara rubbed her eyes. They were becoming sandy, reminding her that she needed sleep. "I hope so. I left the scene tonight feeling optimistic because the EMTs and the fifth cop *seemed* like they were on the level. All of that hope disappeared by the time I got home."

"You received multiple pieces of information from *Herr* Mercer, many of which pertained to great losses you have suffered or to significant threats you face now. You had little time to come to terms with this before you were called on to defend someone in need. It is no surprise your mood changed as you returned home. You are *tired,* Kara. Go rest."

It might have been Kara's imagination, but she thought Grimm's candle glowed a little more warmly than usual, more gently. As though he were putting a hand on her shoulder and telling her everything would look better in the morning.

"Yeah. Yeah, I should. Only a few days until I have to give James Torres his third notice...if the city's still standing by then."

CHAPTER NINETEEN

<u>**Tuesday, January 30, 2091**</u>

The city was still standing by the time Tuesday rolled around. The public outrage around James Torres' allegations had died down as well, thanks to the ever-rolling news cycle.

This both pleased and bothered Kara. On the one hand, it meant the streets were less of a war zone than they had been the week prior. On the other, it meant fewer people cared about holding Commissioner Torres to account.

It was a coin toss whether that would ultimately work in her favor when it came to rooting out his network of corruption. Sarra Palmer still had her nose to the grindstone, and fewer distractions were frequently a good thing, but if the public wasn't clamoring for justice, more of Torres' pawns would be able to slip into the shadows.

Kara had received no more response to the four-week notice than she had to the six-week notice. By all appearances, James Torres had read and shredded them and was paying them no mind. Kara couldn't believe she was thinking it, but she almost missed Willie Marrow's threatening texts. Then, she had known what he was up to.

James Torres seemed to be continuing with business as usual. He'd given a press conference with Chief Harmon, where he had promised his priorities were nothing but keeping the bad apples out of the barrel. His winning smile had won over more than a few suspicious citizens. He seemed like a good guy, and since he couldn't comment on anything that was before the court, you had to believe he had reasons for doing the things that nasty lawyer said he'd done.

It made Kara sick, and not only because she could feel the insincerity oozing out of every pore. Torres was Athemis. He knew exactly what he was doing, and he was so damn good at hiding it that no one could tell who didn't agree with him already.

"How does someone like that get into power, anyway?" Kara wondered while enduring Neo Los Angeles' morning traffic. "Either Torres is a sociopath, or the system's been breaking for a long time, I suppose. I'm not sure which one I would prefer."

The radio made no reply.

Kara was on her way to deliver the third notice, the last one officially required by the Vehmic Court before she could carry out terminal judgment. The other two copies of this notice had already reached James Torres, but as with Willie Marrow, Kara decided to give the last notice a personal touch.

"And if he still doesn't think I'm serious at this point, the man must be stupid." *Or arrogant. Maybe both.*

She would show up at NLAPD headquarters that morning as herself. No subterfuge this time. There wasn't much point, she figured. Her conversation with Luca Mercer had confirmed that Athemis knew exactly who she was, so she would have to bank on them not wanting too much public attention.

Then again, if they exposed her as a vigilante, the NLAPD would be well within their rights to lock Kara away.

Kara had the unsettling suspicion that sooner or later, she

would no longer be able to continue living this double life. She would have to go entirely off the radar, functionally disappear.

"Unless I can take out enough of Torres' network that no one will be left who knows who I am," she mused. "That seems difficult, but maybe not impossible. Of course, every time I show up as myself, it gets a little harder…but then again, when have I ever done anything the easy way?"

Kara's heart was in her mouth as she parked her car along the curb and turned the engine off. She didn't think James Torres was the type to kill her outright in public, but he could start a smear campaign. One way or another, even though her visit was legitimate because she was serving papers on behalf of Sarra Palmer, this visit had the potential to change her life considerably.

Kara smiled politely at the receptionist at the front desk, despite the woman's acidic greeting. "Kara Greims, attorney at law, here to serve papers to Commissioner Torres on behalf of Nestor Palmer Law."

The receptionist nodded tersely. "Of course, Miss Greims. Go right up. I imagine the commissioner is expecting you."

At first blush, it unnerved Kara to think that Torres knew she was coming. Then she realized that as a member of Athemis, he would know exactly when the next notice would arrive. The intimidation tactic served as confirmation that the receptionist was in his confidence. No guarantee she knew about the Vehmic Court, but she was on James Torres' nice list.

Kara made her second trip up to the Internal Affairs department, keeping a low-level *ausklammern* field on the whole way. She was under no illusion that it would make her invisible, but she wanted as few people as possible to pay attention to her or realize she was there. The less scrutiny, the better.

The elevator ride seemed interminable, but at long last the doors opened. In short order, Kara was back in front of Commissioner Torres' office, smiling anew at his personal secretary.

"More legal documents for the commissioner?"

The bags under the secretary's eyes would have incurred oversize fees at any airfield. *I guess it's as good a sign as any that all of this is taking a toll on someone.*

She offered a sympathetic smile. "That's right. Is he available now? I'm afraid I have to give these directly to him."

Wearily, the secretary pressed the intercom button on her desk. "Commissioner, more legal papers for you."

Through the door, the faintest of growls could be heard. The sound made the hair on the back of Kara's neck stand on end. If she hadn't known better, she would have thought there was a wolf behind the door. *It would be just my luck to find out that Commissioner Torres is the most lupine of the Wolf Court.* She swallowed a nervous chuckle. *Good thing Luca told me that Athemis has no magic.*

Torres didn't answer his secretary over the intercom. Instead, based on the noise audible through the door, he pushed his chair sharply back, crossed his office in a few quick strides, and opened the door with enough force that he had to catch it before the knob banged the opposite wall.

The last time Kara had visited, Torres' smile had not reached his eyes. Today, every part of his expression read as perfectly pleasant courtesy, while his eyes promised retribution.

"Miss Greims. I hope you're having a pleasant morning."

"I appreciate that, Commissioner. Traffic was hell, but I have a fantastic coffee waiting in my car. Just have to get this little errand over with first." She favored him with as genuine a smile as she could muster, although she suspected her gaze was more predatory than she might have preferred. She had no need to antagonize him further, especially since it was altogether too evident that the last four weeks had taken more of a toll on him than he had previously let on.

Torres stalked across the room and snatched the envelope from Kara's hands before she could remove it fully from her messenger bag. Kara stomped on the reflexive urge to fight back. Getting into a fistfight with the NLAPD's Commissioner of Internal Affairs would only hasten her retreat into obscurity.

Torres had no such compunction. He remained in Kara's personal space, leering over her in a way that would have made most people nervous. The secretary, Kara noted, seemed fully cowed by her boss' behavior. Out of the corner of her eye, Kara could see that the secretary was averting her gaze, deliberately looking at her computer screen.

"You have some nerve coming in here," Torres hissed in Kara's ear. "I know what you are, and I could have you arrested in a heartbeat."

Kara's heartbeat pounded in her ears, but the sensation was familiar from innumerable sessions in the courtroom. Kara had faced up to nasty witnesses before, people who thought they could intimidate her into giving them a break. They'd been surprised to learn they could do no such thing, and James Torres was about to learn the same.

"On what grounds, Commissioner?" Kara pivoted gracefully out from under his gaze, moving away without moving back. She kept her pleasant smile on, and it only grew wider when a muscle in his jaw twitched in angry response. "I hardly think you'd like Ms. Palmer to file a complaint about harassing her server. I doubt it would look good on you, considering the allegations you're currently facing in court."

"Is that a threat, Ms. Greims?"

"Nothing of the sort. Only a reminder of public perception. I know firsthand how hard it can be to hold onto that perspective when you're buried in as much work as I'm sure you are right now. There's a reason sleep deprivation is considered torture. You look like you could use some coffee yourself, if you don't mind my saying."

Torres gritted his teeth and stared Kara down for several

more heartbeats. Finally, with a grunt that seemed to say, "This isn't a retreat, it's a strategic withdrawal," he turned and strode back into his office and slammed the door behind him.

Kara slowly and gently exhaled, drawing the breath out to lower her heart rate. Then she met the secretary's eyes and spoke quietly. "Sounds like it's been a stressful couple of weeks. How are you holding up?"

The secretary's mouth quirked in a half-smile. "It certainly hasn't been boring, I'll tell you that much. Luckily…"

She glanced at the office door. Kara took the hint and edged forward until she was close enough for the secretary to whisper.

"My position goes through HR, not him," she murmured. "No matter what happens, even if I leave this office, I'll still have work."

"I'm glad to hear that." Kara kept her voice low as well, just a hair above a whisper. "I've worked for hard bosses. I count myself lucky I've never had to be a whistleblower against any of them."

The secretary opened her mouth as though to say more, but movement from the inner office made her spine straighten. She glanced at the office's outer door, and Kara nodded.

I wonder if Renée spoke to her, Kara mused as she rode the elevator back down. *Secretaries are incomparable sources of information, and if you don't treat them well, you can be in for a world of hurt.*

Kara kept the *ausklammern* field up all the way through the building. Nobody gave her a second glance, which was reassuring. She had hoped the slimy knot of dread in her gut would have eased after leaving Torres' office, but the sense that the other shoe was about to drop didn't leave as she got in her car.

"I'm getting paranoid," she muttered and glanced in her rearview mirror as she pulled away from the curb. "At this rate, I'll only ever go out at night in my stealth suit."

Then the driver of the car behind her met her eyes in her rearview mirror, and he sped up to tailgate her.

The tattoos on Kara's arms flared hot. This wasn't a random impatient driver, wanting her to hurry up. The look in the man's eyes told Kara he meant business, and that point was driven home by the gunshot that crashed through her window and the passenger's side window, narrowly missing her head.

Kara's vision blurred for a split second as a scream died in her throat. Then everything snapped into harsh focus, just in time for the light in front of her to turn green.

She hit the accelerator and shot through the intersection. Her pursuer kept pace and was joined a moment later by the car that had been to Kara's left, the one with the shooter. Kara thanked her lucky stars that the road ahead was less congested than when she arrived. Without that, she would have been a sitting duck.

Kara wove through traffic at high speed, clinging to her steering wheel as though her life depended on it. The cars behind her, each a nondescript white sedan with no visible damage, sped up. Kara laid on her horn as she approached another intersection and veered to the right between two groups of panicking pedestrians.

Her luck would not hold. That was a certainty. She would have to evade her pursuers long enough to ditch her car and disappear into the city.

Kara spied a parking garage coming up on her right and left rubber on the asphalt as she turned in and sped up the ramp. The change in direction had been fast enough to lose one sedan, but the other followed Kara in.

Kara groaned as she took a turn a couple of inches too tight and broke her side mirror off. It clattered away behind her. Kara expected her attacker to run over it without remorse, but the gunman in the passenger seat leaned out and blasted it with a shotgun as the driver slowed briefly to allow him to do so.

Kara didn't have time to wonder why. She swung into another aisle of cars, pulled into the first available parking spot, and grabbed her messenger bag before running out the door. She left the engine running and the keys in the lock. If she were very lucky, they might think she was still driving for a couple of seconds. She could get a long way in a couple of seconds.

Kara cursed herself for picking today of all days to wear heels. *I should have known he'd set me up. That was too easy. Kara, you're an idiot.*

She sprinted to the end of the lane of cars and threw herself behind a wide concrete pillar as the headlights of her pursuer flashed around the corner. She covered her mouth with her hand and focused on breathing through her nose, deep and slow.

If I'm lucky, if I'm very, very lucky, they'll see my car and think I've run on. If they get out to check, I'll hit them with an ablenken *that sounds like the door to the stairs over there. Then, I book it back the other way as soon as they're through the door.*

The sedan screeched to a halt back where Kara had parked. Instead of a car door slamming open and shut, however, Kara jumped as automatic rifle fire sprayed over her car. The report of the gun and the impacts on glass, steel, and concrete echoed through the area until Kara couldn't hear herself think.

The gunfire stopped. Kara thought she heard a car door open among the echoes, followed several seconds later by a car door closing. Then tires screeched, and the car shot past her up the ramp.

Kara waited until the car had wheeled around to the next level before ducking out from her hiding spot. Keeping low, she ran between the concrete barrier and the parked cars until she was stopped by an SUV pulled right up to the wall.

She cursed under her breath and glued herself to the car while edging toward the ramp. Her ears still rang from the barrage of gunfire that had presumably destroyed her vehicle.

Can't wait to file that insurance claim. "What happened to your car, Miss Greims?" Oh, nothing much, just got shot up in a parking garage.

Why? No reason. Man, gang violence is really on the rise, isn't it? No, I had nothing to do with the incident...

The thought crossed her mind that she would have to file a police report at the same time an NLAPD squad car pulled up to block the entrance to the parking garage. Kara bit back another curse. *Friend or foe? Won't be able to tell until it's too late.*

The rumble of an engine overhead told Kara her pursuers were on their way back. A glance revealed nowhere for her to hide or escape. Her options were to wait for the gunman and driver to return or take her chances with the NLAPD before they arrived.

Bystanders were gathering around the squad car. One of the pair of officers was doing his best to keep them back, but with little luck. Rubbernecking was hardwired into the human psyche.

Witnesses make corruption harder to hide. I have to take the chance.

Kara clutched her messenger bag and darted out from behind the SUV, doing her best "panicked damsel in distress" impression as she hightailed it for the entrance. She raised one hand and yelled, "I need help!"

The officer not attempting crowd control had one hand on his sidearm and the other shielding his eyes from the sun's glare as he peered up into the dim garage. "We had a report of shots fired in this building, ma'am! Are you injured?"

"No, I—"

A *bang*, followed by a searing pain in Kara's arm, cut her sentence short. She stumbled, then dove to the side, curling around her bag and doing her best to tuck and roll. Alarmed shouts went up from the onlookers, accompanied by the crackle of static and barked commands into the police radio.

Kara's vision swam, and her ears rang. The sedan's tires rolled to a stop beside her, and she instinctively rolled under the pickup truck she had landed beside. The movement sent waves of pain up her arm, but Kara clenched her jaw against the urge to cry out.

More sharp *bangs* echoed up from the entrance to the garage.

The gunman who'd been following Kara responded with more automatic rifle fire. Someone screamed. The officers shouted, and more sirens shrieked in the background.

Chaos reigned for what felt like an eternity before ringing silence descended. According to Kara's watch, it had only been five minutes since the last time she'd looked at her dashboard clock.

Kara peered out from underneath the truck's undercarriage. Two men were on the ground beside the white sedan. Neither moved, and blood was seeping down the concrete ramp. Possibly dead, possibly unconscious.

"Ma'am! Are you injured?" an officer shouted from the base of the ramp. "Paramedics are here and will be with you when we've secured the scene!"

Kara touched the spot on her upper arm that had gone numb. Her fingers came away bloody, and moving that arm hurt. *The bastards shot me. It'd be damn nice if* stählen *handled bullets as well as it does blades, but I guess that would be a bit* too *superhuman.*

"I think they grazed me," she called back. "They're not moving. I think you're okay."

"Please don't move, ma'am!"

Oh, don't worry, no chance of that. Kara kept her eyes open and forced herself to count every bolt she could see on the undercarriage. She felt woozy, probably from a combination of blood loss and adrenaline.

The next several minutes passed in a blur. The officers guarded the unconscious assailants until the EMTs could haul them onto stretchers and take them away, while another pair of EMTs helped Kara out from under the truck and assessed her arm. It was a graze, as she'd suspected, although a fairly deep one.

Kara refused to let go of her messenger bag, even as she was loaded into an ambulance. "This is what they were after," she insisted. "It has to be. I'm not letting it out of my sight."

The cop accompanying her, a man her age with a mop of

curly brown hair and a shadow of stubble, frowned. "Wait. I recognize you. You're Kara Greims, right? The lawyer who's been making waves with anti-corruption cases?"

Kara's heart rate jumped again. *Why do you want to know?* "That's me."

He jerked a thumb toward the other ambulance, where the gunmen were disappearing behind closed doors with his buddy to escort. "You think these guys wanted your legal documents?"

She nodded. "They started tailing me as soon as I left NLAPD headquarters this morning."

His frown deepened. He grabbed a notebook from his breast pocket, where the name Dominguez was embroidered in thick black lines. "Why were you there?"

"I was serving papers on behalf of Sarra Palmer, of Nestor Palmer Law."

Dominguez's thick eyebrows came together. "She's the one going after the Commissioner."

"That's correct. I was serving Commissioner Torres with papers relevant to the case."

Dominguez scribbled in his notebook. He didn't look happy, but he didn't look angry, either. He looked worried. He caught the EMT closest to Kara and asked, "Is she good to stay here for a few minutes?"

The EMT, a short woman with a long ponytail, pursed her lips. "She *should* go to the hospital right away. Why?"

"I want to go with her for her own protection, but I need to wait for my backup to arrive." Dominguez tapped his radio. "They're on their way. It shouldn't be long."

The EMT debated internally for a moment, then nodded. "If that changes, I'm taking her straight to St. Christina's."

"Absolutely, miss."

Dominguez didn't ask any more questions while they waited for his backup. Kara watched him take notes. They were in Spanish, but she had picked up enough from Ana and Maria as of late to work out the gist of what he was writing.

Police-issue guns used on civilians and a lawyer. Who hired the attackers?

Good question, Kara silently agreed. *Aren't I lucky to have found a cop not on Torres' payroll? Officer Dominguez, you've made a new friend.*

CHAPTER TWENTY

<u>**Friday, February 2, 2091**</u>

"*Damn* that man! Damn him to *hell!*"

Kara grabbed the nearest object—a coaster—and hurled it at the wall. It hit, then clattered to the floor. She didn't feel any better.

"I have no doubts that is where he'll end up," Grimm-the-cat remarked. His voice was smooth, but the cat's flicking tail betrayed his frustration. "He is remarkably skilled at circumventing justice."

Kara stared at her laptop screen, where James Torres lurked in the background of the frozen image of the press conference that had just taken place. The anger she had seen in his eyes earlier that week was gone, replaced by calm neutrality. In public, he wore the face of a man whose priority was, beyond a shadow of a doubt, the propriety of his station. He had the best interests of all Neo Los Angelenos at heart. How could anyone think otherwise?

"Tell that to the poor sod who just took the fall for him," Kara muttered. "God *damn* you, James Torres."

"Why are we cursing people, and should I get *Mami?*"

Kara swiveled her chair to face the open door of her study, where Maria was leaning across the threshold with her raised eyebrows conveying curiosity and concern. "Hey. James Torres. And honestly, sure. Your mom's curses are fantastic."

"Especially since she's been hanging out with Ivonne. Can I come in? I was coming to say hi, but it seems like you need someone to talk to."

Kara sighed and motioned at the armchair in the corner, beside the end table stacked high with books. "Sure. Have a seat. I'm not sure I'm great company."

"Better than a screaming baby."

Kara winced. "That bad, huh?"

Maria shrugged, then flopped into the armchair and rubbed her eyes. "*Mami* says it's not unusual. He's five weeks old. All he does is eat, cry, shit, and sleep, and there's not much in the way of rhyme or reason. But yeah, I needed a break. She has him now."

Kara hiked her legs up to sit cross-legged in the chair and leaned back. "You sure you want to hear about the woes of the world, then? That's not exactly a *break*."

"It's a distraction. Also, you don't usually throw things, so I'm worried. What happened?"

Kara glanced toward her laptop. "The NLAPD is using Tuesday's attack as a convenient way to scapegoat someone else for the accusations James Torres is in court for."

"What? They can do that?"

"Well, ultimately it'll be up to the judge and jury, but this will sway the court of public opinion big time. Basically, they've produced evidence linking someone in Torres' office to a number of the complaints Palmer's leveled against him, *and* they've linked him to the attack on me."

Maria grimaced. "Making it look like they were so worried about the truth coming out that they were trying to silence you, and setting Torres up to be the hero that roots out corruption in his own department."

"Exactly. I've no doubt that this poor guy had nothing to do with it—or at the very least, he was *real* low on the totem pole. They're throwing him to the wolves. He'll be lucky to get a job anywhere, even if he manages to weasel out of jail time."

"That sucks."

"Yeah."

Maria thought for a moment, then frowned again. "How likely do you think this will be to *actually* derail the court case against Torres?"

Kara shrugged a shoulder. "Anyone's guess...although it doesn't really matter."

"Why not?"

"Because his deadline is less than two weeks away. Unless he pulls an emergency U-turn between now and the fifteenth, he won't be around to face his sentencing."

Maria's face darkened. "Right. Six weeks and a day, and you gave him the two-week notice on Tuesday."

"I sure did."

Maria tilted her head, struck by a sudden thought. "In that case, why do you care? Maybe I'm being obtuse, but if this doesn't change anything for you..."

A wan smile curled Kara's lips. "I don't *want* to kill him, Maria." She reached behind her and tapped a stack of papers. "I was in the middle of assembling evidence that would link him to the attack. It would have been done and dropped off to the correct authorities by Sunday night, meaning he'd get another dose of pressure to do the right thing and turn himself in.

"Law enforcement agencies are well known for taking their sweet time to get around to anything, *particularly* when it comes to areas where they might be at fault. The last thing I expected was for the NLAPD to get their shit together fast enough to beat me to publication."

"They must be rattled," Maria mused. "Sounds like they're scrambling."

"Undoubtedly. For some, that'll be a solid tick in the 'guilty' column, and for others it won't."

Kara drew a deep breath and closed her eyes while she let it out. Then she opened her eyes again and leaned forward in her chair, meeting Maria's gaze. "I'm pissed off because justice has been perverted even further. The *Book of Deeds* already told me that Torres was indirectly responsible for Tuesday's attack, and I was in the middle of making that evidence actionable. Then he jammed a stick in my bike's wheels.

"If he had attacked me as Nemesis, I'd have no leg to stand on. The rumors are already flying about my takedown of those cops a couple of weeks ago. But he sent his goons after me in broad daylight, and they ended up firing at law enforcement and injuring two innocent people. In no universe is that acceptable, and he should be held to account for it. Now, he won't be."

"Except by you."

"Except by me," Kara acknowledged. "I just wish that didn't have to be the case."

"He's forcing your hand."

"In any other case, I'd say he was calling my bluff. Since he's Athemis, you're right. He knows the stakes are just as high for me. If I don't pursue justice, I die. So yes, he's forcing my hand. My options are to kill him, die trying, or just plain die."

"And he hopes those odds favor him."

Kara nodded. "Unfortunately for him, I have no intention of caving—and not just because I don't relish the idea of my magic eating me from the inside out. I believe in my calling. If I die on this mission, it won't be because I've given up or because I wasn't ready."

Maria's eyebrows rose a degree. "I hope you don't die at all."

"Me too." Kara turned her chair partway and idly leafed through papers on her desk. She was avoiding eye contact with Maria as she continued. "But if the worst happens, you and Carlos will be safe here. Ivonne assured me that the wards and defenses will hold against everything short of a small army. You should be able to hide away here until Carlos is of age to take on the mantle."

Maria didn't reply for long enough that Kara was forced to turn. When she found the young mother looking pensive and anxious, Kara winced. "Uh… Sorry, Maria. Too morbid?"

Maria closed her eyes. A single tear slipped between her lashes and splashed over her cheek. "Yes…and no. I know you walk a dangerous road every day, and I know you chose it as much as Jacob did—which is to say, you didn't feel you had a choice. It was offered to you, and you could have chosen not to take the oath.

"But you *did*, which means you had a choice. And that's honorable of you, it's courageous, it's the right thing to do…but how can I raise my son, knowing the whole time that as soon as some invisible, unknowable magic court decides he's old enough, he'll be thrust into this world? Doesn't *he* get a choice? Don't *I*?"

More tears followed the first, streaking Maria's warm brown skin. "How can I raise my child knowing he's more likely to die than live? And how can I accept that you're…*okay* with that?"

Kara crossed to Maria and knelt in front of the armchair, then clasped Maria's hands in her own. "You're right. I'm sorry. It's not right for me to talk about Carlos becoming a Free Judge as though it's a done deal. He *does* have a choice. Grimm's told me as much."

Kara glanced over her shoulder and frowned. "Speaking of Grimm, he sure made himself scarce. Chickenshit."

Maria chuckled wetly, which brought Kara's attention back to her. "He might *technically* have a choice, but he doesn't *really*. No more than you or Jacob did, and definitely not if I raise him with a sense of honor and responsibility. Fighting for justice is right. There's no way around that. It just breaks my heart that it's necessary…and it breaks my heart that I'm the one who has to let him go."

Kara ran her thumb over the back of Maria's hand. "Nothing about this situation is right. It's *all* fucked up. No two ways around it. And if I have anything to say about it, I'll be alive and kicking as the last Free Judge until he's ready to decide whether he wants the job. Then, who knows? Maybe we'll do, like, aunt and nephew field trips, but instead of going to the museum, we'll kick some bad guys' butts."

Maria snorted with laughter. "Oh, God, what a thought. Please don't put my little boy in Spandex."

"No worries on that. Spandex is terrible for damage protection." Kara gripped Maria's hands and smiled. "Thanks."

Maria sniffled. "For what?"

"Reminding me to quit feeling sorry for myself. Yeah, this job is hard as balls, and sometimes it really sucks. But it's also given me the opportunity to do what I've wanted to do since I was a teenager, more so than my career as an attorney ever would have. Also, I get to use magic and I have a dryad living in my house, all of which is quite frankly bonkers."

Maria smiled weakly. "So you're saying you need to count your blessings?"

"Something like that." Kara let go of Maria's hands and sat back on her heels. "At minimum, I need to focus on the plan rather than the obstacles."

"Want a sounding board?"

Kara bit her lip thoughtfully. "Actually, I might call a Circle meeting on this one. Did your mom say how long she'd take Carlos for?"

"As long as I needed."

"Great. In that case, I think it's war room time."

***

Fifteen minutes later, Kara was pacing the length of the "war room" when the last member of the Circle, Ivonne, walked in.

"Sorry I'm late," she announced as she took a seat in one of the ornately carved wooden chairs. "The hedges in the west zone were getting persnickety again."

"Did you have to go after them with a flamethrower this time?" Cedric inquired.

Kara's eyebrows shot up. "What? *This time?* Has that already happened? Why are you torching my hedges?"

Ivonne waved Kara's concern aside. "It's fine. All under control. Don't worry about it."

"Don't *worry* about—" Kara cut herself off. "You know what, I don't think I want to know. Only one question. Do I need to have the fire department on standby?"

"Of course not. That's what the nymphs in the pond are for."

"We have a *pond?*"

"You *really* need to take a walk."

Kara scrubbed her hands over her face, silently bemoaned her tendency to focus single-mindedly on work, and reset her attention on the task at hand. "Okay. Unruly magical foliage notwithstanding, I need your help coming up with a plan to outsmart James Torres."

Cedric crossed his arms and tilted his head. "Is this about the press conference? If that shrinking violet desk jockey is the guy who ordered those hulks to shoot up your car, I will eat my hat. He had so little confidence he didn't even fill out his suit properly."

"Yes and no," Kara replied. "That's part of it. In short, I don't think there's any universe in which Torres turns himself in. I thought I'd rattled him on the thirtieth, and maybe I did, but it resulted in precipitous action against me rather than anything approaching repentance.

"That means in twelve days, I will have to render summary judgment. In other words, next Wednesday, I have to kill him."

"We can't help you," Ivonne pointed out. "This can't be a group effort."

Kara shook her head. "You can't help me with the execution itself, no. You *can* assist with the planning, which is what I'm asking for. James Torres has a network better than the goddamn Internet, as evidenced by his ability to turn the attempted murder of an upstanding member of the community into an opportunity to shift suspicion off his own scheming, conniving ass."

Cedric arched an eyebrow. "You're *mad* at this guy."

"How could you tell?"

"Suddenly, you're swearing."

Kara's cheeks heated. "Huh. Never noticed that."

Maria tapped a pencil on the long oak table. "How can we help, Kara?"

Kara cleared her throat, grateful for the interruption. She woke the laptop on the table and turned on the projector that sat beside it. Scale plans of James Torres' estate and grounds appeared on the empty wall behind her. "I believe I will have to kill him at home."

"Assassinating someone at NLAPD headquarters does strike me as a *dumb* move," Cedric agreed, doing his best to keep from smiling.

Kara chuckled. "Probably smarter than killing someone at a precinct station, but you're right, it'd still be pretty dumb. Just because most of the folks working there are desk jockeys *now* doesn't mean they always were, or that I could count on them having lost their touch. They're also more likely to carry concealed weapons, and anyone who worked active duty would still remember their training.

"No—unless I managed to get in, kill Torres, and get out without raising *any* alarm, escaping NLAPD HQ would be a nightmare. Too many potential witnesses, too many chances for collateral damage. Much safer to go after him at his house."

"Haven't you already broken in once?" Ivonne queried. "Why do you need to plan? Get in the same way in the middle of the night, slit his throat, and get out."

"Because I don't want it to look like an assassination. Also, I can't just slit his throat. He has to be conscious and aware for the ultimate refusal. Otherwise, I'm jumping the gun."

Ivonne rolled her eyes so hard that Kara was surprised they didn't roll out the door. "That's *such* wood rot. This obsession with fairness makes your job a million times harder."

"Throwing that moral code out the window is what created Athemis. That's a slippery slope I can't afford to flirt with."

Ivonne grunted. "Fair enough. Still. You break in, you wake him up, you ask if he's gonna turn himself in, and when he says no, you carve him up like a Christmas tree. Wait, no. You *don't* want it to look like an assassination. Um…"

"Let him fistfight you first?" Maria wondered. "Get yourself some defensive wounds?"

"I'd still have been breaking and entering," Kara pointed out. "In that case, Torres becomes a murder victim, and the network of corruption at the NLAPD stays safe and sound while it waits for its new leader."

"So, you need to leave his dead body on top of a wall of boxes full of evidence against him," Cedric ventured. "And leave a Nemesis calling card. Let the city know you're coming for criminals, even if they're as well-protected as James Torres."

Kara frowned, but for the first time in a few days, it was a thoughtful frown rather than a worried one. "I didn't get very far into his house last time. I wonder if he has archives of documents hidden somewhere."

"Probably," Cedric agreed. "He wouldn't keep any proof at his office, would he?"

"Not unless it was easily explained." Kara turned to contemplate the projected blueprints. "He's meticulous enough that I can't see there being *no* records, and keeping them at HQ would be a disaster waiting to happen. He's probably paranoid enough that he'd go for home security rather than a safety deposit box—or *in addition to* a safety deposit box.

"And if I were him, I'd probably keep those archives…right there." Kara snatched a laser pointer from the table and shone its red dot on a spot in the basement. "Easy to hide, easy to secure, hard to get at. No one but the food staff would go into the cellar, and they'll be paid enough not to ask questions."

"Could you steal the evidence and go public?" Maria suggested.

Kara shook her head. "It would have been obtained illegally, which would make everything inadmissible in court. That would *add* a rose to his bouquet, not cut its heads off."

Maria scowled. "Damn. And here I thought I'd landed on an easy way out."

Kara tapped the laser pointer on her chin. "Maybe not, but you *have* given me an idea. The biggest factor in evidence admissibility is chain of custody. If *I'm* not the one handing the documents over to the authorities…if, instead, it happens to be one of NLA's finest…"

"Normally, I'd say they'd have to investigate, but how will you make sure the information doesn't fall into the wrong hands?" Cedric countered. "They've already shown they're willing to condemn an innocent man to jail. What's to keep them from sweeping it all under the rug and saying he was murdered in cold blood?"

"I have to make sure the right person is in the right place at the right time." Kara's eyebrows drew together in deep thought, but her lips were curled in a deceptively excited smile. "Luckily, I think I know just the guy."

CHAPTER TWENTY-ONE

<u>**Tuesday, February 6, 2091**</u>

"I'm glad to see your arm's healing well. That was a lot of blood."

Kara smiled and flexed her arm. "Looked a lot worse than it was. A few stitches and a few days of rest, and it'll be good as new soon. Nice scar, though."

Officer Ricardo Dominguez chuckled and saluted her with his hot dog. "I love a lady with a scar. Uh, I mean—" He flushed scarlet and immediately drew himself upright. "Apologies, miss. Sometimes the training room humor comes out at the worst times."

Kara chuckled. "If that's the worst that gets bandied about in the NLAPD locker rooms, I'll take it. Nothing wrong with a good scar. Reminds you you've lived, if you ask me. So, how are the hot dogs here? Any good?"

Dominguez swallowed his mouthful before responding. "Best I've had since New York, miss. You looking for lunch?"

"Sure am. Been a busy morning. I'm starving." She handed the cart's proprietor some bills and accepted the hot dog he offered in return. "I'm glad I ran into you, though. I hoped to. Do you have a minute to chat?"

Dominguez checked his watch. "I have ten minutes before I'm back on duty. Unless someone goes and does something stupid, that is."

"Heaven forbid." She gestured at a nearby bench. "I assume you're walking the beat. Want to sit?"

"I'd love to."

Dominguez waited until Kara sat before joining her on the bench. The man was about Kara's age, as she had guessed before, and he had a keen eye. He was lean and fit, his hair obeyed no master, and he had a hunger in his eyes Kara recognized on sight.

Ricardo Dominguez wanted justice, and he wasn't afraid to seek it.

Kara had quietly tailed the officer for three days, sneaking around in her Nemesis suit while noting the neighborhoods he patrolled while on shift. Two days at the same hot dog stand had been a notable coincidence. Three days clinched it.

"Must have been a hell of a week for the boys in blue, booking that guy in Torres' department," Kara commented. "Everything settling down?"

Dominguez made a noncommittal sound in the back of his throat. "Sure."

Kara side-eyed him. "You don't sound convinced. Or—sorry, am I stepping on toes?"

"It's technically still an open investigation, and you're one of the victims. I shouldn't talk about it."

Kara shrugged. "Fair enough. I don't want to make your job harder. Just…"

She glanced up and down the street, then made a show of leaning in. "Can I tell you something? Something I think you should run down?"

Dominguez's eyes narrowed imperceptibly, not with suspicion but with vindication. "I'm listening."

"Lots of lawyers know the guys at IA, you know how it is. So I asked around, and…well, let's just say there are a lot of people in the legal community who smell a rat, and it's not the one that got thrown behind bars."

Dominguez popped the last bite of hot dog in his mouth, chewed, and swallowed. Then, with a decisive nod, he plucked a business card from his breast pocket and scribbled on the back. "Meet me when I'm done with my shift?"

Kara slid the card into her pocket. He'd written a time and the name of a nearby coffee shop. "I'll be there."

Dominguez was a few minutes late, but he strolled up to Common Ground in jeans and a bomber jacket and smiled when he spied Kara in the front window. The bell on the door rang when he entered, and he ordered a coffee and brought it over to join her.

"The owner here keeps an eye on a few persons of interest for us," he explained to Kara as he sat. "So, we buy lots of his coffee and pastries in return, and we can usually have conversations here that we don't want to be public knowledge."

"Handy." Kara made a mental note. *Could be a good resource.* "What did you want to talk about?"

Dominguez sipped his coffee, then set it on the table and wrapped his hands around the creamy porcelain mug. His fingers were long and slightly calloused, and his nails were clean. *No ring,* Kara noticed.

"I think I should be asking you. You know something more than you're letting on."

"That may be, but I also have to respect attorney-client privilege, and even though I'm not the attorney on record for the case against—well, let's just say it would not be good for my reputation if I started spreading rumors."

Dominguez held Kara's gaze for a long time. "Heard and understood. This is a completely anonymous tip, then?"

Kara nodded. "Any chance you can get yourself assigned to the night shift in Kareno District on Valentine's Day?"

Dominguez blinked, thrown by the seeming *non sequitur*. "That's the district the Commissioner lives in."

"Imagine that."

"Finagling a district transfer for a night isn't exactly *easy*."

"You're not saying no."

The silence stretched. Finally, the doorbell chiming as a new patron entered broke it. Dominguez's gaze flickered to the new arrival, then back to Kara, and he slowly nodded.

"I'll see what I can do."

Wednesday, February 7, 2091

Kara crept along the tall hedges bordering James Torres' estate, moving by feel more than sight. She was grateful for the clouds, which hid the light from the three-quarter moon, and she was grateful that James Torres lived in a neighborhood that wasn't choked with advertising billboards turning the night into day. All she had to do was slip between the puddles of blue cast by the streetlights, and she was effectively invisible.

Torres had a week left on his countdown. Since the public arrest and condemnation of Peter Portman for his role in the conspiracy surrounding the Internal Affairs Commissioner, Neo Los Angeles had quieted down as Kara had expected. The public was content to believe that the issue had been dealt with, and they could trust their police force again.

Inasmuch as anyone in this city trusts the police. Which really depends on your demographic.

Kara would deliver the final notice on Friday, giving Torres the weekend to think about his imminent demise and to allow his conscience one last chance to grow a spine. Then, this time next week, Kara would be waiting for the commissioner to come home.

She already had his duty schedule for the day. He would be late leaving the office, which suited her. Ricardo Dominguez had arranged two weeks of shift changes into this district, and he would be cruising the quiet streets of this rich neighborhood, waiting for a 911 call he suspected would upend his world.

Kara hoped he was right about that.

Right now, Kara needed to get back into the Torres mansion and case it properly. Torres was out of town for two days, at a mid-week conference of commissioners and chiefs. They were discussing restorative justice, of all things. Kara could only imagine that Torres was laughing to himself the whole time.

Still, it was convenient for Kara. She had confirmed through three independent sources that Torres truly *was* out of town, and not luring her into a false sense of security so he could catch her breaking and entering. According to her intel, the Torres mansion was empty tonight apart from a single security guard.

And if my ausklammern *field can't take care of one measly security guard, I'm in real trouble.*

Kara let herself in the contractors' entrance again. Neither the gate nor the lock had changed in any way from her last visit, which was a relief. So far, it didn't look like her previous visit had been detected.

She snuck from topiary to topiary, staying low and keeping to the deep shadows. One searchlight mounted high on the back wall swung in a lazy arc, easily avoided. Meant to deter thrill-seeking vandals and petty thieves, it would not sway Kara from her purpose.

Kara hunkered down behind the last pruned hedge before the entertaining patio and took a moment to examine the back side of the house properly. Below the searchlight, scattered across the wall, seven security cameras blinked their little red lights from on high. It was hard to tell in the dark which directions they pointed, and impossible to tell their model. If they were real, they would have night vision or infrared sensors. Otherwise, they would be useless—except, perhaps, as visual deterrents.

Kara got down on her belly and army-crawled toward the west side of the house, where she had last ascended to James' bedroom balcony. It was as good a place as any to return. *No point reinventing the wheel.*

She hadn't been paying attention to the back wall last time, thanks to the food services contractors, but she had paid attention to the west side. Unless he had upgraded his security since then, there were no cameras between her and the balcony.

Kara paused long enough to verify she saw no blinking red lights before proceeding. She kept her *ausklammern* field at full strength in case she missed one in the darkness, but she felt confident. Even after Kara had dropped his notice in his bedroom, his level of arrogance hadn't changed. *Maybe he thought I magicked it inside. I wonder if I could do that...*

The ascent to the balcony was harder without the benefit of daylight to help her gauge distance, but it was not impossible. Her enhanced senses were by now fully attuned to the low light of the suburb, and Kara could pick out the lines of the railings in dim grayscale.

The sliding door to James Torres' bedroom opened with the same *verschliessen* as last time, and a momentary flash from her headlamp revealed no new tripwires.

Kara stepped into the silent bedroom with dual sensations of triumph and suspicion warring in her gut. *This is too easy. Why hasn't he made this harder? I know I've kept him busy, but this is ridiculous. It's like he* wants *me to break in.*

She tucked the suspicion away in the back of her head and crept forward, distributing her weight carefully to avoid any creaking floorboards. She hadn't picked up the hair-raising sensation of any anti-magic devices, so until she discovered otherwise, her *ausklammern* would go a long way toward protecting her.

Kara paused in front of the bedroom door. The room she wanted to get into most was his study, but the study was also most likely to be trapped or alarmed. Still, it was riskier to explore the rest of the house. If she were discovered, she would get *no* chance to investigate the study.

Guess I'd better not get caught, then.

The knob turned silently, the hinges were oiled, and Kara slipped into the corridor without a sound. *Thank you for having plush carpets, Mr. Torres.*

Top floor. Bedrooms, bathrooms, a library, and a music room. This one gave Kara pause, and she spent a few minutes examining the pictures of Torres and a young boy with several trophies. The grand piano in the center of the room gleamed, and a stack of sheet music sat on a table beside it.

Wouldn't have pegged you for a music lover, but the world takes all kinds. And is that your son? Geez. Talk about surprises.

Back in the corridor, Kara headed for the staircase to the main floor. It was wide, curved, and polished wood. Kara dearly wanted to slide down the banister and kick the front doors open. *Maybe on my way out, if it all goes to shit.*

Step by step, she made her way to the main floor, her ears wide open for any movement. Based on the floor plans she had finagled out of the public records office, the security guard's office was just off the entrance hall. If there was a spot she was most likely to get caught, this was it.

Kara had just put both feet on the hardwood floor when the sound of a door opening made her jump out of her skin. She took two long strides around the back of the staircase and tucked herself in its shadow, then held her breath.

Calm, unhurried footsteps left the guard's office. They did not approach Kara's location, but went down the hall on the other side of the stairs. *Bathroom break.* Kara waited until she heard a door close before dashing out from her hiding spot.

She paused at the door of the guard's office. Standard security kit. CCTV, intercom, hotlines for the police and the alarm company. No controls or boxes that suggested anything more dastardly than loud noises and bright lights. *No hidden turrets? No flamethrowers? Why, Mr. Torres, how boring.*

Water ran from across the entryway. Kara sprinted on tiptoe down the corridor and into the east wing. *Over halfway. Just gotta make sure Torres isn't hiding any more surprises, and I can sneak out and go home.*

Kara quickly realized that a large conservatory took up the east wing. The humidity spiked the moment she slipped through the glass door, and the tropical plants hanging from the ceiling dripped condensation onto her hood. Kara quickly backed out and checked behind her to ensure she wasn't leaving wet footprints.

Kara held her breath again as she approached the closed door to the guard's office, which she would have to pass to continue to the rest of the house. Whoever was inside was evidently watching reels on their phone, however, and paying no attention to anything else. *Must be a cushy job. Maybe working for a questionably moral police commissioner would let me sleep better at night. Next life, I guess.*

Twenty minutes later, Kara had completed her exploration of the main floor and found nothing notable, unless you counted the beautiful set of kitchen knives in the block on the island. Kara returned to the base of the stairs fully convinced that James Torres kept his police work strictly separate from his home life.

Even the office in the west wing had been next to empty. The filing cabinet, opened with a silent *verschliessen* spell, revealed archived tax forms and personal correspondence. For all that Torres flaunted the law, that apparently didn't extend to keeping confidential documents at home.

Which means that unless I missed a hidden door to the basement, or he has a safe in a wall that I didn't find, the only place I haven't looked is his bedroom study.

Kara padded back up the wooden stairs. The guard hadn't moved from their office since their short break half an hour earlier. Torres was clearly confident in the quality of his security system because Kara hadn't found anything inside but cameras. The idea was obviously to keep people out and trust that the guard would handle anyone who tried to get in.

Back in the bedroom, Kara faced the door to Torres' study. She wrapped a hand around the knob and counted to thirty before activating the *verschliessen* spell. The lock clicked open. Kara waited another thirty seconds, in case of delayed or silent alarms that would bring the guard running. When she heard nothing, she opened the door.

She hadn't been far off with her initial guess of a walk-in closet. The room was small, set up more like the hidden room in Jacob's apartment than a true study. Shelves ran the length of the walls, each packed with banker's boxes. A tiny table sat in the center of the room, big enough to fit a couple of stacks of paper.

Kara turned on her headlamp and played it over the boxes. Each box was inscribed with the Athemis symbol, plus a couple of words that hinted at what lay within. Kara recognized the names and dates from the evidence she had gathered and given to Sarra Palmer.

Immediately beside the door, Kara spotted a box labeled *Greims*. The harsh lines of the permanent marker felt like they'd been burned in, and her tattoos flared in sympathy.

Kara slid the box off the shelf. It was a risk, and she knew it. If James Torres truly expected Kara to come back, he would expect her to look in this specific box. It could be trapped. It could have had a pressure switch underneath it, which she had triggered.

She had to know.

Kara balanced the box on the table. It was dust-free, and the lid came off with only a faint hiss of cardboard on cardboard. The inside was almost packed full of papers. Kara pushed them to the back of the box and peered at the papers in front, flicking through them with gloved hands.

Floor plans of Jacob's apartment. Movement logs for her, Jacob, and Maria. Names and addresses of known associates. A list of cases Kara had worked in the last six months.

The contract to kill Jacob.

Ice flooded Kara's veins. Her hand trembled, putting a tiny crease in the paper.

James Torres had a copy of the contract, signed by Brendan Mercer, instructing William Marrow to kill Jacob Greims. Mercer had paid Marrow $75,000 to kill her brother, with an additional twenty-five grand on the table if Marrow managed to make it look like a suicide.

Guess you didn't get your bonus. A helpless laugh bubbled up in Kara's throat, and she quashed it.

Kara smoothed the crease in the paper as best she could, then put the lid back on the box. No doubt the box contained more incriminating evidence, possibly even the orders to attack the safe house in New York and to kidnap Ana, Maria, and Carlos.

She couldn't handle reading any of it now. She hoped she would never have to. However, the existence of this much evidence, unlikely to be faked and verifiable by third parties, gave Kara an idea of how she would finally bring James Torres down.

Kara returned the box to its place on the shelf, taking care to line it up with its neighbor exactly as it had been before she moved it, then locked the door behind her. She let herself out the sliding door, locked that too, then swung over the balcony and dropped to the lawn.

As she slipped between the bushes to the exit, she returned to her discomfort about how *easy* it had been to break into Torres' house and study. Athemis was frustratingly competent. Its operatives were strong, well-trained, and lethal, and its intelligence and reach were impressive. Torres' personal resources were no different. If Kara hadn't gotten lucky in the parking garage, she would have died.

Are you really just that arrogant?

Kara chewed on her lower lip as she let herself through the back gate. *It could be arrogance—not just that he believes his security system will keep me out, but that he doesn't believe it matters if I get in. He's confident that he'll win, even if I know everything.*

She disappeared into the shadows of the street with her hands in her pockets, deep in thought. *I have to trust that my plan will work. That I'll have the right people in the right places at the right time, and the right eyes on the documents when they're made public.*

Kara laughed silently into her mask. *When I went after Willie Marrow, he called himself the Big Bad Wolf. Hell, for a while I thought about calling myself Little Red. Which fairytale is this? I feel like Hansel and Gretel, sneaking into the witch's hut to eat her gingerbread...or maybe it's Jack and the Beanstalk, and I'm doing my best to steal the golden goose.*

She snorted aloud and covered her mouth reflexively, but no one was around to hear. *No. It's the Emperor's New Clothes. I'm about to show the world that James Torres isn't who he says he is, once and for all. Get ready to be stripped naked in front of the entire city, Mr. Torres. Your arrogance won't save you this time.*

CHAPTER TWENTY-TWO

<u>Sunday, February 11, 2091</u>

Kara sat back in her chair and rubbed her temples. "I feel like I'm losing my mind, Grimm."

The candle flame atop the skull flickered. "You are certainly expending a great amount of mental energy on every possible way Commissioner Torres might attempt to hoodwink you."

"Because I keep coming up with more! Something doesn't feel right, and I can't put my finger on it, which means I have to be ready for anything."

"You *cannot* be ready for anything. It is impossible."

"I can try."

"It is a waste of energy. Better to tally your assets and liabilities, and leave it at that. Know what you have at your disposal, so you can act decisively when the time comes."

Kara grumbled under her breath, then sighed. "You're right. It's just that..."

"It was too easy," Grimm supplied for the hundredth time.

"It was. His house is *too easy* to get into, Grimm, and all his Athemis documents were behind a single mechanical lock. Well, after several other doors, but the point remains. No traps. No alarms. No surveillance. Not even a hair in the door!"

"Why would he put a hair in the door?"

"To see if someone had been inside," she wearily replied. "Old detective novel trick."

"Fascinating. But what of it? You yourself have said he is arrogant in the extreme."

"He is, but he's also not *stupid*. No one could build a network like he has without being incredibly smart *and* clever. Plus, he knows who I am! He knows about the Vehmic Court! He *knows* I've marked him for death, he probably has the date circled on his calendar, and he's *not doing anything about it*. He's letting me waltz into his house and poke through his stuff! It doesn't make sense!"

Grimm allowed a moment of silence before replying. "What are the possible explanations you have theorized?"

"The simplest is that he *is* just plain stupid, but that doesn't jive with the rest of his behavior. I spent a day wandering the NLAPD headquarters, and it would be impossible to get to him there. When he's not at work, he keeps to well-populated areas. He's rarely alone. It seems like the only time he *is* alone is when he's at home, and even then he has a guard present at all times.

"My best guess is that he's trying to lure me out, either into a one-on-one confrontation on his turf, or into a situation where I could be exposed or innocents could be hurt. The setup is too perfect otherwise."

"I agree with your assessment. What do you plan to do about it?"

Kara pursed her lips. "That's the thing. I don't think I have a choice beyond what I've already planned."

"Officer Dominguez being on call in the neighborhood on the night in question."

"And hauling out all the boxes from the closet, so Torres is found with the evidence that damns him, even posthumously. But that doesn't change how risky the whole thing is."

"Being a Free Judge is inherently risky. You act against the base instincts and desires of a powerful subset of the global population. You challenge criminals to repent and surrender to authority. No one likes to be told they're wrong. Powerful people like it even less."

Kara drummed her fingers on the table while she considered this, then accepted it with a slow nod. "You're right. I guess it's harder to accept that risk when it feels like I don't have a choice."

"He is forcing you to accept the risk, yes, either to yourself or to others."

"Or both."

"Indeed."

Kara grimaced. "James Torres is a damned bastard."

Grimm chuckled. "By the time a person's name is written in the *Book of the Guilty*, it is to be expected."

"But he has a kid, he plays the piano, and he grows tropical plants and throws parties on his back deck. In some ways, he's normal. He just happens to also be neck-deep in a conspiracy to subvert justice in one of America's biggest cities."

"It is rare that you will find a target who has lost their humanity entirely," Grimm cautioned her. "Exceedingly rare. It is a testament to the complexities of our kind that we may contain multitudes."

"And not all of those multitudes are pleasant. You're right again."

"I typically am."

"Yeah, yeah, don't go getting an inflated head about it."

"If you have suggestions on how to increase the volume or decrease the density of bone matter, that I might *inflate*, I am all ears...despite not being in possession of any cartilage."

Kara rolled her eyes. "Very funny." She gathered the documents spread over the table and tapped them into a neat pile. Then she read James Torres' final notice again, ensuring it was perfect.

"One last kick at the can in the morning," she muttered as she creased the letter and slipped it into an envelope. "Soon, this interminable waiting game will be over."

"For better or for worse," Grimm remarked.

"Oh, it'll get worse again before it gets better," Kara assured him. "No matter how terrible James Torres is, carving out something like twenty percent of the NLAPD in one fell swoop will do a hell of a lot more harm than good in the short term. Whether it serves justice in the *long* term will depend on who fills the vacuum and how well they function while they're spread thin. The next several months will be very interesting, one way or another."

Monday, February 12, 2091

Third time's the charm? Kara wondered as she strolled into NLAPD headquarters, doing her best to maintain an air of professional nonchalance.

The receptionist smiled at Kara's approach, rather like the cat that caught the canary. The gleeful expectation threatened to throw off Kara's groove, but she held her ground and returned the woman's Cheshire Cat grin with a polite smile.

"One of these days I'll find out your coffee order since we keep crossing paths," Kara teased.

"Black," the woman replied without missing a beat. "I'm sweet enough as-is."

Gag me with a spoon. Kara chuckled. "I should have known. I'm sure you can guess why I'm here. Is Commissioner Torres in?"

"He is," the receptionist confirmed, still smiling like she knew something Kara didn't. "Go right up."

"Thank you so much."

"You're so welcome."

Kara managed to keep from rolling her eyes until she was in the elevator. The woman's *Mean Girls* vibe was stifling. Kara still hadn't gotten her name, and she wasn't sure she wanted it. Kara didn't typically allow herself to wish harm on others, but the thought was tempting in her case.

It would be just my luck if she isn't included in the purge if this goes well. Kara clicked her tongue. *I suppose if she hangs onto her job by the skin of her teeth, I'll have to keep an eye on her.*

"Morning."

The word jolted Kara out of her thoughts. She glanced to her right and automatically smiled at the young man standing beside her. He was a couple of inches shorter than her with a shock of untidy brown hair and square-framed glasses in gunmetal gray. His nose was squashed, and the bridge was crooked, as though it had been broken. He was clean-shaven, but his button-down shirt was as untidy as his hair.

"Morning." *Who talks to people in elevators?*

He stuck out his hand and grinned. His teeth were blindingly white. "Daniel Jones."

Kara shook, hoping her moment's hesitation didn't show. "Kara Greims. Do you…make a habit of greeting people in elevators? Or is there something I can do for you?"

Daniel stuck his hands in his pockets and kept beaming at her. Kara immediately filed him away in her head as "sunshine incarnate."

"Just introducing myself. It's my first day. I'm the new tech guy. *Cybercrimes.* It's very cool stuff."

Kara smiled. *First day jitters combined with an extroverted personality. Oh, you poor kid. This job is gonna chew you up and spit you out.*

"Definitely not my area. But congrats on the job. Word of advice?"

"I'll take anything."

"Straighten your shirt and tuck it in. You'll make a better impression. Also, you might consider doing something about your hair."

Daniel immediately set to fixing his shirt. "The hair's a lost cause, unfortunately, but thanks. I appreciate it."

"Any time."

The elevator car slowed to a halt at the Internal Affairs floor. Kara bid Daniel goodbye, then exited with her messenger bag under one arm as usual. This time, she had worn flats instead of heels, and a bulletproof vest under her understated blouse and slacks.

Heads turned and people glanced in her direction as she crossed the floor with purpose. She had opted *not* to use an *ausklammern* field today, in the hopes that enough people would notice her that if she disappeared, someone would raise a fuss.

This was especially important since she was here under no pretense.

The last two times she had visited Commissioner Torres in his office, she'd had legal documents to deliver from Nestor Palmer Law. Today, she had nothing of the sort and was coasting solely on her reputation.

Kara entered the commissioner's office and smiled at the secretary, who was on the phone. She took a seat near the door and waited patiently.

The woman finished her phone call, then smiled at Kara. "Welcome back. We should give you a frequent flyer card."

Kara chuckled and stood. "I hope my regular visits will taper off soon, but I appreciate the sentiment. How are you doing, if you don't mind my asking?"

The secretary shrugged lightly. "He's in a better mood today."

Kara nodded. "Can he be interrupted?"

"We can try." She buzzed the intercom. "Sir? Miss Greims is here, from Nestor Palmer."

Silence on the other side of the door for a long beat. Then the intercom buzzed in reply. "Send her in."

The secretary gestured to the door. "Go ahead."

"Thanks." Kara took a step toward the door, then paused. "Uh… Weird question, but… If you hear *stuff* going on in there, are you allowed to…"

The corner of the secretary's lips curved up in an ironic smile, and she slipped a hand under the edge of her desk. "Response time of thirty seconds."

Relief washed over Kara. She'd been right to think this woman *wasn't* in on Torres' bullshit. *I wonder if she got assigned to keep an eye on him?* "Great. I don't think anything will happen, but it's good to know."

"I understand."

Kara squared her shoulders and opened the door to Commissioner Torres' office. The Spartan room was well-lit by the morning sun. Rays of light refracted through a pointy glass sculpture on his desk. It was an award for policing. Kara suddenly wanted to smash his skull in with it.

James Torres did not rise from his desk when she entered. He was perfectly groomed, and his face held no hint of the frustration or anger she had seen almost two weeks ago. "Good morning, Miss Greims. I take it Sarra Palmer has more tedium for me?"

Kara pulled the door shut behind her. The *click* of the latch echoed through her chest. "Actually, I'm here on other business."

Torres arched an eyebrow. "Other business? What might that be?"

"I think you know."

He didn't reply, but he kept eye contact with her as she slipped the simple envelope from the front pocket of her messenger bag, crossed the office, and set it on the desk before him. Only then did his eyes dip to the unmarked white paper.

"No seal?" he remarked. "I'm surprised. The Vehmic Court is so old-fashioned, I thought this would be parchment sealed with wax."

Kara drew back a step and forced herself to keep her arms loose at her sides when all she wanted to do was cross them protectively. She had the vest. She needed her arms free to react if he tried anything.

She didn't respond to his jab about the Vehmic Court. Truth be told, *she* wouldn't have been surprised to find similar requirements on the books. The Court did like to gild its traditions with a touch of showmanship.

"You should open it," she told him.

Torres had picked up the envelope between his index and middle fingers, and was now flipping it back and forth idly. "I know what it says. Why bother?"

"Do you?" she challenged. "I find it hard to believe you've read *any* of the notices I've sent you. You haven't done anything that would indicate you had."

Torres shifted his grip on the envelope, sat back in his chair, and laughed. "Oh, I've read them. They're so full of shit, I could use them as manure. You have no jurisdiction! You have no power! You are one person, trying to uphold an outdated system.

"What are you going to do? Assassinate me? Please. You barely avoided being gunned down in the street. The only reason you didn't die in that parking garage was because you got lucky."

Kara stared at him. She was speechless.

The moment stretched long enough that Torres' second eyebrow joined his first up near his hairline. "What's wrong? Cat got your tongue? Or have you just realized I'm right, and you're breaking your back for no reason?"

Kara still couldn't think of anything to say. The man was arrogant beyond belief. He truly didn't believe Kara could or would deliver on her promise.

That unshakable belief in himself shook her. *What if he's right? What if I can't do this?*

Kara frowned. *But I have done this. More than once!*

She opened her mouth to point this out but caught herself

before she spoke. Admitting to a murder in the office of a police commissioner was what one might call *a really bad idea.*

Torres' eyes gleamed. Kara wondered if he knew what she'd been thinking.

Kara turned on her heel and headed for the door. Hand on the knob, she looked over her shoulder. "You have two days," she warned him. "It's a tight turnaround, but you still have time to turn yourself in to the authorities and do the right thing."

Torres didn't budge. He laughed again. "I'm hardly going to turn myself in to my own boys, Miss Greims, especially when I've been doing the right thing all along. That would be the definition of a useless exercise.

"In fact, I think it would be much more productive for them to take a look at *you.*" Torres' tone and demeanor suggested good-natured teasing, but the gleam in his eyes had frozen over. "Don't think I don't know where some of that evidence came from in the LBM Holdings cases."

"Perfectly legitimate channels," Kara evenly responded. She'd rehearsed that one in the mirror for hours on end.

"But only if you know where to look, which is the sticker, isn't it? You have to break the law to uphold the law. See? We're not so different, you and I."

Kara's jaw set. The flippant insult chased the nascent fear away, and she opened the door. "Two days, Commissioner. Use them well."

"Oh, I will," he called behind her as the door closed.

Kara stood on the other side for a few seconds with her eyes closed and her hand still on the knob. Eventually, she looked up to meet the secretary's gaze. "I think that went well."

The secretary lifted her eyebrows. "Well, you walked out under your own power and I didn't hear any shouting, so I'm inclined to agree."

Kara nodded. "Now we wait and see."

"My favorite," the secretary commented. "Did I hear you say 'two days?'"

"You did."

"Until what?"

Kara tilted her head, regarding the secretary with curiosity. "Until judgment day," she replied at length.

The secretary pursed her lips and glanced at the door. "Now that, I'd like to see."

"Maybe you will." Kara hefted her messenger bag and turned. "Have a good day, miss."

"You too, Miss Greims."

An hour later, Kara sat in the living room watching snow fall on the maze of topiary on her front lawn. She would swear that two days ago, the one that looked like a dragon had looked like a worm. "Do they change themselves?"

Ivonne didn't look up from the bonsai tree she was trimming. "Of course not."

"Do you change them?"

"They don't change."

"That's crap. They change. That one didn't have wings last week."

Ivonne's head came up, and she squinted at the window. "Huh. Look at that. Weird." She bent back to her work.

Kara groaned. "You're yanking my chain."

"You have no chain to yank."

"Why did I hire a fairy again?"

Ivonne chuckled and laid aside her tiny pruning shears. "You didn't hire me. I volunteered. And I volunteered because I believe in what you're doing, and I don't like it when people think they can get one over on my family."

Kara swirled the dark liquid in the smooth, wooden goblet

and sniffed it. "I am also harboring suspicions that you wanted to get out from under your dad's nose and have a little fun."

"It *might* have been an ulterior motive."

"One that plays into why the cedar tree in my front yard is turning into a dragon?"

"I'll never tell. Unless it sets fire to any of the other trees. Then I'll tell."

"No, you'll only tell if I *catch* it happening. Otherwise, you'll clean it up, and I'll never suspect a thing."

"Now you're getting it." Ivonne nudged the bonsai pot aside. "You're more talkative than usual. Nervous about Wednesday?"

"Incredibly. He just doesn't *care*, Ivonne. He doesn't believe I can follow through, and he doesn't give a damn about justice. He's full of himself, and the worst part is that I can't tell if I should worry."

"If he has something hidden up his sleeve, you mean."

"Exactly. I haven't seen *anything* to indicate that his bluster is more than just that, but if I guess wrong..."

"Then Athemis wins."

"Yeah." Kara sighed and downed the liquid in the goblet. It was smoky and flavorful, mildly alcoholic, and like nothing that existed on Earth as far as she could tell. Ivonne called it *kesvan*. Kara hadn't pushed for details.

Ivonne broke the silence. "I've been thinking."

"About the menagerie you're turning my front lawn into?"

"Well, sure, but apart from that. Why is it your job to keep the entire human world in check?"

Kara raised an eyebrow. "Because I'm the last scion of a system designed a thousand years ago that isn't working very well anymore?"

"Yeah. What if, you know, the system just...breaks? What's the worst that will happen? *Really?*"

Kara narrowed her eyes. "Didn't we talk about this a while back? Humans used to ask fairies for help dealing with nasty people, and the world was a lot worse off for it. The Vehmic Court was created to keep everything on the level."

"I remember. But the worlds have *changed*, Kara. Mine *and* yours. Nobody believes in fairies anymore, so the likelihood of humans asking their fairy friends for favors is way down. What if the Vehmic Court breaks down, and nothing happens?"

Kara thought this over, then shook her head. "I don't think that's how it would go. For one, you're not taking Athemis into account. They *want* the Vehmic Court out of the way so they can manipulate its powers to their advantage. Ordinary humans might not believe in fairies and magic, but you can bet your bark-covered butt that Athemis operatives would start trading favors. That wouldn't end well for anyone."

Ivonne shrugged. "You might have a point. It's just something I've noticed—humans have a real tendency to put more weight on their shoulders than is warranted. There are billions of people on this planet, and billions more in the fae realms. Everyone makes a difference. It's not just you.

"The planet would keep turning if you weren't a Free Judge, that's all I'm saying." The dryad picked up the terra-cotta pot and turned it back and forth. A single leaf fell off the tiny tree, and she clicked her tongue. "Damn. Still haven't got the hang of doing this in the mundane world."

"You need better fertilizer," Kara muttered.

Ivonne chuckled. "Actually, what I really need is *fire*."

"What?"

"Burn it all down, and it comes back twice as strong. That's what forest fires are for. Come to think of it, that might apply to your conundrum about Athemis, too." Another shrug. "Anyway. I'm turning in for the night. Get your roots untwisted and get some sleep, you silly human."

Kara watched her go. Burn Athemis to the ground? Burn NLA to the ground? Burn *James Torres* to the ground? Ivonne's counsel was perennially interesting, but Kara was always mildly stymied by the fairy's approach to interpersonal matters. Apparently, in the fae realm, it was perfectly acceptable to torch your enemy's home if enough people agreed that he deserved it.

It's a fae-eat-fae world out there, I guess. She turned back to the dragon cedar on the lawn. *I hope I don't burn* myself *if I start playing with fire.*

CHAPTER TWENTY-THREE

<u>**Wednesday, February 14, 2091**</u>

Kara triple-checked the zippers and buckles on her suit again while standing outside the back gate to James Torres' estate, bringing the number of checks to twelve. She'd been nowhere near this nervous preparing for Willie Marrow's final moments.

I knew what I was getting into with Marrow. His style was the same as his lackeys' style. Brutish and brutal, but straightforward. James Torres... He's still an unknown.

She had looked up his NLAPD personnel records. He maintained his firearms qualifications in the highest percentile, even though the requirements for a commissioner were lower. His mansion didn't include a fitness room, but he showed up early every morning at NLAPD HQ and put in an hour at the gym. He ate clean. He stayed sharp.

In other words, he stayed at the top of his game even though he didn't have to, and he felt like he had nothing to be afraid of.

For the first time in the seven months since she had become a Free Judge, Kara wished assassination was allowed. Sneaking in and slitting his throat, or slipping poison into his salad dressing, would have been infinitely easier and less nerve-racking than this.

She even thought she would be able to live with it.

That scared her even more than Torres did. It had only been a couple of months since Kara had played verbal Ping-Pong with Grimm about revenge, wondering if she was losing her soul in the name of justice. They'd come down firmly on the side of "necessary evil" at the time, and Grimm had reassured her that if Kara ever seemed like she was veering too far down the low road, he would call her back.

He hadn't done so yet. Then again, she hadn't admitted out loud that part of her longed to put a long-range, high-caliber bullet in Torres' head and be done with it. Granted, most methods of assassination made martyrs out of their subjects. Kara could abide that outcome about as well as she could stand this heart-in-mouth waiting game.

She drew a deep breath and let it out to a count of twelve. The longer she waited, the worse it would get.

Kara unlocked the back gate and slipped through. The night was clear, which meant she had to duck behind the shadows of the hedges to avoid being picked out on the security cameras. The moon was waning from its third quarter, but its crescent reflected plenty of sunlight tonight.

Regardless, by this point she felt as though she knew the route to Torres' bedroom like the back of her hand. Kara darted from bush to bush, easily evading the searchlight making its slow arc across the yard. She hauled herself onto the roof of the west wing, then leapt to catch the balcony railing. Lifting herself hand over hand, she dropped catlike outside the sliding door.

No alarms. No cries for assistance. The curtain was drawn. Beyond it, her target lay sleeping…or so she hoped.

Kara laid her hand on the sliding door's lock and pushed a *verschliessen* into it. It clicked open. This time, she stayed on the "wrong" side of the door, pulling it open rather than pushing it, so she wasn't immediately in the open behind the curtain. She had no idea how lightly Torres slept. The soft sound of the door sliding in its track might wake him, if the lock opening hadn't already.

No sound from within. Kara was grateful the moon shone on the other side of the house. It meant she wasn't silhouetted against the curtain.

No turning back now.

Kara stepped through the curtain into a silent, darkened bedroom. Her eyes adjusted quickly to the lack of light, revealing a person-shaped lump in the bed.

His breathing was quiet and even. Asleep, then. Which meant, since she wasn't here to assassinate him and disappear, she would have to wait.

Kara didn't bother closing the balcony door this time. It might come in handy for a quick exit. Instead, she padded across the plush carpet until she stood on the rug with the Athemis symbol, at the foot of Torres' bed.

She was about to grumble internally at the anticlimax of arriving to find her target peacefully asleep when his breathing hitched. He was awake.

"Good evening, Commissioner."

Torres yawned lazily and slowly sat up. He wasn't wearing a shirt. Kara hoped he at least had boxers on. "Miss Greims. Normally, my overnight companions come in by the front door, but I suppose there's a first time for everything."

Kara scowled behind her mask. "Not funny."

"No? Ah, well. I've only just woken up. Can't be on point all the time." He stretched. "Do you mind if I get my housecoat? I'd prefer to have this conversation marginally clothed."

"Be my guest."

"Thank you." He rose from the bed, pushing the covers aside, and grabbed a terry cloth bathrobe from the chair beside his nightstand. Police blue, like the rest of the fabric in the room. Kara had barely noticed it.

He sat on the edge of the bed again and faced her. "So. Six weeks and one day. I presume you're here to kill me, then."

"Unless you show remorse, yes."

Torres was acting completely unfazed by the sudden appearance of an assassin in his room in the middle of the night. The *wrongness* of it made Kara's heart slam against the inside of her ribcage, but she refused to let her nerves show in her body language.

His shoulders rose and fell, barely visible in the dark. "Then I suppose you'll have to kill me. I feel no remorse for anything I've done, and I'm not about to start now."

Kara stared at him. "Seriously? None at all?"

"None. I don't know how much NLAPD scuttlebutt you picked up on while investigating me for that bygone relic of a justice system, but it's well known among the upper echelons that I'm a clinically diagnosed sociopath. In my case, it lets me get the job done without feeling guilty about it. My superiors have always considered that a plus in my line of work."

"Keeping the police department aboveboard?" Kara couldn't keep the disbelief out of her voice. "That makes *no* sense!"

"Doesn't it?" he challenged. "I don't feel empathy. I don't have compassion. I see a rotten cop, I toss them out on their ass."

"But you *don't,*" Kara shot back. "You've facilitated hundreds of dirty deals over the course of your career. You haven't been upholding justice at the NLAPD. You've made a mockery of it."

Torres' wide smile gleamed in the near darkness. "Ah, but you see, when people trust that you can do the job, they believe the job you're doing is the one they want."

Kara had to take a second to process that. "It doesn't matter if the cops you toss are actually dirty. Whoever's up the chain from you believes they are, because you're 'objective.'"

"Precisely. It's a very tidy system, and it lets me handle my work for Athemis without any pesky NLAPD nonsense getting in the way."

Kara resisted the urge to cross her arms. *Keep your hands free to act. That's much more important than showing him you're not impressed.* "And what exactly *do* you do for Athemis?"

"A little of this, a little of that." He shrugged. "Whatever I'm asked to. It's served me very well over the years to pave the way for Athemis operatives to do what needs to be done. Regulations only cripple progress, in my humble opinion."

"And, what, you didn't think you'd ever get caught?"

"Not until you showed up, no. *Well...*" He rolled his eyes, the movement evident even in the dark. "Until your annoying brother showed up. I caught on to him right away, you know. He thought he was subtle. He started causing trouble, so I nudged the right people in the right direction."

Kara's throat tightened. *He's trying to piss you off. Don't let him get to you.* "You had him killed."

"Eventually, when he'd served his purpose. Then you showed up. I must admit, the last thing I expected was for the stuffy old Vehmic Court to let a *woman* take the mantle of a Free Judge."

"It's happened before."

He scoffed. "For a couple of weeks at a time, and they never lasted long. You, on the other hand...you're *annoying.*"

"Thank you. I work hard at it."

"No doubt. And to be fair, I can appreciate the skill involved. I've studied the history of both our organizations. The reason you're so annoying is that you're very good at what you do."

Kara consciously unclenched her jaw. "The feeling's mutual."

Torres flashed her a grin. "Why, thank you. It's nice to be appreciated."

Kara glared. "You're not welcome. If you're so pleased with what you do, why aren't you more pissed off that I'm here to kill you?"

"Because you won't kill Athemis by killing me. I've done

plenty in my time here, but I'm hardly the linchpin. You won't dismantle everything I've put in place, and my death won't destroy all of Athemis' operations."

"Then why did you threaten me in your office two weeks ago?" This man *mystified* her.

"New tactic. Wanted to see if it would work. Clearly, it didn't."

Kara shook her head. "You are a strange man, Commissioner Torres."

"Again, thank you. Now." He clapped his hands once. "I believe you have a job to do, no? You'd best get on with it. After all, you only have…" He glanced toward the clock on his nightstand. "Oh, we're making excellent time. You have a whole twenty minutes before my people show up."

Kara did a double-take. "What?"

"Come on, Miss Greims. You didn't *really* think I didn't know about your visits, did you? Each lock on the premises sends a record of its usage to the house computer at midnight every day. I knew you were here. You didn't show up on the cameras, but I understand you have ways of avoiding that.

"So, I set an alert on my balcony door tonight. When you opened the lock, it triggered a countdown. We'd have enough time to chat before you tried to kill me, and regardless of your success, you'll be caught red-handed. Elegant, if I do say so myself."

Kara's heart had taken up residence in her shoes. *I knew it was too easy!*

She lunged. He dodged aside, faster than she had expected but not fast enough to avoid her spinning kick. Her boot caught him in the sternum with a solid *thud,* but the angle hadn't been quite right to crack it.

Torres grabbed her ankle as he stumbled back. He twisted Kara's foot, and she was forced to leap and spin to avoid being dragged to the floor.

Torres obviously didn't expect Kara to be as advanced in

martial arts as she was. He didn't see the flying kick coming, and Kara's heel connected with his jaw. This time there *was* a painful crack, and he grunted and let go of her other foot.

Kara landed on her hands and knees and dove forward, away from Torres. Pain wouldn't stall him for long, she was certain.

She was right. He'd scrambled away from her immediately and was reaching under his pillow when she turned back.

It was too dark for Kara to see what he was grabbing, but she would put heavy money on it being a gun. She rolled aside just in time for the bullet to hit the carpet where she'd been.

She sprang to her feet and hurled a small throwing knife at him at the same time. It glanced off his upper arm, slicing through the bathrobe, then bounced off the wall.

Torres' jaw hung at an unnatural angle. She had done a number on it. His gaze was intent, and his eyes were bright. Kara suspected the man was having *fun*.

At least he can't talk anymore.

She dove toward him, aiming for his knees. He sidestepped, but his spatial awareness wasn't as finely honed as Kara's. He hit the bed, stumbled, and went down on his back.

Kara had already tucked and rolled, anticipating that he would dodge her. She caught her momentum on the wall with one foot and bounced upright. Two strides brought her to the bed, and a sharp strike to his wrist broke his grip on the gun. She shoved it off the end of the bed, then pinned him with a hand to his bruised sternum.

"End of the line," she snarled in his face.

He coughed, choking on blood, then spat bloody teeth at her.

Kara didn't flinch. Her tattoos were hot enough she'd swear they would burn through her suit. "James Torres, your perversion of justice will no longer stand unchallenged. You have received notice of your impending judgment, and you have refused to surrender. Therefore, I, Kara Greims, Free Judge of the True

Vehmic Court, hereby sentence you, James Torres, to terminal judgment."

She scowled and brought her wrist blade to his throat. "Rest in peace, you fucking bastard."

She flicked the trigger, and the blade sprang from her wrist and buried itself in Torres' throat. Blood spurted from the wound, soaking the bed in short order and covering Kara's hands.

Torres gurgled, twitched, then let out a rattling, bubbling breath and lay still.

The blood flow slowed, but Kara didn't wait for it to stop before pulling the blade out. A fresh spurt rolled over his chest as the blade came free.

Kara grimaced. She wiped her knife and hands on a clean spot on his bathrobe. *Good thing I wore gloves and the full suit.*

She checked the clock. If Torres' estimation was right, she had fifteen minutes before forces sympathetic to the commissioner would show up. That meant she needed to get a move on.

Kara fumbled for the burner phone tucked in the inside pocket of her jacket. A moment later, the call connected. "911, what is your emergency?"

"I think I heard a gunshot from inside 566 Alvaron Avenue," she reported. "I was out for a late-night walk with my dog, and I wasn't sure at first, but I thought I'd better call, just in case."

"Good thinking, ma'am. Can I get your name for the report?"

"Yes, of course. It's Vita Marconi..."

Kara tucked the phone between her ear and her shoulder as she kept the dispatcher on the line. She would have to feign a service break in a moment or two, but until then, she could keep working.

Torres had said *all* the locks sent reports to the main computer every day. She could see that being the case for the electronic locks, but she *dearly* hoped it didn't extend to the mechanical ones. If he knew she had gotten into his cache of

Athemis documents, there was no chance in hell he would have left them for her to find tonight. He would have burned or shredded them—or both.

She closed her hand around the doorknob between her and the walk-in closet, still blathering to the 911 dispatcher. A *verschliessen* spell opened the lock, and she swung the door open.

The boxes were still there. She would have to take one down to see if they were empty.

Kara slipped a hand onto her phone, then waited until she was in the middle of a sentence to "accidentally" end the call. She grimaced. It would mean the cops would look for Vita Marconi, and there would be questions when they didn't find her.

Oh, well. It's not like it won't be obvious that someone killed Torres.

Kara pulled the first box off the shelf—*not* the one with the documents about her and Jacob. It was blessedly heavy. Her first stroke of luck yet.

She set the box in front of the door to keep it open, then hauled a couple more off the shelves and made a path of "stepping stones" between the door and the cooling body on the bed.

"Won't be able to miss that," she muttered.

Then Kara retrieved a pre-written note from another inside pocket. She considered putting it on top of Torres' corpse, then decided that would be a touch overdramatic. Instead, she set it on the table in the walk-in closet.

A faint siren faded into existence outside. Kara's heart rate leapt, and adrenaline crawled up her arms.

Her initial plan had been to beat feet the moment she had set the scene the way she wanted it. Now, with competing forces on the way, Kara was forced to choose between taking on extra risk for herself or risking continued injustice.

The tattoos had faded to a manageable burn, but they hadn't cooled. James Torres was dead, but there was still a strong chance the wrong people would find his body. The choice wasn't a choice.

Kara gritted her teeth and cursed herself for not coming up with a list of places to hide when she had cased Torres' estate the week before. *Note to self: Never assume* anything *when putting together an execution plan.*

She flicked her headlamp on and checked the soles of her boots. No blood, thank *goodness.* Somehow, she'd managed to avoid stepping in it. She wouldn't leave footprints, wherever she went, and she had wiped most of the blood off her gloves.

The siren was approaching. *There's no time!*

Kara headed for the balcony. It was by no means a perfect hiding place, but she would be able to take off through the back yard if necessary. Better than fighting her way out.

Reminding herself that slow was smooth and smooth was fast, Kara carefully arranged the curtain, slid the door shut, and relocked it. Then she crouched in the corner of the balcony, and upped her *ausklammern* field as far as she could.

The siren was much louder out here. The blue and red lights flashed on the front drive, reflecting off the exterior walls. One loud car door, then two. *Only one car so far. Please, let it be Dominguez.*

Kara waited on tenterhooks for a full two minutes before her enhanced hearing picked up the bedroom door opening within. No surprise there. They would have had to clear the entrance hall first, then they would have split up. She prayed Dominguez had taken the top floor, if it was him.

"Holy shit."

The voice came through the glass clear as day, thanks to the Vehmic Court's magic, and with it came a crashing wave of relief. It *was* Dominguez.

"Reynolds! Upstairs!" he yelled, then he keyed his radio. "Twelve-Lincoln-fourteen, we need an RA and backup at my location. Victim is a middle-aged man, significant blood loss from a wound to the throat."

Kara's shoulders relaxed. The initial report was coming from a trusted source. Dominguez wouldn't let it slide. He would see the boxes, read the note, and make a fuss. She could leave.

As she swung herself over the balcony railing and dropped to the lawn like a cat, she recited the note written in solid Gothic calligraphy she had left on the table in her head.

If the contents of these boxes are not delivered to Sarra Palmer within twenty-four hours, knowledge of their existence will be leaked to Renée Carter.

Corruption in Neo Los Angeles will no longer be allowed to hide in the shadows. All those who would twist justice to their own ends now have an enemy who will not rest until they are brought to the light.

That enemy's name is Nemesis.

CHAPTER TWENTY-FOUR

Neo Los Angeles Times, Morning Edition, February 16, 2091
Vigilante Kills Corrupt Commissioner
By Renée Carter

In a stunning and altogether unexpected turn of events, the Neo Los Angeles Police has admitted to gross negligence and wrong-doing by its late commissioner, James Torres. Even more surprising, it has admitted that his death occurred at the hands of a vigilante using the alias Nemesis.

Torres was found murdered at his estate in the early morning of Wednesday, February 14. Details of the crime scene have not been released to the public, but this reporter has it on good authority that he died of significant blood loss after a struggle with his assailant.

Readers of this paper will remember the exposé published in January, in which this reporter listed a number of detailed accusations against the late commissioner. These accusations, which covered everything from illegal plea bargaining to outright doctoring of criminals' rap sheets, were summarily dismissed as rumor by the NLAPD's Internal Affairs Department.

Sarra Palmer, of Nestor Palmer Law, was not so easily swayed. Even after the arrest of Peter Portman as the alleged superior responsible for the parking garage assault on three civilians, Palmer continued to shake the trees at the NLAPD like a dog with a bone.

She was right to do so.

Nemesis, after killing James Torres, pointed investigators via a written message to a large cache of documents kept under minimum security in Torres' home. These documents cover the entirety of Torres' career, and prove beyond a doubt that the allegations leveled at the late commissioner were true.

Nestor Palmer Law has issued a statement indicating that they will pursue suits against everyone implicated in the Torres papers, regardless of cost or time. They have an open line for citizens wanting to know if their cases were mishandled at James Torres' hands. When asked whether a class-action lawsuit was in the cards, Sarra Palmer said, "It's not out of the question. We're interested in justice being served. Whatever it takes, we'll do it."

The sentiment is shared by many across our fair city. While the outrage at Torres' alleged actions lessened after the arrest of Portman, rumors of Torres' death on social media have sparked renewed calls for the NLAPD to clean house. Certain commenters have challenged law enforcement, saying the vigi-

lante Nemesis did in one night what "NLA's finest" had not done —or had, perhaps, assisted—in decades.

Acting Commissioner of Internal Affairs, Roberta McNally, has called for patience. "We attest to the late James Torres' overreach on multiple cases during his career as commissioner," she said in a press conference late last night. "I'd like to take this opportunity to assure the public that we will be investigating every case Torres was involved in throughout his career, and every officer involved in those cases, with a fair and open mind.

"The NLAPD's job is to maintain security and peace in our beloved city," McNally added. "We do not condone civilians taking matters into their own hands. We do not condone vigilantism. We are searching for the perpetrator of this murder with as much attention and resources as we are devoting to the investigation into Torres' actions. Nemesis, if you're out there, we ask you to turn yourself in. Two wrongs don't make a right."

Given Acting Commissioner McNally's comments, the vigilante is not believed to be in custody at this time. While many on social media are pleased and vindicated by Nemesis' actions, and calls are already going up for the vigilante to target other alleged perpetrators of injustice in the city, others are wary. Who is this stranger? Why do they consider themselves above the law? How did they know about James Torres' deeds, and where will they strike next?

Kara couldn't keep the smile off her face. She folded the newspaper and set it aside, then picked up a piece of buttered toast and took a huge bite.

"Your appetite's come back," Cedric observed with a chuckle. "I don't remember the last time you attacked your breakfast with that much zeal."

Kara grinned around her mouthful of toast. "Renée Carter isn't exactly J. Jonah Jameson, but I can *hear* the editor yelling in the background."

Cedric snorted. "*Bring me pictures of Spider-Man!*"

"You get me."

Kara took another, more contemplative, bite of toast. It was true. The man *did* get her. They got along very well, as it happened, and Kara had become accustomed to having Cedric around.

"I was thinking," she started.

"Always dangerous." He winked and sipped from the straw coming out of his mug. He preferred a South American drink called *yerba maté* to regular coffee. Kara had tried it and didn't care for the taste, but she had to admit it packed a punch.

She stuck her tongue out at him but took the jest in stride. "Yeah, yeah. I was wondering when you planned to move back to your apartment. I love having you around, but you must be missing the gym by now."

Cedric shrugged. "Actually, no."

"Really?"

"Really." He sipped his drink again and savored the liquid before continuing. "I love working as a coach, but running a business has never been my forte. I do okay, but it's more of a pain in the ass than anything else. And…"

Cedric set his mug on the island and leaned in, putting both elbows on the wooden block. "Can I be honest with you, Kara?"

Kara's heart lurched. *Honest good or honest bad?* "Um. Sure."

"The last few weeks have been *insane.*"

She chuckled nervously. "Can't argue with you there. Which is why I would entirely understand if you wanted to go home and never see me again."

He waved off the end of her sentence. "No, no, that's not what I'm saying."

"Then…"

"I'm saying it's been *great*. I know lots of people would, if they got thrown into a world where magic was real and an international cabal was coming after your girlfriend and her sort-of sister-in-law and they controlled half of the local police department… Well, let's just say they'd lose their shit."

Kara stared at him. Had she heard what she thought she'd heard?

"My shit?" He gestured to himself. "Eminently not lost. *Surprisingly* not lost. That day on the sidewalk, when you took those guys out like it was nothing, that was just the teaser. I knew something was up. And when you told me everything…

"When we finished that conversation, I fully expected to come away from it thinking you were nuttier than a squirrel convention and that I should run as fast and as far as I could in the other direction. Instead, I realized there was no place I'd rather be but right here, helping you."

He glanced at the remains of his *huevos rancheros*. "Although frankly, I'd be lying if Ana's cooking didn't tip the scales even further. God*damn*, that woman can cook."

Laughter bubbled up Kara's throat, threatening to escape. She did her best to tamp it down, but a giggle snuck out. "She *is* a very good cook."

"Right? I would have killed a man for last night's enchiladas." He winced. "Shit. Sorry. Too soon?"

Kara shook her head. "No, it's fine."

"You sure? You look a little shell-shocked." Doubt flashed across his face. "Uh, if this was supposed to be your way of graciously asking me to leave, I'll go. I just didn't—I thought—"

"You thought I was your girlfriend," Kara finished. Her heart felt like it was attempting to take flight through her ribs.

Cedric blushed a deep red. "Uh, well—Oh, crap, I said that out loud, didn't I?"

"You did."

The powerful confidence was quickly ceding to flustered

embarrassment. "If you're not interested, um, that's fine. I didn't want to assume, I was just—well, we get along so well, and I really like you, and every time we spar I want to finish by kissing you, and—"

"Cedric."

He swallowed so hard his Adam's apple bobbed to the bottom of the pail of water. "Yeah?"

"Shut up for two seconds."

Cedric sucked his lips between his teeth and bit down on them. It looked so ridiculous that Kara had to laugh again. When his eyebrows creased in regret, she quickly waved both hands, palms out.

"I'm not laughing at you!" Kara promised. "I'm not, I'm *so* not. I'm just…"

She waved at the paper. "I can't believe my life right now. I killed a police commissioner in his bedroom and exposed forty-some years of insidious corruption to the media. Half the city wants to string me up, and the other half wants me to go after the next guy on the list.

"I'm living in a millionaire's mansion, and I have enough money in my bank account that I don't have to work for the next ten years if I don't want to. I have a dryad as my majordomo, and she spends her spare time reinforcing the defenses on my estate with magical topiaries and God only knows what else.

"Those defenses are necessary because, as you so aptly put it, there's an international cabal out for my head. *That's* happening because I'm the last vigilante Judge of a millennium-old court, a position I got because that annoying international cabal killed my brother seven months ago.

"Speaking of my brother, his fiancée-to-be and her eight-week-old son are *also* living with me, along with their mother-slash-grandmother. Why? Because that international cabal tried to kill and kidnap them almost before the poor kid got his eyes open."

"Babies aren't kittens," Cedric interrupted.

"I know that. What I'm *saying* is that I *completely* understand what you're saying about the last few weeks being *absolutely bonkers*. Oh, did I mention that my majordomo hired a bunch of dwarves—sorry, Morians, don't want to be culturally insensitive—to build me a magical railway in my basement? And I'm about to erase my former identity from the face of the planet so I can function full-time as a goddamned vigilante named *Nemesis*?"

"I suppose I don't exactly have the monopoly on crazy lives," Cedric admitted. His acute embarrassment had faded to awkward sheepishness.

"We're in this together, but of all the people here, you had the most choice. You could have said no a hundred times over. You had no stake in my war. Instead, you've thrown yourself in with as much zeal as anyone. You've helped me learn to defend myself. I wouldn't be alive without your help."

The blush came back. "Well, I mean, you're a good student..."

"Don't duck the compliment," she admonished. "My point is..." She cleared her throat. "My point is that every time we spar, I want to kiss you, too, and I really want you to stay, but I couldn't ask you because I didn't want to put you in danger. *More* danger, I mean."

Cedric cocked his head. "Being your boyfriend puts me at more risk than being your live-in sparring coach?"

He was grinning, and Kara was doing the same, but the words landed like rocks falling in a pond. "It does. And before you agree, I need you to think it through.

"Athemis has been hunting my family for over a decade. We're hidden now, but they're not gonna stop because we got rid of Torres. That'll be a setback, but it won't deter them. It would be *incredibly* irresponsible of me not to make sure you understand that hooking up with me paints a target the size of the city on your back.

"And that doesn't begin to touch what could happen if we get serious," she added. "I don't wanna put words in your mouth or feelings in your heart, but if we ever decide to have a kid, they're next in line for my job. Free Judges take an oath to serve, but the position is hereditary. One of my next tasks is pushing Grimm to figure out how we can *change* that, but it's gonna take a while."

The giddy excitement had drained from Cedric's face, but he hadn't turned into a pale imitation of himself. His gaze remained focused on hers, and the set of his jaw was firm. "I'd already thought about that. Hard not to, with Carlos around."

Kara accepted that with a nod, but refused to acknowledge the little hop, skip, and jump her heart had done at the same time. "And you're still in."

His smile turned a touch self-deprecating. "So far in that I *accidentally* called you my girlfriend. I planned to broach the subject early next week, after you had a few days to rest. Guess my mouth ran away with me."

"Guess so."

Kara reached across the island, laying her hand palm up on the smooth wood. "In that case… I'm in, too."

Cedric grinned, took her hand, and gripped it. The callouses on his fingers rubbed smoothly against hers. It felt so intimate and *right* that Kara almost scrambled over the island to kiss him right then and there.

"*Dios mío, ¡ya era hora!*"

Cedric and Kara started, losing their grip on each other and turning to the kitchen door. Ana stood there with her hands on her hips, laughing silently.

"Ana! We didn't hear you come in!" Kara sputtered.

"*Por supuesto.* I am quiet as a mouse. You will never hear me coming unless I want you to. But it doesn't matter—I am glad you two have *finally* opened your eyes."

Kara blinked. "What? You mean—"

"You knew—" Cedric interrupted.

Ana threw up her hands. "It was clear as the nose on

Ivonne's face! The way you two fight in the gym is like *dancing*. Honestly, I thought you'd *already* started doing the horizontal cha-cha whenever Kara was home for longer than an hour!"

Kara blushed a brighter red than the tomatoes in the basket on the counter. She started to say something—although what she planned to say, she couldn't have told you—but was saved by the arrival of Maria and Carlos.

"*Mami*, what's going on?" Maria took in the scene and snorted. "Oh. I *see*. *Mami*, stop tormenting them."

"*Ay*, someone has to." Ana rolled her eyes, then chivvied Cedric away from the island. "Go away. I need to make cake."

Cedric quickly backed away in the face of the Latina whirlwind. "Cake? What? Why?"

"To *celebrate*," Ana replied, exasperated. "*Dios mío*, Kara, are you *sure* about this one? He must be good in bed. His brains obviously leave a little to be desired."

"*Mami!*" Maria scolded, but her eyes were alight with repressed laughter.

Kara slipped off her stool and backed toward the door. "I, uh, am gonna go talk to Grimm. See what the books have to say. Polish his skull. Dust the swords."

Cedric's eyes widened, imploring. "No! Don't leave me!"

"Good luck!" she called over her shoulder as she skedaddled.

Before she turned the corner to head for her study, she thought she heard Maria say something like, "You asked for it. Welcome to the family..."

"You told them you were going to *polish* my *skull?*"

Kara covered her face with her hands and groaned. "I know. I know! Stop laughing at me. It just came out!"

Grimm did not stop chuckling. "I suppose my skull could use

a polishing, now you mention it. It has lost some of its luster with age."

"I am not polishing your skull, Grimm. You can do it yourself."

"How do you propose I do that? In case you haven't noticed, I am rather lacking in the hands department."

"You have a cat. Cats have fur. And tongues."

"That is unsanitary."

"You're a skull."

"A well-preserved one, thank you!"

Kara started laughing, and she didn't stop for a full minute. When she finally caught her breath, she felt relieved and relaxed, as though she'd just gotten out of a hot tub. "Oh, my God. What is my life?"

"I believe the Greeks have a proverb along these lines. Something along the lines of 'May you live in interesting—'"

"Interesting times," Kara finished. "Funny, I always thought it was a Chinese saying."

"I imagine many cultures have articulated the concept throughout history."

"Probably." Kara drew a deep, calming breath, then let it out. "I'm not condemning Cedric by hooking up with him, am I?"

"No more than the partner of any enforcer. You set forth the stakes succinctly, and I believe he has been aware of them for some time, as he implied. He is not entering this relationship blind, nor are you. The more important question is, are *you* prepared for this?"

"Having a boyfriend? I know about the birds and the bees, Grimm."

"I'm aware." The skull's dry wit passed quickly. "The largest reason Free Judges eschewed Circles in the more recent past is that it *does* put members at risk. The lines of multiple Free Judges ended for similar reasons."

Kara inhaled slowly in realization. "They didn't have kids."

"Indeed. Many Free Judges, if they did not already have offspring when they inherited the position, chose not to have families. It is human nature to wish peace and safety for our children. Knowing you cannot promise that—knowing, in fact, that you can guarantee the alternative...

"Are you ready for what this means for *you*, Kara?" he repeated. "If you and Cedric have a son, the line will automatically pass from Carlos. You have said this is something you want, but I am not convinced you have fully considered the implications."

Kara thought about it. Having kids of her own had never been in her plans. She had fully expected to be a lawyer first, and not much else second. Maybe a relationship here or there, but nothing serious. She hadn't thought she would have time.

The idea didn't feel real. She had barely considered juggling her job and motherhood—what about being a vigilante while pregnant?

"I think I might get a prescription for birth control before Kara Greims disappears from existence," she weakly announced. "I, ah, maybe didn't think it all the way through either."

Grimm chuckled again, not unkindly. "That might be wise. Shall we change the subject for the time being?"

"Please."

"Very well. I must commend you for your work these past weeks. Under significant pressure, you built a strong case and delivered a decisive judgment. No innocent lives were lost, and there seems to be a good chance that law enforcement will continue the work where you left off."

"Thanks, Grimm." Kara's heart rate was slowing down. *Funny how I'm much more comfortable talking about vigilantism than I am about kids. That probably says something about me, but I am not in the mood to follow that rabbit hole.*

"You are welcome. I must also applaud your cultivation of

contacts and resources. Ricardo Dominguez will be a valuable asset, as will Renée Carter."

Kara nodded. "I agree. I think I lucked out with Dominguez. He has a good head on his shoulders and a good heart. Hopefully, with the housecleaning at the NLAPD, he'll end up in a position where he can *do* some good. Renée Carter, though…"

"You do not like her?"

"I'm wary of her. Maybe it's a lawyer thing, but I've always been leery of journalists. She has a reputation for telling the truth, though, so I'm reserving judgment for now."

"Always wise. What are your next steps?"

Kara cracked her neck. "I'm gonna lay low for a while. Scout the streets, train, see how things shake out at the NLAPD. If an opportunity presents itself for a takedown that won't get in the way of the NLAPD cleaning house, I'll take it, but I don't want to risk inadvertently distracting from the task at hand. Something tells me the news cycle will be a lot more interested in a vigilante doing their thing than the continued story of a corrupt police commissioner's hold on the city."

"I believe that, too, is wise. And, of course, it has *nothing* to do with your new relationship."

Kara blushed crimson again. "Oh, Grimm, not you too!"

The skull laughed, and while Kara was embarrassed, she had to admit it was nice to hear so much laughter in the house. She would endure the teasing if it meant her Circle was happy. *God, I'll never hear the end of it when Ivonne finds out.*

As she looked out her study window over the subtly shifting trees, Kara hoped the lighthearted interlude lasted a little longer this time. *No disasters, please,* she asked the universe silently. *Just give us a few weeks. Maybe even a few months. I'd really appreciate it.*

MICHAEL'S NOTES

FEBRUARY 10, 2026

<u>**Las Vegas, NV**</u>

First, thank you for not only reading this story, but these author notes in the back as well!

Fifteen Billion Dollars and They Still Can't Hire Enough Nerds

The Pentagon's cyber budget for 2026 just hit **$15.1 billion.** That's a 4% jump from last year, with **$9.1 billion** for core cyber-security operations and another **$612 million** for cyber research. Fifteen billion. With a !@#%! *B*.

And they are STILL short *more than 20,000 cyber professionals.*

Let me repeat that number, because it deserves its own moment: twenty thousand unfilled positions defending the digital infrastructure of the most powerful military on Earth.

Meanwhile, the civilian sector is short **750,000** cybersecurity pros nationwide. Three quarters of a million people we don't have, doing jobs we desperately need done, protecting systems that run everything from power grids to weapons platforms.

Here's the thing that gets me — one of the big reasons they

can't fill these roles? According to Ryan Dunford, a lead infrastructure engineer and veteran: people think cybersecurity requires "superior intellect" and that the certifications are "out of reach."

Meanwhile, I know of gamers who've been running guild logistics, coordinating 40-person raids, managing supply chains in EVE Online, and reverse-engineering game code for fun since they were fourteen.

You're telling me those people can't do cyber defense? Half of them have been doing it *recreationally*.

Don't get me wrong. The Pentagon is also racing to build **post-quantum encryption.** That means they're developing cryptographic systems that can withstand attacks from quantum computers. Computers that *don't fully exist yet*. They're defending against weapons that haven't been built, protecting secrets that haven't been stolen, from enemies who haven't figured out the math.

Which is literally my job description as a science fiction writer. Except I get paid considerably less than $15.1 billion.

I should renegotiate with Amazon. (*Fat chance!*)

The legislation also pushes for baseline cybersecurity standards across all defense contractors, because apparently (and I'm trying not to scream here) we didn't already have those? We're spending $15 billion on cyber defense and the contractors building our weapons systems were operating on the honor system?

This is fine. Everything is just F#@#ing fine.

The good news? The military is pushing hard to recruit veterans into cyber roles, and it makes sense. Leadership training, attention to detail, operational discipline (which they all have) turns out the skills that keep you alive in a combat zone also keep networks alive when someone in Eastern Europe decides to poke at our infrastructure at 3 AM.

So if you're a veteran reading this (or you know one) there's a

SkillBridge program, GI Bill-funded cybersecurity training, and about twenty thousand empty chairs with your name on them.

And if you're a gamer? Maybe put that on your resume. I'm serious. If you have a gamer in your basement then encourage them to do something with a paycheck. It's just a really intense gaming puzzle, right?

Sure, there is the whole 'blow up the world' angle as well, but that's just... details.

Ad Aeternitatem,
Michael Anderle

P.S. - The Pentagon is short 20,000 cyber warriors. My books have entire armies of AI-enhanced hackers. At this point I'm not writing fiction based Author Noter. I'm writing recruitment brochures. Someone owes me a consulting fee as part of that $20 billion.

MORE STORIES with Michael newsletter HERE: https://michael.beehiiv.com/

THE STORY CONTINUES

The story continues in book three, *Convicted*, coming soon to Amazon.

BOOKS BY MICHAEL ANDERLE

Sign up for the LMBPN email list to be notified of new releases and special deals!

https://lmbpn.com/email/

For a complete list of books by Michael Anderle, please visit:

www.lmbpn.com/ma-books/

CONNECT WITH MICHAEL ANDERLE

Website: lmbpn.com

Email List: michael.beehiiv.com/

Facebook: Facebook.com/LMBPNPublishing

Twitter/X: Twitter.com/MichaelAnderle

Instagram: Instagram.com/lmbpn_publishing/

Bookbub: Bookbub.com/authors/michael-anderle